VANISH FROM SIGHT

A HIGH PEAKS MYSTERY THRILLER

JACK HUNT

DIRECT RESPONSE PUBLISHING

ISBN: 9798389544444

For my Family

ALSO BY JACK HUNT

If you haven't joined *Jack Hunt's Private Facebook Group* just do a search on facebook to find it. This gives readers a way to chat with Jack, see cover reveals, enter contests and receive giveaways, and stay updated on upcoming releases. There is also his main facebook page below if you want to browse. facebook.com/jackhuntauthor

Go to the link below to receive special offers, bonus content, and news about new Jack Hunt's books. Sign up for the newsletter.
http://www.jackhuntbooks.com/signup

A High Peaks Mystery Thriller

In Cold Blood

Vanish From Sight

Her Final Hours

After it Turns Dark series

When the World Turns Dark

When Humanity Ends

When Hope is Lost

When Blood Lies

When Survivors Rise

The Great Dying series

Extinct

Primal

Species

A Powerless World series

Escape the Breakdown

Survive the Lawless

Defend the Homestead

Outlive the Darkness

Evade the Ruthless

Outlaws of the Midwest series

Chaos Erupts

Panic Ensues

Havoc Endures

The Cyber Apocalypse series

As Our World Ends

As Our World Falls

As Our World Burns

The Agora Virus series

Phobia

Anxiety

Strain

The War Buds series

War Buds 1

War Buds 2

War Buds 3

Camp Zero series

State of Panic

State of Shock

State of Decay

Renegades series

The Renegades

The Renegades Book 2: Aftermath

The Renegades Book 3: Fortress

The Renegades Book 4: Colony

The Renegades Book 5: United

The Wild Ones Duology

The Wild Ones Book 1

The Wild Ones Book 2

The EMP Survival series

Days of Panic

Days of Chaos

Days of Danger

Days of Terror

Against All Odds Duology

As We Fall

As We Break

The Amygdala Syndrome Duology

Unstable

Unhinged

Survival Rules series

Rules of Survival

Rules of Conflict

Rules of Darkness

Rules of Engagement

Lone Survivor series

All That Remains

All That Survives

All That Escapes

All That Rises

Single Novels

The Haze

15 Floors

Blackout

Defiant

Darkest Hour

Final Impact

The Year Without Summer

The Last Storm

The Last Magician

The Lookout

Class of 1989

Out of the Wild

The Aging

Mavericks: Hunters Moon

Killing Time

1

Friday, November 18, 8:10 p.m.
Adirondack County, Upstate New York

D*eath hung in the air.*

The evening was crisp, the sky clear, allowing the moonlight to cast its cool glow over the surrounding trees. In the midst of fall, the leaves were ablaze in golden yellows and deep reds, signaling the natural cycle of death and renewal.

A single fishing boat glided through the calm waters of High Peaks Lake, the only sounds coming from the gentle lapping of the waves against the hull and the occasional call of a night bird in the distance. As it was the weekend before Thanksgiving, the days were cold, the nights even colder.

"Are we there yet?" Caitlin Dowling said.

"Almost," her boyfriend replied.

Escaping the hustle of city life in Albany, with the hope of enjoying a weekend away, the young couple had opted to head north to experience the beauty and tranquility of High Peaks.

It was a little after eight in the evening when they'd left the Airbnb for what was meant to be an adventurous boat ride across the 5.5-mile lake. The waterfront cabin had come fully stocked with all the amenities, a full-size fishing boat, kayaks and canoes. With his girlfriend too afraid to use a kayak, he'd taken out the fishing boat.

"Billy, let's go back. It's too cold out here." She shivered as she faced him.

He smiled back. "Put your hood up. It will be worth it."

"This is not what I had in mind when you said we were going to get away."

"Live a little."

Caitlin grumbled, wrapping her arms tightly around herself in an effort to stay warm. She'd dressed for warmer weather, not expecting a sudden shift in temperature, now she was beginning to regret her choice of clothing.

With winter on the doorstep, Billy could feel a harsh wind biting at his cheeks. The boat bobbed up and down as water lapped against it. Desperate to stay warm, Billy began to row faster, hoping the exertion would generate some heat. He could feel his fingers getting numb and his teeth chattering. He'd brought a flask of hot cocoa and some finger foods. It was meant to be romantic — a kind gesture—proof that he hadn't lost the touch. That the work on Wall Street hadn't consumed his soul the way it had others'.

A light mist hovered over the surface of the water like a ghostly apparition.

Even as he focused on the task at hand, all he could think about was the cold.

"We should have gone south... No one knows we're out here. If something happens..." she said.

"Chill."

"Is that meant to be funny?"

He snorted, finding humor in the moment.

"Nothing will happen," he said as the oars cut through the still waters.

Finally, after what seemed like an eternity, they got close to the outcropping of rocks he'd told her about. The air became still. He felt a sense of unease wash over him. Billy heaved a heavy sigh as he brought the oars into the boat. The sound of the clattering against the hull echoed across the water.

He turned to Caitlin with a grin.

"Well, we're here," he said, gesturing to a rocky outcropping. "This is where she's supposed to be seen."

Caitlin squinted. "I don't see a damn thing, so let's go back."

He chuckled, reaching for the flask and handing it to her. "Take this. Get some of that in you. It will warm you up."

"It would be better if we drank it around a fire."

Another cool breeze blew across the surface of the lake, rustling the leaves and carrying the scent of nature toward them.

"We will. Just give it five or ten minutes. You're always listening to those spooky ghost stories. I figured you would get a kick out of this one." He poured himself a cup and clambered over to her end to sit beside her. He wrapped an arm around her shoulders, pulling her in close. "Okay, so back in September 1933, a well-known teacher from around these parts supposedly disappeared while rowing across the lake. No one had any idea where she went. She was the dean of an illustrious college. Apparently she was vacationing out here, a bit like us."

He grinned and Caitlin slapped him on the leg. "Billy Crawford, you better not be pranking me."

He laughed and she summoned a smirk.

"Shh. Let me finish. So, police dragged the lake, searched the surrounding mountain trails and came up empty-handed. Not a sign. She was there one minute and the next, gone. The only thing they found was her capsized boat near the shore. Then get this... thirty years goes by and this diving group is out here on the lake, you know, doing their thing, having a little dig around to see what they could find, and they come across her preserved remains on a shelf about 95 feet down below the surface of the water."

Caitlin listened intently, her eyes wide with wonder and fear.

"It seems there was a weight attached to a rope around her neck. They think it was suicide but no one could be sure. Too many years had passed to determine if she was murdered. Anyway, since that night, tourists and locals swear that the ghostly figure of a woman is seen hovering near that outcropping of rock over there. They say the spirit of the Lady of the Lake still haunts that spot 'til this very day."

As she squinted to make out if she could see anything, Billy startled her by shouting, "Boo!"

Caitlin slapped him again and he roared with laughter.

"Billy!"

"You are so easy to scare."

He studied her expression as Caitlin took a sip of her drink.

"Did you make that up?" she asked.

"No. I swear. It's a true story."

Caitlin shook her head. "Poor woman."

"Apparently, she had a lot of bad luck in her life. Family and whatever." Billy surveyed the surface of the rock, his eyes slowly descending before he glassed the lake. "Goes to show you that you can achieve a position in life but that career, money, none of that really matters if..." He trailed off, as he began squinting.

"What is that?" she asked.

"Can you see that?" he replied.

"Oh, stop, Billy."

"No. Seriously Look out there," he said, pointing toward a strange shape floating in the distance.

Caitlin followed the direction of his finger. Billy took out his flashlight and shone the beam outward, its warm light danced across the ripples. "Here, hold this," he said, taking out the oars and paddling as fast as he could toward it.

"Billy. C'mon. Let's go back."

"I just want to get a closer look."

"This better not be a joke."

He didn't answer. He was too focused on what was up ahead. As they approached the unusual object, he soon realized that it was a lifeless body floating face-down in the water. Billy took an oar and touched the tip of it against the shoulder, turning the face, just enough to see it wasn't a mannequin but a woman. In fright, he almost dropped the oar.

"Holy crap."

Frightened and unsure of what to do, he rowed back while Caitlin took out her phone and called the authorities.

2

Friday, November 18, 8:30 p.m.

It was a mystery.

Under the glare of the floodlights, Noah Sutherland stood beside the realtor, unable to believe it was true. He'd only been back in High Peaks a mere two weeks, living out of Aunt Gretchen's spare room until he could find a place, when he received a call at his work from a local real estate broker. As Kerri was in real estate, he'd been having her handle the search for a property. With a limited budget, his options weren't extravagant.

That's why this was baffling.

An upscale realtor called him out of the blue, presenting an unbelievable offer to live in a five-million-dollar waterfront property, completely free. He thought it was a prank, that Hugh or one of his siblings had staged it, but as he stood on the edge of the property on the north side of High Peaks Lake, he realized it was very real.

She was already there when he arrived, standing beside a sleek, fancy SUV that was a reflection of her taste for luxury and success as a broker. The realtor was the epitome of class and sophistication. She wore a navy-blue suit that fit her like a glove, paired with black heels that accentuated her long, slender legs. Her dark hair was pulled back into a neat ponytail, and her makeup was impeccable.

It was clear she took pride in her appearance and her vehicle, knowing that first impressions meant everything to clients.

A quick shake of the hand and she opened the mammoth door and led him in. As she turned on lights, one after another illuminated a magnificent abode.

"As mentioned before, my name is Suzanne Gilford, I'm a broker representing Harland and Stafford, one of the world's leading real estate agencies specializing in the brokerage of premium residential and commercial properties. If you have any questions, please feel free to ask."

With that, she began the tour.

The house was breathtakingly beautiful, with floor-to-ceiling windows that offered a panoramic view of the lake, hickory flooring and several cozy fireplaces throughout. There were three spacious bedrooms, each with its own bathroom, and a fourth bathroom on the main floor. The master bedroom had an unobstructed view of the nearby mountains, a private balcony with a fire-pit, and a skylight above a queen bed for stargazing. The primary suite spanned the entire second level, offering a walk-in closet as well. "Who lives here at the moment?" he asked.

"No one. It's been on the market for over a year. All the furniture you see comes with it. It's brand-new. So, no need to buy anything. Did you have furniture?"

"Not much. A few things in storage. I sold most of it."

She led him through a state-of-the-art kitchen, a stunning

living room, and then out to a private dock where there were three water bays with motorized boat lifts and two slips, along with a high-end Duffy 21 boat and a smaller one for fishing. "And these boats?"

"For your use."

"And what's that over there?"

"A sauna, a bathroom, a changing room and another covered dock."

Noah had questions. Lots of them, but he could barely form words. His eyes widened; his jaw went even wider as he soaked in the view from the main deck. "You should know that it comes with a built-in sound system and a gas hookup to the grill for those nights you want to throw on a steak or entertain guests. And who can forget the 180-degree view of the lake and the Adirondack Mountains. Come along..." she said, leading him from one spectacular view to the next. "Not bad, right?"

"Stunning."

"You get half an acre. The property has a guest house with two bedrooms, two baths, two kitchens and a single-car garage. So basically you are getting a lakeside house, a large cottage and... did I mention the boats too?"

"You did."

The realtor smiled and led him back into the house over to a kitchen island where she had some paperwork. "Okay. All I need is a few signatures and the keys are yours."

Noah scanned the paperwork. "Let me get this straight. I would own this place?"

"Not own. You would use it. Ownership still belongs to our client."

"And this client. Who are they?"

"Client confidentiality. It's an LLC. All I can tell you is the benefactor wishes to remain anonymous."

He nodded slowly, puzzled. "May I ask, what is it they expect from me?'

"Nothing. No strings attached. Of course, like any rental property you would ensure it remains tidy and clean. Any repairs that are needed would be covered by management unless of course you wish to do them. You would pay for heating, water, electricity and so on but there would be no monthly rental charge. In the event our client wishes to change the agreement, you would be notified three months in advance by letter."

Noah looked around the kitchen. It was astonishing. Considering some of the dives Kerri had walked him through, it would have been insane to turn down the offer, and yet he knew nothing was truly free.

"Did they give you any reason why they are offering this to me?"

She unbuckled a sleek briefcase and handed him an envelope. He opened it and pulled out a single sheet of paper. There was no official letterhead — it was typed — nothing to indicate who the writer was.

Mr. Sutherland,

I'm sure you are a little taken aback by the offer you've received today and we would be surprised if you didn't need some time to think it over. So, please, take all the time you need. The keys are ready whenever you are. As for why? I would like to say that associates of mine were very pleased to learn of your involvement in the recent case that saw not only narcotics driven out of our county but also those who might wish to continue to taint the good name of this town. It came to our attention that you were in need of a place to stay while you establish yourself in the region again. We hope this property will suffice. If there is anything more you need, please feel free to get in touch with us through Harland and Stafford. They handle many of our properties in the area and I'm sure they can find you something else if this place is not to your taste.

For now, kindly enjoy.

Noah closed the paper.

"Well. Will you be accepting the offer?"

"It's hard not to be impressed by the extravagance of it all. I certainly don't wish to stay with my aunt any longer than I need to." He looked around. In the years he'd grown up in High Peaks, he wanted to live in a home like this, but he couldn't have imagined it would be possible. Close to accepting, he felt a nagging feeling in his gut. Who was this anonymous benefactor? What did they really want from him in return? No one but no one gave away something like this without wanting a little something back. He wanted to run it by Kerri. If anyone might know who was behind the offer, it would be her. She had her finger on the pulse of those who were buying and selling.

Noah turned toward Suzanne. "I will need some time to think about it."

Suzanne smiled sympathetically and said, "Of course. Take all the time you need. But if I might offer a suggestion."

"Go ahead."

"I've been working in this business for close to twenty-three years. Our company deals with a lot of high-end clients. People with deep pockets and even deeper ties to the community. They are successful because they know their worth and can leave properties on the market for years until the right buyer comes along. This is a rarity. A once-in-a-lifetime opportunity."

"That's what concerns me," Noah replied.

He thanked the realtor for her time and headed back to his black Ford Bronco.

As he climbed in, his phone chimed. The caller ID came up for Savannah Legacy.

THE STEADY THROB of emergency lights from High Peaks Police Department cruisers and an EMT van illuminated the night. Noah swerved into the lot of the marina just as several uniformed officers were hauling a body bag out of a boat.

They had cordoned off the area with yellow tape that was flapping in a gentle breeze. Curious onlookers, illuminated by the flashing blue and red lights, strained to catch a glimpse of what was happening inside. They whispered among themselves, speculating.

High Peaks Marina was normally a bustling hub of activity during the day, with boats bobbing up and down in the water, and tourists laughing and chatting across the docks as they prepared to take one of the tours in the famous enclosed pontoon boats. But now, it looked very different in the darkness, it was eerie and foreboding.

Police officers paced, some talking on radios, a few taking down statements and the rest conferring with each other in a hushed tone. As Noah worked his way through the crowd, he caught the eye of his older brother Ray.

"Looks like we might be working this one together," he said, lifting the yellow crime-scene tape so Noah could duck under.

"This isn't going to be good for business," Noah muttered. "Is it a drowning?"

"Not exactly."

Ray fell in step as they made their way over to the ambulance. EMTs were loading the body to be taken to the medical examiner. Ray asked for a minute or two. The crew walked a short distance away as Noah climbed into the back of the ambulance. Ray unzipped the black body bag just enough to see the victim's face.

"Unknown female. Married by the looks of the wedding band on the finger." Ray unzipped the bag a little more to reveal rope tied around the victim's waist and legs.

"That's a lot of rope," Noah muttered.

Noah snapped on some blue latex gloves, then moved some of the soggy hair out of her face. She was middle-aged, no more than forty-five, if that. Her once vibrant brunette hair clung to her face, a tangled mess, her skin was a ghoulish shade of blue.

Having seen numerous floaters, he estimated from the state of the decomposition and bloating of the body that she'd been in the water for longer than a few days. Of course, other factors came into play such as water temperature, body weight, size, and if there were any injuries. The bloating occurred due an accumulation of gases from bacteria that originated as the body's tissue broke down. The gases would then cause swelling and the body would eventually rise to the surface.

As Noah scanned, a bullet wound in her chest caught his attention. He rolled her and noted that it had gone straight through. A clean shot.

"Someone shot her," Ray muttered. "Then dumped the body."

"Maybe. Or she offed herself in the hope someone wouldn't find her," Noah replied, glancing out across the lake. Both were possible theories that would need to be explored by forensics techs, who would check to see if there was any water in the lungs. That would allow them to see if she was dead or alive when she went in.

"Whereabouts was she found?" he asked.

"Near Pulpit Rock." Ray lifted a piece of colorful rope. "We figure this had some kind of weight attached to it. We have divers out in the lake right now to see what else they can find but with night and the depth, they'll probably have to go back out in the morning."

Noah took hold of the rope, noting the end. "Looks clean."

"Yeah, like it was cut or the weight came loose," Ray said. "Which would explain the body rising."

"Interesting style," he said, noting it wasn't the run-of-the-mill kind of rope but was bright blue with flecks of orange and other colors in it. Noah noted the amount of work that had gone into wrapping the waist and legs. It was tight, all on top of her clothes. Overkill for someone trying to take their own life.

Noah lifted his eyes, his gaze landing on a young couple huddled together near the front of a cruiser. The girl was crying, her face buried in her boyfriend's chest.

"They the ones who found her?"

Ray glanced out. "Yeah. Caitlin Dowling. Billy Crawford. A couple of tourists from Albany. They are renting an Airbnb for the weekend on the north side. A quick getaway. They were out for the evening on the lake. They spotted the body and called 911. Crawford said he wanted to show his girlfriend the lady of the lake."

Noah cut Ray a glance.

"I know. I know. But it is what it is."

The lady of the lake was one of the many stories that had worked its way into the region's history. The death was true, the ghost story, debatable.

"That will be a memory they won't forget," Noah said.

"That's for sure."

"Did they touch the body?"

"Only with the oar."

"Were they the only ones on the lake?"

"That we know so far. We've got officers canvassing the surrounding area, questioning home owners and businesses around the lake and trying to gather what information they can."

"Check the department for reports of a missing person."

"We're looking into it," Ray replied.

"I'll contact County and see what they have." Noah looked back down at the victim, wondering who she was and how she came to find her way into the murky depths of High Peaks Lake.

3

Saturday, November 19, 9:45 a.m.

Crime sold almost as much as sex.

Lena Grayson sat at her cluttered desk, pecking the keyboard as she wrote the story that wouldn't hit the print newspaper until the following day. She was surrounded by stacks of papers and files, and in front of her was an oversized coffee cup with the remnants of a second pour. Although she usually took the weekends off, the news never stopped at the *Adirondack Daily Enterprise* and that morning was no different.

Timing was everything.

Whoever got out the news first received the lion's share of hits and ad revenues, but that relied upon tips. Most of their sources didn't come from law enforcement; the cops liked to stay ahead of the media and only utilize them when they thought it could benefit a case.

Until Lena had arrived at the newspaper two years ago, the

ADE was old school. There was nothing on their website to motivate people to send in tips. She was quick to remedy that by arranging with one of the local diners to offer a free coffee to anyone who sent in a solid tip. Maggie had laughed at it. Said it wouldn't work. Days later, she ate her own words and the local diner was overrun.

Now the only problem they had was being one of the first in the region to get the news out. So much had changed since she'd gotten involved in journalism. With the birth of social media, everyone with a phone could take a photo or video or tweet out a message, and within an hour, thousands would know.

Newspapers were going the way of the dinosaurs and with it the revenue of the print newspaper. Few people wanted to shell out the money when they could load up the internet on their phone and get the news on-demand as it happened.

Lena knew if they didn't evolve, they'd all be out of a job. That's why she'd been urging the newspaper to update their website, offer financial incentives for tips, and create a way for readers to request coverage of stories that weren't getting enough attention. It was a chance to generate original content that could only be accessed through an online subscription or purchasing a paper. Still, it was a hard sell and she was already starting to rethink the future of her career. Maybe she could go it alone as a freelance journalist. Others she knew had. At least that way she wouldn't be tied to one region and she could cover whatever she wanted and for whoever she wanted.

"I'm pretty sure I recall you saying that Noah used to work too much," Maggie Coleman said, grinning from across the room.

Not taking her eyes off the screen, Lena typed at a feverish pace. "Maggie, we received the tip late. If I let this slide until Monday, it will be old news."

"I admire your drive, Lena, but you don't have anything to

prove. You're not on probation and this isn't the big city. Remember, folks here move at a snail's pace."

"Doesn't mean I have to."

Maggie chuckled, shaking her head as she walked over.

"Even if you had gotten it out this morning, locals won't read it until Monday. They are days behind. Heck, I only check my mailbox once a week."

"Uh-huh," she said, half-listening.

"And seriously, another story about death, so soon after the Sutherland case? Why don't you let me give this one to Carl?"

"Carl?" That got her attention. She pulled off her glasses and leaned back in her leather chair. "Are you kidding me?"

Maggie smirked.

Lena knew she was yanking her chain. Carl McNeal was a cocky reporter who had been working with the newspaper for far longer than she had. He'd cut his teeth in journalism with a position over at *The New York Times* until he opted to retreat to the quiet life of Saranac — though that wasn't exactly the truth. After a little digging, Lena discovered the NYT had canned his ass for lying. Still, Maggie didn't see any harm in it. She said the news wasn't truth, just poorly bended lies.

Anyway, instead of inspiring up-and-coming investigative journalists, he preferred to slither around the office, slurping coffee, throwing in his two cents where it wasn't needed and spouting stories of his time in the field as if he was some Pulitzer Prize winning journalist. It was a pathetic sight but somehow, he managed to do no wrong in the eyes of Maggie.

The phone jangled, interrupting her train of thought.

She expected it to be another tip or an update on the breaking story of the unknown woman pulled from the lake over in High Peaks.

Lena lifted a finger and Maggie winked at her before walking away.

"Good morning, *Adirondack Daily Enterprise*," she said, holding the phone in the crook of her neck while continuing to type.

"Is this Lena Grayson?"

"It is."

"My name is Hannah Chang; I was hoping I might be able to get your help. I saw on the website that you are accepting ideas for stories that you would look into."

"Go Public. Yes."

"I emailed you a story but no one replied."

"Oh, I'm sorry, we're a little backed up at the moment."

"Two of my dogs have been stolen."

Lena stopped typing; she chewed on the inside of her cheek. "I'm… sorry to hear that. Um. Well, we generally investigate stories that aren't getting much attention and are of interest to the public. I can't guarantee yours will be selected. We get a lot of people submitting ideas and…"

The woman groaned. "And this is why it continues."

"Continues?"

"Gangs stealing dogs. My dogs are not the only ones that have been taken. Zeus and Penelope are just two of many. And no one is doing anything about it."

Lena picked up a pen and jotted down on a sticky note a few items she needed to collect from the grocery store before she forgot. "Um. Have you alerted the police?" she asked, distracted.

The woman laughed. "The police don't do anything. They treat pets like a lost phone. It means nothing to them. And even if these good-for-nothing A-holes get caught, they would just slap them with a fine and send them on their way."

"Well, to be honest, I'm not sure how we can help."

"I've seen your pieces. The news gets the attention of people. You shed light on wrongdoing and hold the powers that be accountable. These people need to be held accountable."

"Sure, but..."

"But what? You're desperate for stories, aren't you? I'm handing you one on a silver platter, and video footage to go with it."

That got her attention. "Video?"

"Yes. They took my dogs straight out of my yard."

"Have you shown that to the police?"

"You're not listening. They don't do anything." Hannah released a heavy sigh. "I'm sorry to be so sharp. I... I haven't slept well since they were taken. I just can't believe anyone would do this."

Lena understood how deeply attached folks were to pets. Ethan had been asking for a dog since Noah had brought Axel around. The problem was they lived busy lives. Dogs needed stability. Not someone who would see them for a few hours in the evening and then leave them all day. That wasn't fair. That was also the reason why shelters were full of animals. People got caught up in the adorable phase, when a dog was just a pup, and then realized fast that they weren't just a lot of work, they were costly. Vet bills. Food. Grooming. In many ways it was like raising a child.

Lena took a gulp of her coffee only to realize it was cold. She grimaced as she swallowed.

"Are you still there?" Hannah asked.

"Yes. Yes. Your two dogs. What breed are they?"

"French bulldogs. Listen, I understand you're busy but I don't know anyone else to turn to. I figure the more people who know, the more eyes there will be out looking for those who do this."

"Do you know anyone who might have wanted to take them?"

"No."

"Look, I know a few people in the police department. I could have them look into it. If you want to send over the video, your address, the date of when they were taken and a photo, and let us know any identifying features the dogs have, I will see what I can do. No promises."

"Thank you."

She hung up and sat there chewing it over.

"Who was that?" Maggie asked.

"Uh?"

"On the phone."

Lena leaned back in her leather chair, twiddling a pen between her fingers. "A woman wants us to cover a story of dogs being stolen in the region, specifically two of hers. You heard about anything like that happening around here?"

"For sure. As of late though?" Maggie shook her head. "Nothing. I mean I've heard of dog thefts happening around the country but not around here for a while. There you go. Maybe you should look into it."

Lena scoffed. "With this case of a missing woman on the table right now, I've got a better idea, have Carl deal with it."

"No. I think you should."

"Maggie."

"Don't Maggie me. Since you've been back, you've barely taken any time off."

"That's because I have two kids to take care of."

"But now you have Aiden to help."

"We're engaged. Not married."

"Still. I saw the way that last case chewed you up."

"It was Noah's brother. My ex-brother-in-law."

"Carl will handle the missing woman. I want you to deal with this lady's situation. We need the people of the town to know that we care and there isn't anything better for that than you breaking wide a story of dogs being thieved."

"Maggie. C'mon. I'll do it after this."

"You're not a cop."

"Nor is Carl."

"But he's handled more crime stories than you."

"I can't believe you just said that."

"It's true. You're good, Lena, but..."

She closed her eyes tight as if someone was raking nails down a chalkboard. "Don't say it."

"He's more experienced."

She popped her eyes open and stared at her screen. "At least let me get this article out."

"You write it. He'll edit and publish."

"C'mon."

Maggie placed a hand on her shoulder. "You know I have your best interest at heart." She walked off, leaving Lena feeling deflated. Across the room, she saw Carl enter the office, fashionably late as he would call it. He sauntered in with an air of self-importance, surveying the room with a sly grin. He had a full head of carefully crafted dark hair, which he was constantly running his fingers through. If that wasn't bad enough, his thick and well-groomed mustache and designer glasses gave him a touch of old-world sophistication.

His sharp, tailored suit hugged his frame perfectly, and the top button of his shirt revealed a hint of gold peeking out from underneath. His dress shoes clacked against the floor, echoing through the open space and drawing attention from those within earshot. As he made his way over to his desk, he addressed a few colleagues with a causal nod and some random comment before he tossed his sleek leather messenger bag down with a sense of nonchalance.

Lena couldn't help but notice a few disapproving glances from the more reserved nearby as he settled into his chair, leaned back, put his feet up on the desk and took a bite of a green apple.

He saw her staring, pointed at her and winked as he continued to munch.

"Asshole," she muttered under her breath.

She shook her head and turned toward her monitor. Despite being taken off the missing woman case, she couldn't help but be intrigued by the call.

Lena brought up Google and did a quick search on puppy thefts.

Article after article came up reporting dognapping on the rise. It was estimated that over 200 million pets were stolen each year, with many purebreds snatched out of the hands of owners at gunpoint. Investigative reporters had found it to be one of the world's fastest growing illicit markets, coming in third behind narcotics and weapons.

As her eyes surveyed each article, she could see the bigger story.

It was massive and one that few newspapers covered in depth.

Once glance at the going prices for dogs, and it was clear why. Many of the dogs were being sold off in the high thousands.

While smaller breeds like French bulldogs, Pomeranians, Maltese and Chihuahuas were stolen because they were easy to carry, larger breeds like German shepherds and Golden retrievers were still being taken because they were purebred.

Thieves were skirting past the breeding phase and stealing pets out from under the noses of owners at a time when the animals were most valuable. Others were used for breeding.

It was unthinkable.

Most of the pups taken weren't loose or tied up in front of a store. No, the brazen thieves were going so far as to break in or use violence against the owners.

As the minutes rolled by, Lena found herself nose-deep in

watching surveillance footage online from cameras in businesses, homes, and streets. One showed a man taking puppies right out of a pet grooming salon. In another, a man broke into a dog kennel, and a third showed someone snatch a dog from a woman at an outside bar in Florida. The worst was of a dog walker being shot.

Lena clicked off the browser and returned to finishing the article. As her fingers were poised over the keyboard, and she considered her next words, she heard the ding of an email notification that she'd been expecting. It was the video Hannah promised, a short grainy shot that she hoped would provide crucial evidence or a lead for the story, as without something to go on, she could see herself coming up empty-handed.

She clicked on the email and without hesitation opened it and watched in horror as the crime unfolded. All of it was captured at night. The act was brazen and fast. Two individuals worked together, one clambering over a fence. The other waited for the dogs on the other side. Fortunately, there was no sound as she could only imagine the dogs' whelps. They were clearly distressed. Within seconds, the dogs were lifted over and the masked individuals hurried back to a waiting car.

Lena felt anger well up inside.

Being a police officer's ex-wife, she was all too familiar with how cases like this might have been handled. Theft was theft, whether it was a pet or not. Law enforcement was probably treating it like any other theft. The incident report would be assigned to an officer, but without anything to go on, and now with a woman pulled from the lake, a few missing pets would go to the bottom of the pile.

It was going to take some digging but Lena had a few ideas of where to start. Scooping up her phone, she began to make calls.

4

Saturday, November 19, 1:15 p.m.

To say they were behind the curve would have been an understatement.

After local PD finally managed to get a coroner out to the lake to pronounce the death of the Jane Doe, EMTs transported her to Adirondack Medical Center that evening for an autopsy by the medical examiner.

They couldn't notify next of kin until they could identify the victim.

That was the problem, there was no ID found on her.

As Noah and Ray strolled down the hallway, his OCD kicked in, something had been bothering him. "So what was the deal with the delay in getting a coroner last night?" Noah asked Ray.

"Laziness."

"What?"

Ray glanced at him with a grin. "Ah, that's right, brother, you're a big city boy. You're used to large cities where everything works like clockwork. Well, welcome to small-town bullshit. There's been an ongoing debate between the coroners and town officials. The budget pays for four coroners to cover jurisdictions, but best of luck trying to get one of them to show up, let alone pick up the phone. You should talk to Oscar Westborough if you want the full skinny."

"Who?"

"The coroner you saw last night. Metal head. The one that showed up looking like he'd just rolled out of bed or walked out of a heavy weed session." He chuckled. "He's forever ranting about the others. Apparently, one coroner heads off to Florida in the winter, one disconnects his phone, and the other makes it hard to reach them. And yet the crazy part is, they still get paid. It's a real shit show."

"Why don't they just fire the others?"

"It's an elected position. There really is no oversight and they have few other options. Eliminating or changing things up takes work, lawyers and time that no one really has. As long as one shows up, they don't care."

"Insane."

Ray stopped at a machine to get some coffee. He tossed in a few coins and stepped back. "In other states and counties, it may be different, but around here, Noah, the coroners are for the most part funeral directors. They decide if an autopsy is necessary. They pronounce the person dead and often bring the deceased to the hospital. For that they get paid around $4,400 a year. It's pocket change. But hey, you already know this."

"I was just curious."

"Coffee?"

He nodded.

Ray turned to him. "Well, you got extra change?"

"You hard up?"

"Who's not, right?"

Noah handed off a few coins and Ray leaned against the machine. "So, did you smooth things out with you and Tanya?" He asked because when he arrived back in High Peaks a few weeks ago, he'd asked if he could stay in one of Ray's spare rooms until he found a place. Ray couldn't put him up. He cited issues with Tanya.

"Oh, you know us. Smooth is rough, and rough is smooth," he replied before shaking the machine and giving it a kick. "Come on, you piece of crap!"

Noah placed a hand on his shoulder. "Ray. It's fine. I'll get one later."

"No. The damn thing took our money. Hey, miss!" he hollered down the hallway to a nurse. "You think you can get someone to open this up? It ate our change and never spat out the coffee."

The young woman looked perplexed.

"Ray. Leave it." Noah waved off the nurse and pulled him away but not before his brother gave the machine a good kick.

"Piece of crap!"

"What the hell has gotten into you? It's just coffee."

"It's not just coffee. It's money. I'm tired of people ripping me off and taking every dime." He forged ahead and Noah regarded him, wondering what else he was dealing with to cause such an outburst. They took the stairs down to the bowels of the hospital, passing staff on the way. The hustle and bustle of doctors, nurses and other medical professionals filled his ears. Machines were beeping and hurried footsteps echoed as patients were wheeled past on gurneys.

Eventually they made it to the medical examiner's office, located at the far end of the hallway. Pushing in, they were hit with a wave of cold air from an overhead air conditioning unit as the sterile and refrigerated environment made itself known. The walls were lined with stainless steel cabinets, and the air was thick with the aroma of disinfectant and formaldehyde.

At the center of the room was a large steel table surrounded by a variety of medical instruments and tools. Above that, a huge bright light illuminated the space with a clinical intensity. Noah scanned the cabinets. Rows upon rows of refrigerated drawers lined the walls. Each one held a body that had been brought in for examination. It was a sobering sight to say the least.

"What the heck…where's Burt?" Ray asked, sounding confused.

A woman glanced over her shoulder and placed a finger up to the Bluetooth tech in her ear. "Hold on a second, Darla." She raised her eyebrows, addressing Ray. "Can I help you?"

He shrugged. "Burt? Where is he?"

"Retired two weeks ago."

"You know when the new M.E. arrives?"

"You're looking at her." Once again, she tapped her right ear. "I have to go, Darla. I'll call you back."

She turned, tapping a tablet in her hand. There was something unique and eccentric to her personality, from her red hair sticking up like a troll doll's to her brightly colored lab coat covered in cartoon characters. She had the front breast pocket adorned with a collection of quirky pins and neon brooches that conveyed her love of the '80s.

"The name's Dr. Adelaide Chambers. Though call me Addie. Most do."

Noah extended a hand as Ray gawked. "I'm from State. Noah Sutherland."

"I know who you are," she said, holding his hand for an uncomfortable amount of time. "Followed the case here in town. Sorry about your brother." She took a deep breath and stepped back. "So they convinced you to return?"

"Something like that."

"Sucker for punishment. Just like me," she added with a smile before threading her way between the two of them over to the examination table where the victim was hidden below a white cover. She pulled back the sheet to reveal the pale-skinned woman with stitching down her chest where a preliminary examination had been performed.

"So, what were you able to find out?" Ray asked, placing one hand on his duty belt.

Addie handed over the tablet to Noah with the digital pathology report.

"Well, she didn't drown. She was dead before her body hit the water. The lungs were clear. No fluid inside so she wasn't breathing when she went in. The shot to the chest went straight through the heart and out the back. It was taken from close range. No bullet was in her but it's more than likely a .40. I figured from the lividity I would be able to determine if she was tied up after death, you know, if someone had killed her then tied her up to make it look like it was a suicide, however, based on the deterioration of the skin it's hard to know. It could have been either."

"So you think it's possible she shot herself?" Ray asked.

"Was a canoe, kayak or any other empty boat found nearby?"

"No."

"Then it's possible." She mimicked what the woman could have done by holding her hand up to her own chest as if she was wielding a gun. "But as there weren't any powder traces on the hands because of the deterioration and being in the water..." She trailed off, her gaze washing over the woman. "Who knows."

"How long was she in?" Noah asked.

"Estimation. Between four and seven days. There were no traces of skin or hair on the rope, however there was some red fiber twisted into it. It was barely visible. It doesn't match her clothing but it could have come from her vehicle, home or wherever she was when she died. If you had something to match it to, that might give you a lead. We won't have the toxicology report back for a while."

"Fingerprints?" Noah asked.

She pointed to the tablet. "A week makes it hard as the skin wrinkles badly, but I did take them. You can check the system for a match. If it comes up empty, you would have to expand it to state level and then national level."

The M.E. was alluding to the fact that even if the woman hadn't committed a crime, her prints might exist with the FBI if she had ever enlisted in the military, or had prints taken for licensing, security clearance or some kind of civil service employment.

"And dental records?"

"I can provide you with the mold. If you check dental places in the area, you might get a hit. Alternatively you might be able to see who she is through DNA using a hair shaft, but I expect it would be faster to match dental records if she's local."

"And has a dentist," Ray added.

Addie lifted the lips to show them. "For a woman with teeth in this shape. I'd say she has one."

Noah nodded as he stared at the victim. It might take a while but at least it was something.

"Anything else?" Noah asked.

Addie pulled the sheet back a little further. "She has a tattoo on the back side of her wrist." The two of them leaned forward. In calligraphy was the word SONNY.

"A possible lover, ex-boyfriend or husband?" Ray said, spitting ideas.

"Talking of husbands. The wedding band on her finger. Any engraving?" Noah asked.

"None. One other thing I should mention." Addie rolled the woman onto her side. "These slightly faded marks were obtained a few days before death. Now either the person who killed her or someone close to her put her through a lot of pain."

"Or she was into BDSM," Ray added.

Noah scrolled through the report to see a close-up of each of the marks. It almost looked like a whip had been used.

"Looks like you have your work cut out for you," Addie said as Noah handed back the tablet.

"Thanks."

"No problem. Oh, and one last thing," she said, turning back to them. "She was pregnant."

They left the hospital that morning with more questions than answers. While they could expedite getting dental records, and search databases for prints, toxicology would take much longer to get back.

"Thoughts?" Ray asked as they headed back to their vehicles.

"Where do you begin? If she wanted to off herself, why go to all that trouble with the rope if you had a gun? Most of the suicides we've been called out to involving firearms are either at home or at a cheap motel. Somewhere they can be found."

"Maybe she didn't want to be found," Ray said.

Noah contemplated his answer. "Or... someone wanted it to look that way."

Ray got this faraway look in his eyes, he slowed his pace. "Hey, uh, this is probably a bad time to mention this but you've got to come to Thanksgiving dinner this week."

"Of course," Noah replied.

"At pop's."

Noah glanced at him as they continued walking down the corridor toward the exit. Ray continued. "I know what you're going to say but I think it's best."

"Ray, you act like I'm avoiding him."

"Does he know you're back?"

Noah's lip curled. "I wanted to get myself settled before I told him."

Ray rolled his eyes. "Yeah, well, I'd say you're settled. Our father is a smart man. He'll find out soon enough if he doesn't know already."

"All right," Noah replied, pushing his way out into the bright afternoon sun. "I'll be there."

5

Saturday, November 19, 2:35 p.m.

A hard sun flooded the once serene lake, casting a warm glow across its rippling surface. But peace was far from sight with the presence of police cruisers and the forensic team. They were decked out in white hazmat suits and carrying an array of equipment around the lake. Uniformed officers secured the area, trying to prevent anyone from getting close — a feat that was virtually impossible due to the size of the lake.

In less than one day, High Peaks Lake had turned into a circus, attracting the curious, the oddballs, and the morbid vying for a glimpse or the opportunity for internet fame. The media had already caught wind of the death, and a fleet of vans and a slew of reporters from different news organizations had descended upon the scene.

Many were close to the yellow tape, pushing their luck with cameras and microphones at the ready. They jostled for position, trying to get the best shot or a soundbite from anyone willing to talk.

It was crazy.

Drawn back to the marina that afternoon, Noah wanted to see if the divers or officers searching had located any further evidence. With the lake falling into county jurisdiction as well as the town, it was no surprise to see Adirondack County sheriff's deputies on site.

Noah smiled upon arrival at the sight of a familiar face.

He parked, climbed out and crossed the lot, working his way through the crowd.

She had her back turned to him and was addressing a cluster of reporters who were swarming her for a quick soundbite.

"And your name was?" a reporter asked.

"Deputy Thorne," she replied before Noah was quick to add, "Be sure to include an E on that surname. Causes all manner of problems."

Callie turned and a broad smile emerged. "Excuse me," she said to the media. As she made her way out, local PD officers stepped in and instructed the media to move back.

Noah stuck his hands in his long tweed jacket. "Didn't they tell you at the academy about rule number nine?"

"And that would be?" she asked.

"Never talk to media."

"Is that so? And what are the other eight rules before that?"

"I haven't the foggiest," he said with a grin. "How you doing, Callie?"

"Better for seeing you. I thought you weren't coming back until early next year."

"My lieutenant fast-tracked things. Seems they're desperate for boots on the ground up here."

He extended a hand but she bypassed it and gave him a hug.

"Couldn't have arrived at a better, or let's say a worse time," she said, pulling away and glancing over her shoulder.

He nodded. "I know, I was here last night when they brought the victim out."

"Explains why local PD didn't contact us until after."

"Wasn't much that could be done. It was pitch dark out there." He glanced off toward the crowd. "So, what's the deal with the group?"

"Oh, them. Yeah, this has really drawn the oddballs out of the woodwork. That couple over there, the ones performing what looks like an EVP, they are—"

"EV... what?" he asked, cutting her off.

"Electronic voice phenomena. It's a paranormal group. They think they can pick up on the dead with tools that look more suited for finding studs in a drywall than a ghost."

He chuckled as she continued. "Then of course we have social media influencers looking to capture the action for likes and follows. I swear, social websites and apps have become the home for the mentally disturbed."

"And them?" Noah pointed to a cluster of people who had attached a map on the side of a van and were drawing red circles while they sipped on lattes.

"Those are your armchair detectives."

"Doesn't that mean they try to solve a case from home?"

"Oh, well, yes but things have changed, Noah. Evolved. Progressed. We aren't supposed to call them that anymore. Citizen detectives, I think is what they prefer. Terminology is everything nowadays, otherwise folks get all offended."

"Isn't that the truth." Their laughter waned as they walked toward the dock, considering the task ahead. "So have they found anything interesting?"

"Not so far. It's a big lake, right? Without knowing where she went in and now with the body out, I'm not sure they will drag the lake. A dive team is focusing on the area below Pulpit Rock though the body could have drifted there from its original entry point."

He squinted to the outcropping. "That cliff is a good 65 feet up. It certainly would have made the most logical place to dump a body along here if they didn't bring her out in a boat... but... reaching it..." he trailed off.

"Difficult. Yes," Callie said, cupping a hand over her eyes to block the glare of sunshine. "You ever leaped from it?"

He nodded. "A long time ago."

Pulpit Rock was a popular landmark for cliff jumping. Way back when Noah was a kid, he and many other teens looking to test their bravery and courage had taken their turn jumping off the heart-stopping spot. It stood tall and imposing, jutting out over the shimmering lake. For years, teens and twenty-somethings had been daring each other to leap from it, prove their mettle and earn bragging rights. Few did it once. Even less tried a second time. Those that didn't jump from the top did it from a few feet lower down.

Most used a kayak or motorized boat to reach the area. They would anchor it at the bottom and climb up the west-facing wall. As one who could attest to the magnitude of taking the leap, Noah knew it was anything but easy. The climb alone was treacherous. Some opted to go through the dense underbrush at the top but finding the exact spot was harder than it looked, as there were no trails.

Then, reaching the top, that's when the fear really took hold. Noah recalled his heart pounding with a mixture of excitement and terror. The sight of dark water far below was enough to make his knees wobble. The surface seemed impossibly far away, and the rocks that lined the shore or hid beneath the depths were like razor blades waiting to slice skin.

But still, there was something about it that continued to

draw teenagers back year after year. A sense of camaraderie and adventure, one chance to prove you were fearless. He'd leaped from it six times, and never once could he say it was easy, but it had left him with a sense of triumph and elation.

The location had seen its fair share of accidents. The cliff held more risk than guaranteed success. One wrong step and the consequences were dire. And out there, if you were alone, no one would hear you scream.

"Is it as scary as people say?" she asked.

"One hundred percent," he said as he focused on the top. "Any officers been up there?"

"Not that I know of. The focus is on the lake and areas that are more accessible. Waterfront properties on the west side and so on."

"Come on then," he said, turning back toward the Bronco.

"What?"

"Let's check it out."

"I... uh... should probably get this squared away with my sergeant. I'm meant to be securing the scene."

He turned, smiling. "You are. Just elsewhere."

"Noah, it's not like last time."

He waved her off. "Just tell them I've asked for your assistance."

"You know we have a new detective."

"Good. I'd like to meet them when they show up."

She pursed her lips with a smile and got on her radio to update the powers that be. Noah had her hop into his vehicle instead of taking a cruiser.

~

FIVE MINUTES LATER, as the Bronco weaved down a narrow road, hugging the lake, Callie chimed in. "You know you can't get close to that cliff by vehicle."

"Uh-huh."

"Which means the chances of them bringing her up this way would be slim."

She wasn't far wrong, there were only two roads that came close to the area: Mount Whitney Way and Ruisseaumont Way that looped around inside the forest area where a few waterfront properties lined the shore. The difficulty came with the hilly terrain. To reach the edge of Pulpit Rock from the top required traversing the Saranac Lakes Wild Forest that surrounded Mount Whitney and butted up against the Sentinel Range Wilderness. Vehicles could only go so far; the rest of the way required a hike.

"I know. But who's to say anyone brought her here?"

Callie regarded him through skeptical eyes. "You're buying the suicide theory?"

"No. But it hasn't been ruled out either."

As the sun filtered through the trees on the crisp fall afternoon, Noah pulled the Bronco up to the end of a quiet country road. Trees loomed overhead, casting long shadows across a pathway that disappeared into the dense forest.

He exchanged a quick glance with Callie before pushing out of the vehicle.

"I hope you know where you're going," she said.

"Oh, these were my old stomping grounds. You don't forget."

"Has much changed?"

"These homes weren't here," he said, pointing to some of the million-dollar waterfront properties nestled in the woodland and set back from the lake.

With the season in fall, the forest had transformed into a breathtaking display of color. The once sea of green had burst into a riot of red, gold and orange. As they trekked through, their feet rustled the carpet of fallen leaves and pine needles. A crunching sound accompanied every step.

"So have they managed to elect a sheriff yet?" he asked.

"No. Are you kidding? It's been a couple of months. Things don't move that fast around here," Callie replied, stifling a laugh. "The undersheriff, Avery Rivera, is at the helm. She's the acting sheriff right now. She's not bad actually. Nice to have a woman calling the shots for once."

Noah turned to the hilly terrain full of hardwoods and evergreens; maples, oaks and birches were the most dominating species. The maples were ablaze in shades of scarlet and orange, while the oaks shimmered in deep russet and burgundy. Birches offered a striking contrast with smooth white trunks standing out amid the colorful foliage.

Despite the beauty, they remained vigilant, knowing that the wilderness offered its own set of dangers. Slick leaves, cool temperatures, and a real chance of getting lost, plus hypothermia if they did get lost. Noah took out his phone to check if he was getting a signal. One bar. Not great but it would do if push came to shove.

"How are things with your ex?" he asked.

Callie groaned. "Ugh. It took a lot of arm-twisting and the heavy hand of my lawyer but it's all signed off. Feels nice to start a new chapter. What about you? Are you staying with Ed?"

He chuckled. "Ed? I would never sleep. Him and his fitness regime, and his mad theories. No, I opted for my aunt's until I find a place."

"Any luck so far?"

He paused for a second or two. "I have received one tempting offer."

"Where?"

"Are you familiar with that five-million-dollar home that's

been on the market for a year? Over on the north side. The one with red accents."

She stopped walking and cocked her head.

He turned and she shoved him. "Get out of here!"

"No. I'm serious. Someone's offered it to me."

"To do what? Be their pool boy?"

He laughed. "That's the thing, I don't know."

She sidled up beside him. "Well, you've got to take it. It's incredible. You are taking it, right?"

"Haven't decided yet."

"But you will?"

"Haven't decided yet."

"C'mon, Noah. If anyone offered me that, I would be there faster than a New York minute."

"That's what I think they expect." He stopped and swiped a hand across his forehead, wiping sweat away. The first twenty minutes were easy, but soon their breathing became labored as they climbed uphill over fallen trees and boulders, each step becoming more treacherous than the last. As they moved further into the forest, the underbrush became thick, and their pace slowed. "I mean, who offers a stranger free rent in a home that only a small percentage of society could ever afford without strings attached?"

"Who cares?"

"I do."

She narrowed her eyes. "Someone with more money than sense," she muttered. "Or someone trying to buy you off."

"You hit the nail on the head."

Noah continued to use his phone's compass to keep them on track. Even though he liked to think he remembered the area, twenty years away from his hometown had all but dulled his memory.

Still, it wasn't long before they arrived.

As they approached the cliff-jumping spot and could hear police divers yelling, his heart pounded in his chest, his legs ached with each step. Callie's face was flushed with exertion, and her breathing was ragged as she tried to keep up. "I'm telling you, Noah. There's no way someone carried or dragged a body through here."

"Unless they had help," he replied, glancing back. "Or had a reason to be here."

A minute or two later, Noah stopped abruptly, cocking his head and raising a hand. "Shhh!"

"What is it?"

A distant sound pierced the stillness — the unmistakable barking of dogs. At first, it was faint, barely audible over the lapping of water and rustling of leaves, but without them moving, the barking grew louder.

"It's just people walking their dogs," Callie said.

"Exactly."

She frowned. "You think our vic was walking her dog here?"

He continued on. "Perhaps. It's out of sight. A good mile from the nearest home. No one is going to bat an ear to a gun going off, let alone a scream."

"That is, if she was killed here," Callie added.

As they hiked toward the edge of the cliff, their gaze was fixed on the view before them. High Peaks Lake sparkled in the afternoon sun. Far below they could see a group of divers in full gear searching the water, while a few officers remained on a motorized boat. The divers slowly and methodically scoured the depths, searching for a gun or if they were lucky, the bullet that had killed the woman.

Callie unintentionally kicked a few loose stones. They went over the edge down into the water below. Divers that surfaced glanced up; they exchanged gestures before disappearing in again.

Turning away, Noah and Callie began to search the surrounding area for evidence that might suggest the woman had been dumped from that spot. As they combed nearby boulders and bushes, they panted for breath. Callie's radio crackled to life with updates from the dive team in the water.

So far nothing had been found.

Undeterred, they moved through the forest with a sense of urgency, their gaze focused on the ground, branches and underbrush. The forest was dense and overgrown, making it hard, but it was clear others had been there, maybe climbing up to the top to jump. Footprints, discarded food wrappers, a few cigarette butts. Noah snapped on blue latex gloves and bagged whatever he could find. Callie took photos. While it might offer a clue of what transpired and eventually form a picture of the woman's final moments, that alone wouldn't be enough.

Every time an investigation started, Noah felt like he was entering chaos and had a job of creating order and a clear picture.

They continued to work in silence.

They were out there for over forty minutes, moving back and forth, until Callie spotted something out the corner of her eye — a hint of red against the green forest floor. "Noah!"

He charged across to find a dog leash and collar tangled up in the thicket of brambles. The brush was pressed down as if there had been a struggle, as if someone of a significant size had fallen there. He scanned and noted several droplets of blood on the underbrush and leaves. Nearby, a bullet casing. Noah bagged it all, noticing what he could only imagine were blonde dog hairs wrapped tightly around several sections of the leash, and caught in the collar.

Excitement didn't surge through him like it might a new officer. In the past he'd seen found items lead to nothing, but still, with the faint sound of dogs deeper in the woods, he couldn't help but wonder if the two were connected.

With renewed energy, the two of them set off, determined to pursue the sound of the bark, if only to rule out that the owner hadn't lost a dog or misplaced a leash. Connecting the leash to their missing person would have been nothing more than assumption, an attempt to bend the narrative to support it.

6

Saturday, November 19, 5:10 p.m.

The interaction with those in the forest only confirmed that people frequented the area to walk their dogs. No animals were missing. No one had lost a leash. With evidence needing to be returned and a chance for Noah to meet the new detective for the county, they returned to the office later that afternoon.

It was strange to step back into the Adirondack County Sheriff's Office after all that had transpired months ago. A heavy heart from the loss of Luke was replaced by the knowledge of those who had been brought to justice and the warm welcome from those at the office.

"Do I need to get my specs replaced or is that really you, Noah Sutherland?"

She grinned. The familiar sight of Maisie Callaway, the receptionist at the front desk, garnered a smile. To those who worked there, she was a mother figure and source of comfort and support, far beyond the assistance she offered.

Having worked there for over thirty years, she'd seen it all. She had witnessed young and old officers come and go, and had offered a listening ear or a word of encouragement to those who needed it.

In many ways she was the face of the Sheriff's Office. When the public walked through the doors, Maisie was the first one they saw. Her disarming smile and friendly demeanor made even the most pissed-off local feel at home.

Despite her age, she was as sharp as a tack, and always seemed to know what was happening in the office. Her desk was a hub of activity. Younger officers would often be found chatting with her or asking for her two cents on an incident.

She was more than a receptionist.

"How are you, Maisie?"

"Depends what time you ask." She grinned as she hit a button under the desk. There was a loud buzz as the heavy door unlocked and they entered.

She was quick to slide off her stool and envelop Noah in a warm hug, the kind that only a mother or grandmother could give. Although short of stature, she still stood tall and proud, with a wiry frame and sharp features that belied her years. Her curly short hair was a silver-grey and styled in a bob that framed a face lined with wrinkles and creases earned from a lifetime of experience. There was a mischievous glint to her eye and a playful spirit beneath her calm exterior.

She stood back from Noah, smiling broadly. "Please tell me they hired you."

"Unfortunately, no, he's still riding the fence over at B Troop," Callie replied.

"And there was me thinking you were here to take Rivera's position."

"Not today," he replied.

"But one day," Maisie said, gripping his arm tightly as her eyes lit up.

"You've been listening to Hugh again, haven't you?"

She laughed while returning to her seat. "He comes in from time to time to shoot the breeze."

"And toss in his two cents."

"Of course," she replied.

As they moved through the active office, Noah noticed the buzzing energy. Deputies moved quickly, radios crackled, and some darted in and out of rooms. A few phones were ringing, keyboards clicked as reports were typed up and filed away. There was constant chatter as deputies discussed run-of-the-mill incidents and coordinated efforts. The smell of coffee wafted through the air; the fuel of choice that kept them charged throughout long twelve-hour shifts. Passing the break room, Noah heard the microwave ding; the aroma of someone's dinner made his stomach grumble.

The atmosphere was one of organized chaos, as the continued day-to-day strain bore down on deputies striving to maintain order and justice in the community. The sights, sounds and smells of the office were similar to his department, which was located just off Route 86 and sandwiched between High Peaks and Saranac Lake. But his location was one big revolving door as troopers and State officials came and went.

The door opened to the sheriff's office and Avery Rivera stuck her head out. Noah had yet to meet her.

"Thorne. When you have a moment. I would like to see you in my office."

Callie nodded.

Rivera caught Noah's eye; she stepped out to greet him with a smile. "Ah, Mr. Sutherland. We haven't had a chance to meet. I'm the acting sheriff, Avery Rivera."

Without knowing her, it was hard to overlook her physical attributes. She was an attractive Hispanic American with striking features that reflected a blend of cultures. Her dark, expressive eyes were framed by thick lashes and a warm olive complexion that radiated health and vitality, or one too many trips to a tanning salon.

Her long, silky, wavy dark hair was pinned up. Her body was curvaceous with a narrow waist. For a second, he forgot to breathe.

"Mr. Sutherland?"

"Uh. Yes." Noah extended a hand and immediately could tell from her grip that beauty wasn't the reason why she had the position. It was firm, self-assured. She carried herself with a sense of confidence and grace, yet he could sense a hint of fiery spirit that was only tempered by love for family and a strong sense of community. "It's a pleasure."

Still holding his hand, she looked a little confused. "Are you just visiting?"

"Assisting."

"Really? I'm unaware of the office calling for State assistance. Did...?" she said, trailing off and glancing at Callie.

"No. Local PD did," Noah said quickly.

"Ah. Right." She smiled. "Yes, the lake crosses into their jurisdiction. It looks as if we will be working together on this one. Though I have to say it seems a little premature to be requesting State's assistance when we still haven't identified the victim."

"That's a conversation you'd need to have with the chief of police in High Peaks."

"I will. In the meantime, we're certainly grateful for any help."

She released his hand, turned and went back into her office.

Callie hollered to another deputy and had them take the evidence, tag it and book it in. "Well, I should..." Before Callie could finish what she was saying, they were startled by a rowdy noise. They turned to see two men enter the lobby. One was short, a burly man with a scraggly beard. The one behind him was bald with a ginger goatee.

"I did nothing wrong!" the burly man cried, his voice echoing through the room as he was pushed toward the front desk. "You've got the wrong guy."

"Aye, just keep moving before I put you on your ass," the second man said firmly and aggressively in a Scottish accent, but with a hint of playful humor.

"Who's that?" Noah asked.

Callie smiled with amusement. "That's our detective."

Despite his small stature, the man had a wiry strength and quickness to his movement. He was in his early fifties but moved with the agility of a younger man. He was sporting a drab grey suit with a red tie. His shoes were polished to a high shine and from all the pushing back and forth, Noah noticed his socks peeking out were mismatched, a bright plaid.

"Settle down, sir," the detective hollered. "You're making a fool of yourself."

The suspect didn't hear him or refused to listen. He shouted and pulled away; his face red with anger.

The struggle only intensified as the larger man pushed back.

"Stop resisting!"

Several bystanders waiting in the lobby glanced over in alarm, but quickly looked away as Noah swung the door open and charged in to help.

"Ah, I don't need help, lad, I've got this."

Noah chuckled, hearing his thick Scottish accent. "Looks like it," Noah said, helping him bring the guy to the front desk to book him in.

The suspect let loose with multiple curse words and then followed up with, "I can't understand a D-damn word he's saying," he said with a stutter. "And I don't think he U-understands me either. Can you tell him I haven't done anything wrong?"

"What's he here for?" Noah asked.

The detective regarded Noah. "Not that I need to explain to you, but dog theft."

"I didn't steal any dogs. I keep telling you that."

"Oh no, so those mutts in the back of your van are yours? You're a dog walker, is that it?" He roared with laughter. "You must think I'm an idiot. You can explain this to a judge on Monday. Until then you can think about changing your story in the comfort of our county jail. We'll book him in, Maisie, on theft."

"I didn't steal. I keep telling you that."

"You sure do," he said before calling for another deputy to take over so he could straighten out his suit which was now a crumpled mess.

"Noah Sutherland. State investigator." He extended a hand.

"Angus McKenzie. But folks call me Gus." He looked down at his clothes. "Damn, idiot ripped my shirt. I'm going to bill you for that," he shouted over Noah's shoulder.

"Bill me for this!" the guy replied, sticking up two fingers while his wrists were cuffed and he was hauled away by a deputy.

Noah laughed. "Uh, some things never change."

"Nope. No they don't."

"I don't recall seeing you here a few months back," Noah said.

"That's because I was working in the Big Apple. We got word they were needing a detective up here to deal with all the crap. So far, the only crap I've dealt with is folks like that moron." He pushed through into the office. "Meant to retire in five years, this was supposed to be a sweet gig. I'm starting to think I might take that early package."

Callie cracked a joke about all that package containing was coupons to the local Piggly Wiggly, a grocery chain store.

"Aye, I expect so. But hey, at least I can take you out, sweetheart." He winked at her.

She laughed. "In your dreams, McKenzie."

"Aye, a man can dream."

Callie excused herself to go speak with the sheriff while Noah followed the Scotsman as he stormed into the break room to get himself a coffee.

His face immediately darkened with anger as he noticed there were no more capsules for the coffee maker. He let out a frustrated growl and slammed his iron fist down on the counter, causing a spoon to fall and clatter on the floor.

"What is this, a game?!" He charged to the doorway where he shouted out to no one in particular but seemingly addressed the entire office at once. "Where the hell is all the coffee?" he demanded to know, his accent becoming thick as his annoyance grew. "I can't work in this shit hole without my evening cupper."

Noah observed him with curious amusement.

He'd worked with all types over the years. Hard-nosed guys who hardly ever broke a smile, jokers who saw their shift as nothing more than preparation for a future career as a stand-up comedian, through to those who walked the line, nervous that one mistake would be their last.

But this fella. He was a wild card.

McKenzie clenched his fists at his sides and returned to the coffee maker. "In my day they used to have coffee vending machines. It might have squirted out sludge but in all my years I never saw them run out. This. This right here, is government cutbacks. Why pay for a machine when you can get this cheap piece of Chinese crap! This is unacceptable." He went to the doorway again, as if expecting someone to rush in with the solution. "I'm paid to solve crimes. That requires a proper caffeine boost. Where do I get that now?"

"The local café," Maisie said.

"On my salary?"

She shrugged.

"You know how much they charge?" He grumbled, returning to search the cabinets, and letting out a string of curses that would make a sailor blush. He finally fished out a dirty-looking tea bag that someone had already used and plopped it in a cup. He turned on the kettle and retreated to a table where there were a few chairs and slumped down with a defeated sigh, realizing that he'd have to make do with weak seconds.

Noah exchanged a look with Maisie who lifted her eyebrows and stifled a laugh before he turned to the Scottish detective who was fuming.

Noah figured he would throw fuel on the fire of his foul mood. "I didn't see you last night down at the dock."

"No, because that would require local PD doing their job and picking up the phone."

"So, you'll be tackling the case?"

"Haven't been assigned it."

"But when you are?"

McKenzie got up as the kettle reached boiling point, a smile dancing. "When, when, when. That's an interesting word, sums up this place quite nicely. When will I be asked to help? When will I have answers to another crime? When will there be a report on my desk?" He raised his voice, yelling toward the door. "I'll tell you when... when you stock the bloody coffee box!"

Noah figured he wasn't going to get much more from him while he was feeling short-changed so he queried him about the guy he'd brought in.

"The suspect you brought in. What's the deal there?"

"A woman in the community asked us to look into her dogs being taken. As if we don't have enough on our plate. Anyway, I get a report of someone acting suspicious around a local park. I headed out there expecting to find you know, some pervert spying on single mothers, only to find out that he'd apparently taken off with someone's dog. I drove around for a while and ended up finding the little rascal walking three dogs in some field over on the south side. He said he hadn't stolen them. That he came across them without any owner and planned to drop them off at the shelter in town." McKenzie threw up his fingers, creating quote signs in the air. "That he was just 'giving them a walk' before he did that. Anyway, I was able to confirm one of the dogs inside belonged to a couple back at the park. They'd taken their eyes off the dog for but a second and turned around and it was gone. So you do the math. I figure the other two are someone else's, perhaps the woman who phoned in."

"Have you called the shelter to confirm his story?"

"Aye, you're a pushy little bastard, aren't you? I just got in the door." He took out a pack of smokes and tapped one out.

"Um," Noah pointed to the wall to where a No Smoking sign was.

He pulled a face. "I wasn't going to light it. It just eases my nerves. I haven't lit one in two years."

Noah raised an eyebrow. "I'd like to speak with this guy. We found a leash and dog collar out near Pulpit Rock. I'm curious to know if he's ever been out that way."

"Knock your socks off. Just know he's not all there. If you get my drift."

"Right," Noah replied before heading out.

On his way over to the county jail that was on the same property as the Sheriff's Office, his phone lit up. The caller ID was Lena. She was the only one that knew, other than Maddie, Ray and Aunt Gretchen, that he was back in town. He tapped accept, passing a few deputies on the way out. Their eyes lit up and they patted him on the arm as if he'd done them a huge favor.

"Lena. You good?"

"I'm fine."

"The kids?"

"They're well. I was hoping you might help."

"If you want the skinny on who the victim is, they haven't identified her yet."

"No, I'm not working on that."

That took him off guard, he expected her to be all over that. "You're not? Everything okay?"

"Fine. Maggie assigned someone else. No, I was wondering if you could ask Ray and County if they've had any reports of dog thefts in the past month. I've already tried to get the information but I'm not exactly the most popular person over there with the articles I've put out."

He snorted. "I heard. Why?"

"You know why."

"No, I meant why do you want to know about the thefts?"

"Well, I had a woman phone me today. She said she wasn't making much headway with police regarding her two missing French bulldogs."

Noah stepped outside and saw two officers assisting with the removal of dogs from the back of a blue van. They were small.

"You got a description on them?"

"I can send over a photo."

"Go ahead."

"Now?"

"Yeah, Lena."

"Hold up a second," Noah said to the deputies. The timing seemed too good to be true and the odds were low as French bulldogs were a common target for thieves. A second or two later, his phone dinged.

"You got that?"

"One second." He opened his inbox and pulled up the photos with descriptive details. He held up his phone and compared them to the dogs in the back. "Well, I'll be damned. Hey Zeus. Penelope." The pups' heads turned. "Looks like you've lucked out. We've got them."

She was all surprised. "What? You do?"

"Yep, and the guy who took them. Have her come down to County. I'll be here."

7

Saturday, November 19, 5:40 p.m.

Adirondack County's 120-cell jail was adjacent to the County Public Safety Building, which housed the Office of Emergency Services, County Sheriff patrol and civil offices, an enhanced 911 center and even Troop D State Police. The jail, which had at one time been located in Elizabethtown, was overseen by seven sergeants and fifty-six correctional officers.

Noah tracked down the deputy who had completed the booking and had him bring the suspect over to the sallyport which was a special garage where inmates entered and completed processing. The new inmate had just finished up getting showered and changing into orange jail clothes and flip flops when Noah arrived.

"You think I can talk with him?"

"We weren't done processing," the deputy replied.

"A few minutes, that's all."

"You want me to take him back to the station?"

"Is he a danger?"

"Only to himself," the deputy added before chuckling.

The deputy brought him into a holding room where there was a simple desk and two chairs. No one-way mirror. A clock on the wall. Noah didn't sit, he leaned back against the wall, observing the man.

"Aren't I supposed to g... get a lawyer?" he said with a stutter. Noah got a sense he was a little slow.

"Do you need one?"

"Is that a trick question?"

Noah glanced down at the open folder. "Thomas Green. Thirty-two. Never finished high school. Got your GED later in life. You now work as a cleaner at the high school in High Peaks. Father, Gerald Green, deceased. Mother, Abby Green. Your brother is Eric Green, who did a year inside for breaking and entering. You are a resident of Saranac Lake. The owner of a blue Chevy van. Mid '80s. That's old."

"Belonged to my father."

"Custom?"

He shrugged. Noah had noticed how the classic American vehicle that at one time symbolized freedom and adventure stood out from modern vans on the road with its sturdy build. They were often used by families for long road trips. His van had a sleek yet simple design to it, with bulging side windows and a cool zig-zag decal on the side that added a touch of style. Unlike the new ones that were glossy, bold, his was weathered and faded. Noah had peeked inside and nosed around, noticing the plush seats had comfortable cushions. The dashboard was simple yet functional, and it was sporting an old cassette player and radio.

"The rear was stripped," Noah said.

"I had no use for the seats or carpet. I need it for carrying cargo."

"Like dogs you don't own?" He closed the folder and held it by his side.

"I haven't done anything wrong."

"Look, I'm not here to grill you." He crossed the room and took a seat, leaning forward. "I actually might be able to help you."

"And why would you do that?"

"Because I spoke with the shelters in town. Seems your story about dropping off dogs from time-to-time fits."

"I told him I wasn't lying. I don't steal dogs."

"Then why pick them up?"

"Because someone should." He paused, staring at Noah. "I told the other guy but he wouldn't listen."

"Was that before or after you resisted arrest?"

The man avoided answering that. "Have they contacted my mother?"

"I wouldn't know."

"Can you please find out? She's bedridden. I look after her."

"You ever carry anything else in the van?"

He shrugged; his brow knit together. "From time to time."

"You give people rides?"

"No."

"And only you use it?"

"Yeah. Look, if you've spoken to the shelter, why are you asking these questions?"

Noah didn't answer that but continued to pepper him with questions, not just for answers but to see how he would react. Everyone was different under pressure, some would clam up, others would tell you more than they should. Stories changed. Suspects tripped over their own words. "You ever been out to Pulpit Rock?"

"Everyone has."

"I meant through the forest?"

"Of course."

"You ever found a stray or two out there?"

"I want to speak to my mother."

Noah leaned back. "Listen to me, Thomas. I can help you but I need you to help me. Those dogs you had in the van. Where did you find them?"

He rattled off the locations and how he'd stumbled across them without any owners nearby.

"Were you on your way to drop them off when the detective arrested you?"

He nodded.

"The shelter closes at five thirty. I managed to catch them before they shut for the rest of the weekend. What do you do with the dogs you find on the weekends when the shelter is closed?"

He was hesitant to respond but eventually did. "I take them home."

"Any there now?"

He glanced down into his hands, rubbing dark calluses.

"Oh, Thomas?" Noah said, clicking his fingers.

"Three."

"Three?"

"I… I kept hold of three, for a couple of weeks."

Noah narrowed his gaze. "Did you find any of those in the last week over by Pulpit Rock?"

He hesitated. "One."

"What's the color?"

"Golden. It's a retriever. It had been out in the rain for a long time. It was matted. Dirty. Bleeding and hungry. I just wanted to hold on to it and keep it safe until…"

"Until you could drop it off?"

Thomas let out a heavy sigh and nodded.

"So, it was raining the day you found the dog?"

"Um, uh..."

"Why were you out there in the rain?"

"I like to hike."

"Not an easy place to hike. There aren't any trails around there."

"I prefer places out of the way."

"You see anyone else while you were there?"

"No."

"Was the dog wearing a collar?"

"No."

"And you didn't hear anything? See anyone?"

"I just told you. It was just me out there."

"What day did you find the dog?"

"Um." He looked off toward the clock. "Last Wednesday."

Noah was about to ask a few more questions when there was a knock at the door. A deputy stuck his head in.

"I'll just be a minute longer," Noah replied.

"Oh, take your time. Officer Thorne was asking where you were, said there are two women here to see you."

"Right." Noah looked back at Thomas. "We'll continue this later."

"I thought you said you could help?"

"We have to confirm a few things first, Thomas. Trust me. If you haven't done anything wrong, we'll have you out of here ASAP. Excuse me, I need to go," he said, heading out and leaving the deputy to continue processing him. There was a good chance it would all be thrown out on Monday morning but for now he would have to be treated no different than someone stealing property until proven otherwise.

Once Noah made his way back around to the front of the

building and into the Sheriff's Office, he found Lena waiting with a middle-aged Chinese woman.

"Hey," Lena said. "Noah. This is Hannah Chang."

The smaller woman with dark black hair offered a hand.

"Give me a second, we'll bring out the dogs."

A moment later the two pups appeared, carried by Noah and another deputy, and it was clear from the moment they saw the woman that she was the owner. They hurried over, whining and panting. She scooped them up with tears in her eyes, saying their names over and over. A scowl formed. "Is the man who took them in jail?"

"For now."

"For now? He's not going to be released, is he?"

"Did you see him take the dogs?"

Almost at the same time, Lena and Hannah replied.

"No," Hannah said.

"Yes. We have a video," Lena replied, hoping to clarify. She took out her phone and showed him. The first thing Noah noted was there were two people taking dogs and the van wasn't the same. It was a bad recording and certainly didn't offer a good look at the kind of dogs stolen.

"Ma'am, where did you get this video from?" he asked.

Lena was quick to answer that. "She got it from her surveillance."

"Um. That's not exactly true," Hannah said.

Lena offered her a confused expression. "You told me it was from your house?"

"I didn't say that. I just said I had a video of people stealing French bulldogs."

Noah sighed. "Ma'am, where did the video come from?"

"The internet."

Lena rolled her eyes. Hannah picked up on it and defended her actions. "They wouldn't have believed me or taken action if I didn't show them something. Anyway, it doesn't matter. My dogs are back. You have someone in custody."

"It matters a lot. Where were you when your dogs went missing?" Noah asked.

"At my house."

"And your dogs?"

"Out in the yard."

"Was the gate open?"

Hannah stared back.

"Ma'am?"

"He could have taken them from my yard."

"And you live where?"

She reeled off her address. Noah shook his head.

"According to him, he found them at a park miles from there."

"You believe him over me?"

"You're free to go, ma'am. If we need to ask any further questions we'll be in touch."

They waited until she left before he turned to Lena. She was quick to clarify. "Hey look, I'm sorry. I assumed what she gave me was related. If he didn't take those dogs in that video, that means those men are still out there."

"If that video is even from local surveillance. It could be from anywhere. So is this what Maggie has you working?"

"She did. I might have to go back and have another conversation about getting involved with the woman who was pulled from the lake. By the way, any luck with that?"

"You know I can't tell you."

"I'm your ex."

"Exactly. Who works for the media. Once we know more, you'll know more."

"Yeah," she said, chuckling. "What are you doing for Thanksgiving?"

He scratched the side of his face. "I promised Ray I would be at my father's. Would you like to join us?"

"Please. Been there, done that. No thank you." She turned to walk away and looked back at him. "It's good to have you back, Noah. The kids are over the moon."

"And Aiden?"

She smiled, looking off to a cruiser that rolled in. "He's fine with it."

"So have you set a date for the big day?"

"No."

"A long engagement?"

"Haven't decided."

"Not getting cold feet, are you?"

"As if I would tell you. See you around, Noah." She lifted a finger. "Oh, by the way. Ethan was hoping he might see Axel at some point. You think you could arrange a get-together?"

"I'll speak with Kerri."

"He keeps talking about getting a dog but I've told him it may not work for our lifestyle, besides, there's the cost of food, the ongoing vet bills for checkups and then you've got to get them chipped and..."

"You're a genius." Noah wagged his finger at her.

"What?"

He waved her off. "Nothing. I'll catch up with you later."

Noah hurried back into the station to arrange to get a key to Thomas' home in Saranac or have him go with them to collect the three dogs.

"Everything okay?" Callie asked. He brought her up to speed on what he'd learned from Thomas and the conversation with Lena.

~

Thirty minutes later, they pulled up to an old, weathered, single-wide mobile home just off Margaret Street in Saranac. Paint was peeling off the sides and the roof was sagging in the middle. Surrounding the yard was a chain-link fence. From the moment they approached, Noah could hear dogs barking.

Eager to expedite his release from jail, Thomas was more than willing to take them there so they could collect the animals. He inserted a key and the door creaked open, revealing a small, dimly lit interior. A Yorkshire terrier jumped up at Thomas. Not far behind were a bulldog and the golden retriever he'd mentioned.

Once removed, the dogs would be checked for signs of neglect or mistreatment, to make sure they were healthy and well-fed. At a glance they appeared to be in good condition.

"What do you call him?" Noah asked, eyeing the retriever and petting him. The dog responded by licking his hand.

"I haven't given him a name yet. Didn't want to if I was going to take him to the shelter." Thomas kept emphasizing that, as if he wanted to ingrain in their psyche that his motivation was purely to help. Unfortunately, because of his ties to the dog and his confession, they would have to keep him a while longer to ensure he wasn't involved in the disappearance of the woman.

Out of sight but clearly heard, his mother called out. "Thomas?"

"It's me, Mom."

"Who's with you?"

"Just some friends," he said, his voice wavering. He lowered his voice to speak with Noah. "Can I see her before I go back?"

He nodded and walked with him through the cramped single-wide home. One of the things that struck Noah was the musty, damp smell mixed with stale air. The space was small, cluttered, with barely enough room to move around. The tiny kitchenette had a small sink, stove and refrigerator crammed against one another. The cabinets were stained and chipped, and the countertop cluttered with food containers and takeout boxes. The odor of stale food lingered, giving the impression that sanitation wasn't a strong point and that it hadn't been cleaned in a while. The sink had a few unwashed dishes, the trash looked as if it needed to be emptied.

The light above them cast long shadows across the worn linoleum flooring, past a faded couch covered with a threadbare blanket and lumpy, worn cushions. Noah navigated his way past a rickety coffee table that took up most of the space. He eyed a few framed pictures on the walls, old and faded; one had fallen off a hook and was on the floor.

They continued past a small bathroom, with a tiny sink, a toilet and a shower stall that would allow for one person only. The tiles were cracked and stained and there was the faint smell of mildew in the air. Not the best environment for someone that was ill but times were hard for many, and government didn't offer much in the way of health care for those without good insurance.

Further down, they passed a smaller bedroom and another cramped bathroom before arriving at his mother's room which was just big enough to fit a twin-sized bed and a small dresser. The walls sported old '80s style floral wallpaper. The air was stuffy. The bed was covered in worn, mismatched sheets and surrounded by medical equipment and supplies. There was an IV pole to one side, with a big bag of clear liquid hanging from it. Various tubes snaked away to the arms and nose of the woman. She was frail, her eyes open. Her skin was pale and translucent, making her look almost ethereal.

She reached out a gnarled hand.

"Hey Mom," Thomas said.

Noah gave him a moment. He couldn't help but feel pity. His mother was only one of thousands of parents and elderly people throughout the country who suffered in silence and would often slip away without anyone noticing. It made him think of his own father, and the fears he had surrounding him losing his memory. Who would take care of him? At least they were in a better position financially to bring in a caregiver, but someone like Thomas?

He sighed.

Once they collected the dogs and Noah placed Thomas in the back of the cruiser, Callie closed the door and turned.

"Now what?"

"We'll have a vet check the chip in the dog and perhaps that will give us the name of the victim and her address."

"You really think it's hers?"

"Only one way to find out."

8

Sunday, November 20, 7:15 a.m.

Answers were within his grasp but getting them was slow.

Noah was supposed to meet with a local vet later that morning to get the RFID chip in the dog scanned in the hope that it might lead them back to the owner and perhaps put a face to the missing woman.

At least now he had something to latch on to, a guiding light for the next step of the investigation.

As the sun rose over the quiet suburban street across from the museum his mother once worked at, the Bronco bounced over the curb when he pulled into the driveway of Kerri's home. It had been months since he'd last visited. He was eager to catch up with his sister-in-law and see how his niece and nephew were doing.

Noah climbed the front steps and knocked, his pulse racing

with anticipation. Kerri opened the door and greeted him, her face no longer etched with sadness, only relief at a familiar face.

"Noah."

He gave her a big hug. "Hey Kerri." She invited him in and led him into the kitchen, where she had prepared a hearty breakfast of scrambled eggs, bacon and toast. The savory scents made his stomach grumble.

He took a seat.

"Coffee?" she asked.

"Please."

Noah looked around, his eye catching a framed photo of Luke and the family. Better days. He smiled. "Where are the kids? Axel?"

"Oh, they took him for a walk. I figured I would get out all that pent-up energy before he sees you and goes berserk."

"I've missed him."

"I bet." She turned and handed him a coffee, then took a seat. The kitchen was bright and sunny, with large windows that let in the natural morning light. There were even more photos of Luke and the kids on the wall, and a bowl of fruit at the center of the pine table.

"You look well. How have you been?" he asked.

"I have my good days. The others I tend to hide from the kids."

He nodded. Grief was difficult to process. Kerri smiled. "But enough about me. What's happening with you? You've taken on a new position, moved back here. Where are you staying?"

"With Gretchen for a while."

"Ah, I love her. She's done so much for us since the funeral. She takes the kids some weekends, and dropped off meals in the first month."

"Sounds like her." Noah twisted and reached into a leather briefcase. He took out all the paperwork related to the waterfront home and slid it across the table. "You familiar with this property?"

Kerri had been in real estate for so many years, there was very little that escaped her eye. Even if an agent wasn't working for the same company, they were usually aware of homes and businesses on the market, how long they'd been there, and some of the history. What they didn't know usually only required one phone call to find out. She took a sip of her coffee, set the cup down and opened the folder.

Her eyes widened. She glanced at him before continuing to scan the paperwork. "Suzanne Gilford, a broker for Harland and Stafford. I know the group. They only handle high-end properties. Nothing under a million dollars. That's way out of the budget of a police paycheck, Noah."

"You're right. They said it's an LLC that purchased it. Do you know who owns it?"

"No. But with a little digging, I should be able to find out. So many properties are hitting the market at the moment. They come and go pretty quick. Then of course there are those premium ones that barely get any bites because they're priced too high. What's the interest in it?"

"Someone's offered to let me stay there for free. Of course, I would pay for the amenities, gas, electricity, water and so on but..."

"Free?" She clasped her coffee. "That's unheard of."

He nodded, eyeing her.

She glanced back down. "And you said?"

"I had to consider it."

She snorted. "Whoever owns it has more money than sense, that's for sure. A place like that tends to linger on the market because no one has deep enough pockets to pay for it, but even so, there are other options like renting it out. Some folks do that. They're usually relying on the monthly rent to cover the cost."

"Apparently it's all paid for."

"Still, it's cash in the pocket."

"Cash they obviously don't need."

"Then it begs to be asked. What is the need?" she asked. "You know they wouldn't offer you that if there wasn't some kind of ulterior motive."

"That's what I'm trying to find out. At least if I knew who owned it, it might give me a sense of who and the real reason why they were offering it."

"They didn't tell you?"

He gave her the letter that was provided by the realtor. Kerri sat quietly, sipping her coffee and scanning it. She folded it. "An anonymous but generous benefactor who appreciated what you did." She bit down on her lower lip, puzzled. "The question is why? What kind of heat did you take off them? Or what do they think you might do for them?"

"I know."

Kerri handed back the letter. "These things have a way of being turned around. Maybe not today but eventually. One thing I have learned in real estate, Noah, is that the rich aren't rich for giving free rides. They nickel and dime everyone. That's not to say they can't be philanthropists but around here I've yet to see one that didn't benefit on some level from what they gave." She sniffed hard and cast another glance at the paperwork like it was tainted material. "I'll see what I can find out."

"Thank you."

Over the next ten minutes he ate breakfast and chatted about what was new in her world. Then, as they sat in the kitchen, Noah heard the side door opening and the jingle of a leash. Moments later, he caught the familiar padding of paws on the tiled floor, and he knew that Luke's German shepherd, Axel, had returned from his walk.

As soon as he was off the leash, he came tearing into the

kitchen, a ball of fur and excitement. Noah grinned from ear to ear as he reached a hand down and Axel licked him before bouncing around the kitchen like a madman, his tail wagging furiously and hitting the lower cabinets. Axel ran up to Noah again, his wet nose nuzzling into his face. He whined loudly. "I know, buddy. It's good to see you too." Noah laughed as Axel licked at his face, his tail wagging so hard it almost knocked over a nearby chair.

"Axel. Calm down," Kerri said.

The dog's scent filled the room, a combination of wet fur, grass and the fresh air of the outdoors. Noah felt the warmth of the dog's breath on his face as Axel continued to whine and then followed up with barking loudly, overjoyed.

"All right, all right," Kerri said.

Noah glanced over to the doorway where Willow and Austin were standing, their eyes fixed on him. He could only imagine they were again struggling to see him without thinking of their slain father, his twin. He saw a flicker of pain in their gaze, and for a second, they hesitated before coming over and greeting him. Noah rose from his chair and opened his arms to embrace them. A lump formed in his throat. Willow had long blonde hair and was tall in stature. She reached him first, her arms wrapping around his waist tightly. Austin, with his stringy build and quiet demeanor, followed, embracing him with a shy smile.

They were the next generation of Sutherlands, a reminder of the love and legacy of Luke. They were just another reason why he'd returned. He felt a deep sense of responsibility to protect and support them, and even as they pulled away from his embrace, he knew he would do everything he could to keep them safe.

~

Later that quiet Sunday morning, Noah sat in the Bronco outside a local vet's office, feeling anxious about his brother not showing up. He fidgeted for a moment with his phone before calling Ray's number only to be met by a voicemail message each time. Eventually he called Ray's home and got his ex, Tanya.

"Tanya, is Ray there?"

"And hello to you."

"Sorry. Just he's supposed to be meeting me this morning."

He'd never really gotten along with her. The constant back and forth in the relationship between her and Ray was enough to give anyone whiplash. Though he couldn't fault her entirely, Ray wasn't the easiest person to live with and Noah assumed he'd acquired a few skeletons in his closet over the years.

"Well if he hasn't shown up, then more than likely he's still at the casino."

"The Akwesasne Mohawk Casino Resort?"

High Peaks was in the middle of nowhere; the only casino even close to it was in Hogansburg about seventy to seventy-five miles north. A good two hours' drive.

"No. The Ashford Royale. Near Whiteface Mountain Ski Resort. It's a new build. He goes there a lot. I thought he would have told you."

"No."

"Well if you see him, tell him that I'll be at my mother's."

With that said, she hung up. She was clearly fuming.

Whiteface Mountain Ski Resort was a good fifteen minutes northeast of High Peaks, nestled in the valley. It was one of the top ski resorts in the region. For the longest time, High Peaks had fought against having a casino built in the area. People felt it would only bring the small-town atmosphere down and lead to all manner of trouble. But where there were tourists there would always be opportunity for deep-pocketed individuals to profit from it.

About to try Ray's number again, he looked up to see the vet arriving. A white Tesla pulled in and a petite woman in her late thirties with a kind smile got out. She strode over to the small building; a sign above the door indicated that it was the Westside Animal Hospital. The office was a simple brick structure, with a small parking lot out front and a place around back for dogs to run in an enclosed area.

Noah got out and she gave a wave.

"Come on," he said to the golden retriever he'd collected only ten minutes earlier. The one that had been found in the single-wide trailer. Inside he was greeted by the echo of barking dogs and the scent of antiseptic. The waiting room was bright and airy, with large windows that overlooked the street. The walls were lined with posters, ads for pet food and reminders to give them their yearly shots.

"I appreciate you opening today."

"It's all good. Is that our boy?" she asked.

"Yeah."

She crouched and the dog wagged his tail hard. The vet gave him a treat from her pocket and ruffled behind his ears. "This shouldn't take too long. Especially if he doesn't have one. Where was it you said they found him?"

"Out near Pulpit Rock."

"Long way. I have a few clients who go there though."

The vet led them both into an examination room at the back. The room was clean and well-lit, with a steel examination table in the center and tools and supplies on shelves and lining the walls. The vet returned with a small handheld device which was used to scan the dog's microchip between the shoulder blades. "Well, let's see if we have anything."

"What kind of information will that provide?"

"It's not a GPS device. It gives basic details, the company that made the chip and account number. From there, we can get in contact, provide that number and then they usually will contact the owner that they have on file if the dog is lost. That information isn't usually given directly to anyone else or vets but it depends on the situation."

"It won't give you the name of the owner immediately?"

"Oh no. Not that easy. The unique identifier in the chip has to be registered with the national pet recovery database. They prefer to only work with the owners but since this is a police matter, I imagine you could speak with them."

The device beeped, indicating it had found a chip, and the vet quickly pulled up the information on her computer then made a phone call. Noah stood there running his hand over the dog who was panting. A moment later she returned with the phone.

Although it was highly rare that they would give out the information, under the circumstances, the woman on the other end of the line was more than helpful. A quick conversation and he was able to obtain the license number of the breeder, dog's name, gender, date of birth, breed and the owner's address and contact details including a cellphone.

As soon as he heard the name Sonny, it all fit together. The tattoo on the victim was the dog's name.

"Did they give it to you?" she asked.

"Uh, huh. Name and address."

"Good to hear."

"It's registered to an Alexander Hawthorne at this address," he showed the vet.

"Alexander. Huh."

"You know him?"

"He's the rector at the private residential school. High Peaks Academy."

"Is he married?"

"I believe so."

He could only assume that this was his missing wife.

As Noah walked out, he chewed over the information. *High Peaks Academy.* He couldn't recall a private residential school being in the area back when he lived there but that was a good twenty-plus years ago. Then again, he'd attended a public school. Now that he knew who the dog belonged to, he left the animal hospital with a sense of relief that they were no longer searching in the dark.

After returning Sonny to the station, he figured he would swing by the casino.

~

WITHIN HALF A MILE of Whiteface Ski Resort, he could already see the Ashford Casino. The building was truly impressive, with towering columns, a glass façade and glittering lights that beckoned people inside. The sprawling parking lot was packed with cars even on what he would have considered a sleepy Sunday.

After parking the Bronco in one of the many spaces, he approached the entrance, feeling excitement in the air. Laughter and conversation carried on the chilly fall wind as groups of people were milling around outside, bundled up in warm jackets and hats, smoking cigarettes.

Not far away he could see ski gondolas running, and the nearby slopes covered in fresh powder snow. They'd only been open a few days and with the weather so mild, they'd had to resort to using snow guns to jet crystallized water onto the slopes until there was a good dumping of snow.

Stepping inside the warm casino, Noah was taken aback by the opulence of the interior. He gazed around the lobby, staring up at the towering ceiling and gilded chandeliers that sparkled overhead. It was bustling with activity, people chattering, music playing. Slot machines rang out while other players gathered around roulette and card tables. It was grand and luxurious; no expense had been spared.

The atmosphere was one of opportunity and anticipation, the chance to walk away with thousands, even though most would lose. He'd seen places like this. They were rigged, designed to give people a sense that they could win only to pull the rug out from underneath them when they started getting lucky.

Trying to find Ray in there would have been like searching for a needle in a haystack. Noah opted to stroll over to the information center and see if they could be of help. There was a short line of people. As he waited, it felt like an eternity. Getting impatient, and irritated at his brother, he heard his name.

"Noah Sutherland."

Noah turned to see a tall and well-built man in a suit approaching him, flanked by two bouncers. He had a commanding presence. His skin was a deep, rich brown, and his hair jet black, styled neatly and professionally. He wore a sleek and modern navy-blue suit that accentuated his muscular physique, and a patterned silver tie that added a touch of tribal design to his outfit.

Noah noticed heads turn in his direction as he strode confidently toward him. His expression was calm, collected and confident, as if he wore the casino like a second skin.

"I've been looking forward to meeting you," the stranger said.

"Sorry, you are?"

"Gabriel Ironwood. The manager of this establishment."

"Ah, right." Noah extended a hand and felt the authority and pride in the shake. He exuded a sense of respect, and those around him, visitors and staff alike, took notice of his self-assured demeanor. "I'm looking for my brother."

"Ray." He thumbed over his shoulder. "He's in the VIP room. Come, I'll take you there."

As they threaded through the casino, Gabriel continued. "Your brother said you had returned. I must say the county and this town are grateful for what you did. Corruption is a hard thing to weed out, those who seek to cover it up even more so. Do you gamble, Mr. Sutherland?"

"It's never been my thing."

"Well, if you ever change your mind. The house would love to extend to you a thousand dollars. Incentive. Of course."

"Of course. I wasn't aware the city had approved a casino."

"Progress always wins the day. Besides, it's a win-win situation with the ski resort. That place is only open between November and April. This opens up hundreds of jobs and will bring even more wealth into the community."

"As long as that's all it does," he said.

He caught a glint in Gabriel's eye as he opened a door and led him into a VIP room at the back of the casino. His brother was sitting at a large green table, surrounded by other players, most of whom looked like wealthy businessmen. Ray turned, his eyes bloodshot and glazed over, clearly under the influence.

Some might have thought Noah would be embarrassed by his brother's behavior, but he was used to seeing his father in all manner of states growing up. Still, Ray had never struck him as a heavy drinker.

"Oh shit, call the cops!" He laughed aloud then cried out, "Come. Come. Have a seat. Everyone. This is Noah. My little bro. Back to bring justice to all, isn't that right!"

He took a bottle and began pouring two fingers of bourbon into it.

"Ray, c'mon."

"C'mon what?" He continued pouring.

"It's Sunday morning."

"It's Friday evening somewhere," he said. "Hey boys!?"

They chuckled and shook their heads. If he was trying to win their approval, he was failing. "I think you've had enough to drink. Let's go."

"I'm not going anywhere. I'm just getting into a groove. Okay, a few thousand down but I can feel my luck turning." Noah tried to get him to leave. At first, his brother resisted, but Noah kept at it, reminding him of his responsibilities, that others were depending on him. "Ah you're such a buzz kill. Just like Tanya!"

Gabriel regarded them both with amusement.

"Another time, Mr. Sutherland," Gabriel said.

"Always," Ray said, passing him by and swigging some more of his drink. Noah took the glass out of his hand and set it down on the table as he assisted his brother out, his legs almost failing him.

"Remember my offer," Gabriel said. Noah looked back over his shoulder and Ray whispered in his ear.

"How much are they giving you?"

He ignored him.

"C'mon, Noah. What did he offer you?"

"Weren't you supposed to be somewhere this morning?" Noah asked, changing the topic.

"Somewhere?"

"The vet's. The dog. Remember?"

"Oh, I thought Callie or you were handling it."

"You said you wanted to be there."

"Did I?"

Noah grumbled, shaking his head. This was a side of his brother he hadn't seen. When they were younger, he'd watched him go off to parties but he usually saw him in the morning after he'd sobered up. "If you are trying to follow in pop's footsteps, you're doing a good job," Noah said as they headed out into the bright daylight. Ray groaned, shielding his eyes with a forearm.

"Shit, that's bright!"

"Have you been here all night?" Noah asked.

"Time flies when you're having fun, brother."

"Yeah, and so do women. Tanya has gone to her mother's."

"Ah, Tanya is like a yo-yo, she'll come back. Always does."

9

Monday, November 21, 9:20 a.m.

A lead was worth its weight in gold, even if it came to nothing.

Noah's Bronco rumbled down a long, winding driveway flanked on either side by towering trees that dappled the sunlight through a vast array of golden leaves. The dense forest surrounding the historic, elite boarding school — High Peaks Academy — framed the campus and cast a serene yet imposing presence.

Callie was riding shotgun.

As they emerged from the wooded canopy, Noah was greeted by the sight of a vast expanse of meticulously manicured grounds. Rolling lawns stretched out in all directions, dotted with elegant, century-old buildings, each one crafted from red brick and grey stone. The majestic structures, with their ornate carvings and soaring towers, exuded a timeless refinement.

The academy's main building dominated the central quad,

an imposing edifice with multiple wings and grand archways leading to highly polished stone hallways. Its entrance sported tall columns, each one intricately designed. It felt more like a grand European estate than an American school in the middle of the Adirondacks.

Noah drove past multiple dorms, athletic fields and a full-size outdoor swimming pool, the edges softened by carefully tended gardens and lush vegetation. He observed students walking between classes, most in preppy uniforms, a few in casual clothes. Some rode bicycles, others dashed to classes with books in hand. All revealed a sense of shared purpose and drive that came from routine and structure.

As he continued following the winding driveway, the distant sound of bells ringing from the school's chapel echoed across the campus. It was clear from one glance that this was a place steeped in tradition, where history and modernity blended together.

Gravel crunched below the tires as he left asphalt and arrived at the front entrance. He pushed out of the vehicle, soaking in the picture-perfect campus as he downed the remainder of his morning coffee. There was something about the place, something intangible that spoke of the academy's rich heritage — a sense of community that bound the faculty, students and alumni together throughout time.

"You know McKenzie is going to be pissed," Callie remarked.

"I already called him. He said he had a backlog of cases to wade through. Besides, I cleared it with Rivera."

"I thought Ray was assisting?"

"You could say he's a little distracted."

"So why me? There are other deputies who have been with the office longer."

Noah stopped outside, gazing up at the hall.

"You amuse me."

With that he stepped inside.

He couldn't help but feel a sense of natural curiosity and anticipation for what he would learn about the victim. Their footsteps echoed against the stone floors as they meandered down a long hallway following instructions on where to find the rector's office.

"Seriously, Noah, why me?"

"Maybe for the same reason Luke worked with you."

Her eyebrows shot up and the corner of her mouth curled.

"So. Were you ever sent here?" she asked.

"I didn't even know it existed."

The door to the office was already open when they arrived. Conversation flowed out. Alexander Hawthorne's nameplate was on the door, a symbol of his authority and status within the institution. It was made of gleaming gold metal, polished to a mirror-like finish. The engraved name was elegant, with each letter standing out in a sharp black. It read RECTOR HAWTHORNE in bold capital letters, giving off an air of importance and distinction.

Inside, a tall, imposing man in his late fifties, with a full head of salt-and-pepper hair, was holding a stack of folders and inserting them into a filing cabinet.

"Tomlin, Whelan, any further issues, and I will have you expelled, do you understand?" he said to two boys who were standing to attention.

"Yes sir."

Noah rapped the door with his knuckles.

The man turned and they got a better look at him. He was clean-shaven and carried a look of authority. He was dressed impeccably in a brown suit, complete with a white shirt and a navy tie that accentuated his stern appearance.

"Deputy. Everything okay?"

"You mind if we—" Noah said.

"Please, take a seat," he said, directing them to two chairs in front of a large oak desk, then dismissing the two teens. Their heads hung low as they strode passed him. Noah gave them a glance, thinking back to his own education. He would have hated to be stuck in a boarding school.

The room was spacious and well-lit with bookshelves lining the walls from floor to ceiling. Noah extended a hand before taking a seat. Callie remained standing. Hawthorne sank into a comfortable-looking leather chair. His gaze darted between them, his expression remaining stoic. "What brings you here?" he asked in a deep, commanding voice.

Noah cleared his throat and began to explain the situation about the dog, while Callie took out a notepad to take notes. Hawthorne listened attentively, his expression betraying no emotion. When Noah was finished, Hawthorne leaned back in his chair and clasped his hands together.

"I see," he said in a measured tone. "Sonny was originally mine but with work and a change in my personal situation, I was planning on giving him up. A faculty member here offered to take him. I assumed she would have updated his registration."

"The colleague's name?"

"Katherine Evans. She worked here as a residential counselor up until six months ago. She stepped down from her position. Is everything okay?"

Noah stared back at him and the rector's expression changed.

"The woman pulled from the lake. That's her, isn't it?" Hawthorne asked.

"We don't know that yet. Would you have a photograph of Katherine?"

"Yes. Um. Give me a moment." He got up, looking a little washed out in the face. He crossed the room and dug inside one of the filing cabinets. "This is... just... dreadful..." He trailed off, clearly taken aback by the news. A moment later, he pulled out a folder, opened it and handed Noah a school photo. Although the body they pulled out was bloated, the resemblance was clearly there.

"Was that her?" Hawthorne asked.

"Would you happen to have her home address, and a name and number for next of kin?"

"We should." He shook his head, his demeanor shifting to one of worry. "I can't believe this. I was only talking with her a few weeks ago."

"In regards to?"

"Private matters pertaining to the academy." He sighed. "Nicholas will be devastated."

"Her husband?" Noah asked.

He nodded, returning with an address for a home in Keene Valley. Noah tucked the address into his pocket. "How well do you know her husband?"

"Uh. I've met him a few times. Always came across as kind and personable. He's a manager at a bank in town."

"You mentioned Katherine stepped down from her position. Any reason why?"

"Personal choice. You'd have to speak with her but..." He took a deep breath.

Noah looked around. "Did you find a replacement?"

"We did."

Noah eyed some of the pictures of alumni and staff on the walls. "How many faculty members are there?"

"Thirteen and roughly a hundred students."

"Hm. A small group. You know, I grew up in these parts," Noah said, rising from his seat and perusing the room. He glanced at Callie. "I don't ever recall hearing about this place."

"It's not your typical private school. We cater to a very specific kind of individual."

"And that would be?"

"Our students range from twelve to twenty-one years of age. It's coeducational. We mostly focus on those with emotional and learning difficulties that have impacted their ability to perform at home or in public schools."

"Emotional?"

"Students who struggle. There are any number of reasons but mostly it comes down to learning and social needs. We try to take a holistic approach to education, including outdoor-based programs and spirituality to address things such as social trouble, special education, anxiety, lack of motivation, trauma, depression, difficulty conversing with family or peers, ADD and ADHD. We're state approved, of course, and keep our numbers low to ensure we can work closely with individuals. Everyone who is accepted here is usually referred by social services, probation departments or special education agencies." He glanced off to see Callie taking notes, his brow furrowing. "Our staff is comprised of educators, counselors and clinicians who are more than capable of helping these young individuals develop positive, healthy coping strategies as well as improve their behavior and academic results."

"So, Katherine counseled students?"

"Among many things. We work closely with the students and the family as we have found that usually gives us the best success."

"But you cover regular classes?"

"Of course. Writing, math, reading but we also combine that with hiking, skiing, climbing, rope courses, multi-day expeditions. We have wilderness staff that assist with the outdoors. It's been very effective."

"Do you recall any problems... people that Katherine said she was having difficulties with or felt threatened by in the days leading up to her stepping down?"

"None that stand out."

Noah nodded. "Did you have any problems with her as a counselor?"

"None. Trust me when I say that Katherine was by far the best we've had here."

"Well, thank you for your help. If we have any further questions, we'll be in touch," Noah said, rising and shaking his hand again. The firm grip Hawthorne had when they arrived had weakened. He could sense worry.

Leaving the campus that morning, Noah couldn't help but wonder what was the reason behind leaving the job and if there was more to the rector's story.

As they got into the Bronco, Callie asked, "Do you think he's telling the truth?"

"I have no reason to think otherwise. Thoughts?" he asked, leaning against the vehicle on the driver's side as she held the door open on the passenger side.

Callie glanced back at the building. "None right now but I've always had my doubts about private institutions."

KEENE WAS a small town southeast of High Peaks, a speck on the map with just over a thousand people. It sat along the East Branch of the Ausable River and the foothills of Mount Marcy, the mountain with the highest peak in all of the Adirondacks and New York State. The area included the hamlets of Keene, Keene Valley and St. Huberts.

Most locals agreed that Keene Valley had some of the best views of the region, so much so that it was referred to as "The Home of the High Peaks." Noah recalled visiting the area with his school to go climbing. With so much rock and ice on both sides of Route 73, and the famous Beer Walls, it drew in climbers from out of state, and was considered the go-to for avid outdoor enthusiasts.

"Have you seen Alicia since you've returned?" Callie asked, reaching forward and turning up the heat.

Noah adjusted his grip on the steering wheel. "Haven't had the time between searching for a place and work."

"I figured she would put you up."

"How so?"

"Oh, you know, the history you have."

He glanced over as they got nearer the Evans residence.

"What do you know of that?"

"A little. Mostly from what Luke told me."

"You see her around much?"

"From time to time. She's seeing someone."

Noah cut her another glance. "And that would matter to me because...?"

"Oh, I just thought you two were an item." Callie said it as if she didn't care but Noah had a sense she was digging for information.

He chuckled. "Don't let her ever catch you saying that."

The Bronco rolled into a gorgeous property framed by acres of woodland. It had 180-degree views of the highest peaks. The home was mid-century modern with a steel roof and sleek, minimalist architecture that seamlessly blended in with its natural surroundings. From the outside, the front of the home featured clean lines and floor-to-ceiling windows. The exterior was a mixture of natural wood, stone and glass, creating a sense of harmony with the environment.

As they rolled up the driveway, Noah was taken aback. It had a spacious outdoor deck that was perfect for lounging or taking in the views. It was full of comfortable and stylish outdoor furniture and had a stainless-steel BBQ grill for cooking.

"Quite the property," Noah muttered. Still, it faded in comparison to the five-million-dollar abode he'd been offered.

"Puts my place to shame," she said.

Stepping out, Noah glanced off to his right toward lush greenery and towering trees. It all led away down a gently sloping hill toward a shimmering lake.

Noah knocked while Callie walked around the side, speaking into her radio to update dispatch on her whereabouts.

"Noah."

He glanced her way and she motioned for him to follow. He came around and could see a man down near the lake, working away clearing weeds and tossing them into a wheelbarrow. Noah squinted as the light of the day shone in his eyes.

"Morning," Noah said, taking in the sense of peace and serenity that could only be found far from the hustle of city living. The man dumped the long weeds in his arms into the barrel. He cupped a hand over his brow, squinting at them. He was dressed in a faded T-shirt, well-worn jeans and gardening gloves, a change from the suit-and-tie attire that came with the hectic world of finance.

"Mr. Evans."

"Yes?"

"I'm Senior Investigator Noah Sutherland, State Police, and this is Deputy Thorne. Could we speak with you inside?"

"Whatever you need to say, you can say it here."

Noah caught an edge to his voice and nodded. He glanced at Callie who raised her eyebrows. It wasn't uncommon to find folks who were leery of letting police inside their home, let alone speaking with them. Then again, it depended on what they had to hide and what their past history of interactions had been with the law.

"What is this about?" he asked.

"Would you know where your wife, Katherine, is?"

"Your guess is as good as mine."

"You're saying you don't know?"

"I'm saying she never told me." He stared at them both, then scoffed before saying in a quiet voice, as he took off his gloves, "Let me guess. Katherine decided to file some bogus charge against me. Is that it? You know this isn't the first time she's done this — run away — but I didn't think she would go this far."

"No charges have been filed against you, Mr. Evans."

He gave them a confused look. Noah tended to hold back from releasing information because a lot could be gleaned from the reaction of someone before they found out the truth. Some would be quick to tell stories, to come up with alibis on the spot even when he hadn't said a crime had been committed.

"Then what's happened?"

"That's what we were hoping you might tell us," Noah said.

Again, he fed him a line, a last chance to see what he might say.

"She's been gone for five or six days. I assume she is staying with a friend, her mother, or..." He looked away, a painful expression masking his face. "At the shelter." He dropped his chin.

"A shelter?"

"For women. Like I said, this isn't the first time she's left without saying where she was going. Last time it happened, over a year ago, she didn't even tell her parents. Of all places, I found out through her work. I figured she'd done the same again."

"What was the reason for leaving last time?"

"Work stress, loss of someone in the family, and tension in our relationship. Look. Whatever she's told you, take it with a grain of salt because I've never once laid a hand on her. Argue. Sure. We've done that. Who hasn't. But I sure as hell know where to draw the line."

He paused to wipe sweat from his brow and stretch his back.

"And this time?"

"I couldn't tell you. I mean, things were good, as good as they could be between us. Her work. That was another thing entirely."

"And that's why you never filed a missing person report?"

"Why would I? She returned last time. A few months later, but she eventually came home."

Noah glanced across the sparkling lake. "Last time. How long after she left was it before you found out she was at the shelter?"

"Within a day. I got worried. I called her parents. They hadn't seen her. I phoned a few friends. No luck. I then got a call from her work. Alexander Hawthorne told me she was there and she didn't want to see me but she wanted me to know she was safe."

"And this time? You didn't think to call the workplace?"

"Like I said. I figured it was the same." He paused. "Detective, do you know how humiliating it is to call a prestigious school and ask where your wife is because she hasn't come home? Then to find out that she was staying in a women's shelter?" He shook his head. "Even after she came back, it wasn't the same. The way people looked at me. Oh, they might have said they understood but somewhere in the back of their mind, I know they were thinking — did I lay a hand on her? What did I do so terrible that she felt she had to go to a shelter? The truth is, Mr. Sutherland, I don't even know. But one thing I do know, is I didn't lay one finger on her. I never even got up in her face. The only reason she didn't go to her parents was because they would have sent her right back to me. And she wasn't in the frame of mind to be here. I'm not excusing my contribution to her mental decline but I am saying that I wasn't the sole reason why she upped and walked out that door. Yet it was made to look that way because is she really going to blame her job or a loss in the family?" He took a deep breath. "Look, has she told you when she might be back? Given you a number? I tried to contact her cell but never got a response."

"Mr. Evans. You have a dog, yes?"

"Sonny?"

He nodded.

Noah continued. "Your wife never updated the registration."

"Registration? I don't know about that. It was her decision to bring the dog home. I was against it. You know — what with our busy schedule and all."

"You work for the bank in High Peaks."

"That's right. And she..."

"Was at the Academy."

Nicholas nodded, his gaze bouncing again.

"I mean if we had children, maybe I would have been all for keeping a dog. Especially if the kids were old enough to look after it but... look, what is going on and where is Sonny?"

"In good hands."

He got this puzzled look on his face. "He's not with Katherine?" There was a moment of confusion and then he staggered back as if a picture was forming in his mind. "Oh God. No. No. She didn't."

"Mr. Evans?"

"Did she do it?"

"Do what?"

"Harm herself. The woman recently pulled from the lake. Was that her?"

"What would make you think that?"

"Well, it's been in the news. Please. Is it her?"

"We still need to confirm through dental records but... based on a photo from her work, we have reason to believe so." Right there and then, Nicholas broke down. His legs buckled beneath him.

10

Monday, November 21, 10:45 a.m.

As steam swirled above their cups, Noah and Callie studied Nicholas' face, searching for any sign of guilt or deceit after being told that his wife's body was pulled from the lake.

Although they'd assisted him inside, now his demeanor was composed, almost eerily so. Shock could give the illusion that someone didn't care even if they did. Nicholas sipped his coffee quietly, avoiding their gaze. Noah cleared his throat and leaned forward, breaking the uneasy silence.

"Is there someone we can call to be with you?"

"No. Well. My parents are in town but I wouldn't want to burden them with this."

Noah nodded. "Mr. Evans. What can you tell us about the last day you saw Katherine?" His tone was gentle but probing.

Nicholas looked up, meeting Noah's gaze. For a moment, his

face betrayed a flicker of emotion — was it fear or regret? It was gone as quickly as it appeared. "It was like any other morning."

"What day?"

"Wednesday. I believe that was the sixteenth, I think."

"So, two days before her body was found." Noah glanced at Callie; she scribbled it down. It meant she had to have stayed somewhere, a motel, a friend, with parents, or perhaps the shelter.

"I brought her a coffee then left for work. She is usually here when I come home. I arrived back here just after five thirty. The SUV was gone and so was Sonny. I just assumed she'd taken him out for a walk to one of the parks in the area."

"Was that normal?"

"Yes. The time that she took him out varied."

"Did she ever head into High Peaks?"

"No. I mean. Not to take the dog for a walk. We have lots of trails and parks around here. With the fall it gets dark soon. She doesn't like the dark. That would have taken her a good thirty-minute drive." He sighed, then took another sip of coffee. "When I hadn't heard from her by six thirty, I texted but got no answer. Ten minutes later I tried to phone. No answer. Around eight, I was starting to get worried. You know, that perhaps she'd been in an accident or something. I phoned multiple times. I checked to see if she was online. You know, because you get a green dot beside a person's name on social media if they are online."

"And?"

"It was greyed out. By nine, I..."

He paused.

"Mr. Evans?"

He closed his eyes. "I was beginning to think she had done the same thing as the previous year."

"Why would you immediately jump to that conclusion versus thinking she could have been in an accident?"

"I assumed if it was an accident, she would have contacted me, or the police, or the hospital would have." He set his cup down on the table and laced his fingers together. "By the following morning, I figured she was taking time away."

"You said you never called her parents, work or friends this time?"

"No. But then again, things had been a little tense in the days leading up to her leaving."

"And why was that?"

"Where do I even start? She lost her job at the Academy six months before."

"Lost? We were told she stepped down."

He chuckled. "Stepped down, my ass. They gave her no other option. She was told in no uncertain terms that if she didn't leave of her own volition, she'd never get another job in counseling again. They forced her out."

"Why?"

"In the months leading up to her exit from High Peaks Academy, several accusations had been brought to the attention of Alexander Hawthorne. Rumors, you might say."

"Of what kind?"

"Sexual in nature." He sighed. "Several students were saying that she was..." He looked uncomfortable. "Interfering with them."

"But you don't believe that?"

"Not for one minute. Katherine was a good woman. She loved her job. She loved those kids but not in that way. She would have walked over glass for her students. She liked to think of herself as an advocate for the ones who couldn't speak out or were struggling with life. The trouble is her job placed her alone one-on-one with students. If someone didn't like her, or wasn't getting what they wanted, then it would have been easy to create a false narrative about her. It's not like their sessions are recorded."

"Was a report filed with the police?"

He set his cup down. "No. Oh no. High Peaks Academy is a prestigious school. They wouldn't want that kind of heat. No. She was told to step down to avoid bringing the school's name into disrepute."

"But still, parents wouldn't have let that slide."

"It never made it that far. Like I said. Katherine told me there were rumors circling around the school. Whoever was behind it was trying to mar her name. Alexander Hawthorne gave her an option. Leave or face the consequences of what not only could land her in jail but could destroy the reputation of High Peaks Academy. After that, her mental health declined. She was depressed. I tried to encourage her and tell her that she could find another job, but it was like that wasn't what mattered to her. She felt as if she had been hung out to dry and had no recourse."

"Did she ever mention a name, someone that she felt was behind it?"

"Not exactly. I mean, a few weeks before leaving she was working closely with one student. A boy. Sixteen. I can't remember his full name. It was Charlie... something. For some reason she seemed disturbed yet hopeful by the conversations. As if she was going to make a big difference."

"She never told you what it was about?"

"Client confidentiality. She was very particular about not sharing what students had divulged to her. It's mostly anxiety, inability to cope, issues with parents and whatnot. I mean, all of the students they deal with down there are problems. They are there because no one else can deal with them."

"So, you don't think there was any merit to these rumors?"

"No. Absolutely not. Not for one minute."

Noah nodded as he looked around. "How long have you been married, Mr. Evans?"

"Just over twenty years." He ran a hand over his jawline.

"And no kids?"

"Not for a lack of trying. I'm infertile. That was also the cause of a few arguments this year."

Noah exchanged a glance with Callie, silently communicating their doubts as Nicholas continued. "We'd considered going the route of sperm donation, in vitro fertilization and even adoption, but we just didn't get around to it."

"Do you own a firearm?"

"No. I have a license but Katherine didn't want us to have one in the house. Was she shot?"

"Again, until we can confirm through dental records, I can't say."

He shook his head.

Noah rose. "Would you mind if I took a look around?" He figured that if her husband had anything to do with her murder, this was the best opportunity he would get to explore the house without a warrant and before Nicholas might try to cover his tracks if he hadn't done so already. It also gave him a chance to see what his reaction might be.

"By all means," Nicholas said. Noah wandered off as Callie continued to question him, hoping she might uncover a clue or inconsistency that might shed some light on the final day before she vanished.

Noah made his way around the house, scanning the living room and kitchen for any signs of a disturbance, damage or suspicious activity that might indicate a violent fight. Everything seemed normal, almost too normal, given the circumstances. The furniture was neat and tidy, the dishes washed. With blue latex gloves on, he opened cupboards and made a mental note of items. He wandered upstairs, entered the bathroom and opened the medicine cabinet. He noticed there were antidepressants, Prozac and Zoloft, prescribed to Katherine by a local healthcare provider. There was also a bottle of Ativan for insomnia or anxiety.

Right then, Noah felt his phone jangle in his pocket. He fished it out.

Continuing to browse, he answered. "Hey, Kerri, what's up?"

"I did some digging on that waterfront property you asked me to check out," Kerri replied, sounding serious. "I'm sorry to say, I haven't had much luck finding anything on the LLC company that owns it. Whoever is behind it is really good at covering their tracks. From what I can tell, the name of the company is a front for conducting business without personal responsibility for debts or liabilities. My advice is to be careful and not accept the offer. Like the old saying, if something is too good to be true, it probably is."

His suspicions had been confirmed. Whoever the mysterious benefactor was, they must have known he would look into their background.

"Thanks for letting me know. I appreciate your help. Do you think speaking with the real estate agent directly would give you any answers?"

"Suzanne Gilford? No. She's a closed book. The trouble is, no one wants the competition. Having another agent sniffing around, could mean a cut in pay if I was to find someone for the property. No, Harland and Stafford keep all matters related to clients strictly confidential." She paused. "Noah. I know it seems tempting. Heck, if someone offered me that place, I would be hard pressed not to take it, but without knowing who's pulling the strings behind the curtain, you could find yourself getting into more than just a house. And who knows if you'd be able to get out."

Noah knew Kerri was a reliable agent. She was the tip of the spear when it came to real estate in the region, her warning was enough to make him cautious.

"Thanks, Kerri," he said before ending the call. He would have been lying to say he didn't feel disappointed. Thoughts of all the crap homes he'd toured in the last two weeks came back to his mind. He'd considered contacting Alicia to see if she'd managed to have the cabin rebuilt. He could get into something new, modern, and probably work out a deal that was far better than what he could ever hope to find elsewhere.

Still, there would be strings attached there. He still hadn't called her since he'd returned. Noah brought up his contacts, his thumb hovered over her name.

He hit dial. It rang a couple of times then she picked up.

"Alicia Michaels, Fish and Game."

"Hey."

"Noah? Huh. I almost didn't answer. Five months without a peep."

"How you doing?" Noah went into the hallway and opened a towel closet and fished around inside.

"Busy. You?"

"Always. Hey, um, that cabin. Did you get it rebuilt?"

"Why?"

"Just curious."

The line went quiet.

"Alicia?"

"You're back, aren't you?"

"Did you do anything or not?"

"Don't dodge the question."

"Yes. I'm back."

He heard her scoff. "No. It's not. I mean, it won't be for a while. You know how these things go with insurance companies. Trying to get them to pay out is like squeezing blood from a stone." She paused for a second. "Where you staying?"

"Gretchen's for now."

"I'm sure there are other properties out there."

"Did you have a cash-out option?"

"I think so."

"Then I have a proposition for you. I will buy the land from you."

"Why would you do that?"

"I like the view."

"And the neighbor?"

"I would be living beside him, not with him."

She chuckled. "Do you have the money?"

He didn't reply with the answer she wanted. "Do we have a deal?"

"I'll think about it. I need to talk to the insurance company."

"So, I heard you're seeing someone."

"Who told you that?"

"It's High Peaks."

"Right. People are either tight lipped or flapping their gums." She went quiet for a second or two. "Yes. I am. Why, you jealous?"

He laughed. "You flatter yourself too easily."

"I gave you plenty of opportunity."

"I didn't call to talk about us. Just wanted to ask. I'll catch up with you later."

He hung up and stood there, clutching the phone tightly. Thinking about that moment back at the cabin, and what might have become of them had he gone a different way.

Noah pushed it from his mind and turned toward the main bedroom.

It was clean, the bed made. He looked in the closet, lifting clothes, pushing items aside. Nothing indicated that Nicholas was falling apart without his wife around. He noticed on her side of the bed a couple of books, along with a photo of the two of them when they first got married. There was a folded-up newspaper on the floor. He picked it up and flipped through it but saw nothing out of the ordinary — just the usual mix of national news, sports scores and local events. Beneath that one was an older newspaper, going back several years. This one had an article circled in red:

Adirondack Daily Enterprise lead reporter accused of workplace harassment by 'Jane Doe'

He made a mental note of the name of the person who wrote the article, and the one accused, before setting it back down. He continued his sweep of the room but found nothing else of interest.

Back downstairs, Noah entered just as Nicholas' calm exterior had begun to crack, revealing his desperation. "I don't know what else to tell you. I swear I had nothing to do with this," he said, his voice trembling. "I loved Katherine. She meant everything to me." Noah observed him closely, his experience had honed his instincts. It wasn't uncommon to hear similar protests from suspects, but something about Nicholas' tone and body language felt genuine.

"The newspaper upstairs seems old," Noah said.

"Oh, that. Yeah, after leaving her job, she kind of became obsessed by any local or international cases related to harassment. She was considering taking the Academy to court but..."

"But?"

"We didn't have the money for that. A case like that would have been dragged out for years. There was no guarantee she could even win, and what would be gained without ruining our reputation?"

"Our?"

"Well, it wouldn't have just been her reputation, my name would have been dragged through the mud. I work at the bank. I see locals every day. Can you imagine if something like that hit the news?" He groaned. "And really, what proof did she have? Or as I said to Katherine, what evidence did they have against her that made them so convinced that if she didn't step down, it could jeopardize the name of the Academy?"

Noah regarded him, studying his mannerisms. "Mr. Evans, while I can understand why your wife might feel under stress, you said your wife did the same thing a year ago, can you share why that was?"

"Like I said, work stress. I think whatever happened this year was already in the works back then. I just think it finally came to a head." He teared up. Noah sensed that they had reached the limits of what he could tell them for now. Noah thanked him for his time and promised to keep him updated of any developments in the case.

Stepping off the porch, Noah turned. "Would you have the name of the shelter Katherine went to last time, and the address of her parents? We'd like to notify them once we have a positive ID. For now, please keep this to yourself."

Nicholas nodded before heading back in to scribble down the information. He returned a moment later and handed them a scrap of paper.

"I will be in touch to collect Sonny."

With that he turned and went back inside.

As they walked back to the vehicle, Callie asked, "You buy his story?"

"I don't buy anyone's story. But right now, we just follow the breadcrumbs and see where it leads."

11

Monday, November 21, 12:15 p.m.

Lena was no stranger to arrogance but Carl McNeal was on a whole other level. She had encountered her fair share of self-important individuals in her career as a journalist, but there was something about the way he acted that rubbed her the wrong way. He strutted into the break room like he owned the place, his smug grin and dismissive attitude made her wonder what he thought he had to prove.

The lack of self-awareness was unreal.

"I hear you found that lady's dogs, or should I say, the cops did." Carl chuckled as he poured coffee into a cup then grabbed some cream out of the fridge. "Win some, lose some, Grayson. Always got to check your tips before you waste your time following them, even those you think are credible. But you knew that, right?"

He slurped coffee.

She rolled her eyes at him, knowing that he was just trying

to get a rise out of her, but she refused to let him. "Don't you have to be somewhere?"

He leaned back against the counter, eyeing her. "It's in the bag."

"Hardly. I'm sure the victim's family would appreciate if you put in a little more effort," she retorted, trying to remain neutral and calm. Carl laughed, as if her comment was nothing more than a joke.

"Don't you worry your pretty little head," he said, his voice dripping with condescension. "I've been at this game for a long time. I'm on top of things."

She smiled. "The cops haven't told you anything, have they?"

He didn't want to answer that but she knew it was the truth. Two advantages she had was that folks knew she'd been married to Noah, and was a local. Carl on the other hand was an outsider. No one recognized his journalism awards or achievements here. Maybe that's why he was trying too hard to impress people.

"There are other ways to get information," he said.

"And how do you expect to get that?"

"Like I said. I have my ways."

"Sure you do. Pity you don't have connections."

"Didn't exactly help you, did it?"

She offered back a confused expression.

He sipped at his drink. "Finding the truth relies on more than running with every theory that springs to mind."

Lena bit her tongue, resisting the urge to give him a reason to complain to Maggie. As Carl strutted around the room, she couldn't help but wonder how such an arrogant man had become successful as a journalist in the first place.

"What's that supposed to mean?" she asked.

"Oh, I don't know, just my observation after reading the article you did about the woman pulled from the lake before they put me on the story. I should mention, it looks as if someone needs to proofread their work a little better," he sneered, eliciting a few chuckles from a few of the others in the room. Lena bristled, feeling a surge of indignation at the way he was belittling her hard work. "It seems as if Maggie brought me on just at the right time."

"I'm glad you find that amusing." She gritted her teeth, wishing the microwave would heat the food faster. It dinged and she removed her lunch. "Perhaps you should focus on your own job," she added. Lena took a deep breath, trying to remain calm, but she could feel her patience wearing thin.

Carl smirked, clearly enjoying the power dynamic between them. "I'm just yanking your chain, Grayson. If you need help writing those obituaries, just give me a shout."

Another reporter snorted.

"I don't need your help with anything," she snapped, her voice rising. "And if you can't take this job seriously, maybe you should retire."

The room fell silent. Jokes aside, it was clear her frustration and anger had crossed the line. Carl looked a little taken aback. Then he just shrugged, as if her comment was nothing more than a childish comeback. "Why do you think I'm here?" he said.

His insinuation that the *Adirondack Daily Enterprise* wasn't work was noted by the others who had busted their asses to get a position at the paper. They got up and walked out. "Come on guys, you know I didn't mean it like that," he said as his face flushed.

"Hey, it's okay. They might not understand but I do," Lena said.

"You do?"

She pulled a face, nodding.

Lena shifted gears, figuring she would play her own games.

"Yeah, I mean, I understood from the day I saw you pull up out front."

"What's that supposed to mean?"

"BMW." She held up her little finger and wiggled it as she walked backward out of the break room. "Got to find a way to compensate, right?"

She gave a cheeky grin as she strolled back to her desk, unable to hide her amusement. She was just about to take a seat and eat lunch when Maggie called to her.

"Lena."

Her head swiveled.

"My office."

Lena's eyes darted to Carl who was still in the break room. His eyes widened and he put a hand over his mouth as if to indicate she was in trouble. She scowled then swallowed and wiped away some food that had landed on her black skirt. She cursed under her breath, snatching a napkin off a co-worker's desk to work out the mess on her way over.

"Yes?" she asked.

"Close the door."

She could tell by the edge in Maggie's voice that she was in a foul mood. It was unusual for her. She was for the most part a pillar of strength both in the office and in the community. Her no-nonsense attitude and fierce dedication for truth had seen her rise in the ranks from a reporter to co-owning the newspaper. Maggie had seen the changes, felt the challenges, and encountered most of the pitfalls common to reporting news. She had been editor for over thirty years, and everyone in the town knew her by name. Regardless of her age, she was a formidable figure, with short-cropped hair that was a shocking white and piercing forest green eyes that seemed to penetrate. Although she liked to convey a tough exterior, Maggie had a kind heart and deep love for those around her. But cross her, and hell had no fury like hers.

She'd been through a lot. Five years ago, her husband, Jason Coleman, the mayor of High Peaks, had been killed in a car crash up in the mountains. The case had yet to be solved. It remained open with signs pointing to Jason being deliberately driven off the road. The loss of her husband had hit Maggie hard, and she'd thrown herself into her work to distract herself from the pain.

Perhaps that's why she was so adamant about solving cases, leaving no stone unturned and ensuring that whatever crossed her desk was given due diligence.

Nervously Lena tried to recall if she had said or done anything that might have given Maggie cause for concern.

"If it's about Carl..."

"It's not."

Maggie motioned for her to take a seat, and Lena's palms started to sweat. She began speaking before Lena had even settled. "I want you to keep working on the dog theft story."

Lena frowned slightly. "But I told you. That was resolved. The police found him."

Maggie's expression darkened. "That was one of many. Take a look." She turned her monitor and showed Lena a slew of emails she'd filtered that went back several years, incidents of missing dogs. Lena scanned them and realized she was right — there were too many reports for it to be a coincidence. She wondered what had changed to cause a spike in thefts. "We've been getting these emails for a while, Lena. I just haven't had the manpower, time or resources to dedicate to it, but with Carl here and the public demanding answers, I think this is just as important as a missing woman."

Lena leaned back in her seat, regarding her. "Is everything

okay, Maggie?" she asked tentatively, sensing she was more frustrated than she had ever seen her before.

Maggie sighed. "No, not really. We're dealing with a lawsuit from a former employee we fired a few years back for harassment. It was a little before I took you on. In fact, you ended up filling his spot."

"No wonder you were keen to hire me."

"Anyway, I guess he's not done dragging this newspaper's name through the mud. He's seeking compensation, and it's turning into a nightmare. I'm sorry. I'm not usually like this but..."

Lena felt a pang of sympathy for her. She had always been a tough but fair boss and it was clear the lawsuit was taking its toll on her.

"Well if you fired him, you must have had good grounds."

"It's not about winning, Lena. He knows that. This is punishment. The cost of paying for lawyers to fight in court is going to be a drain on the company. Between me and you," she said, glancing over her shoulder and bringing up two fingers within a few inches of each other, "the paper is this close to closing."

"But the website. The lead generation."

"All of it I've appreciated," Maggie said. "But it's not enough. The world is changing too fast. The way people consume media is different. The older generation of people who would buy a copy are either dead or dying off. The rest are going elsewhere. And advertisers, who for many years paid to keep the lights on, are going with them. They can get better advertising results elsewhere. Weekday circulation has fallen by 17 percent and Sunday readership by 14 percent. If the trend continues, they say a third of newspapers will be gone by 2025. Newspapers are closing at roughly two a week. We just don't have the numbers we once did."

Lena nodded.

Maggie blew out her cheeks. "That includes reporters. At one time that room out there would have been crammed full. Folks typing away, answering calls, the buzz was electric. That's why I got involved. It was exciting." She looked down at the report. "That's why I'm trying to change things up. Bring out a story that few others are paying attention to, in the hope it might hit a nerve with readers and make them see that the *Adirondack Daily Enterprise* isn't just another newspaper but it's the heartbeat of this region. That it cares for the people beyond providing weather, sports scores, obituaries, and local news that few give a damn about."

Lena took a deep breath and let it out. "I'm sorry to hear that. If there is anything I can do to help..."

Maggie looked back at the monitor and smiled gratefully. "There is. Dig into this dog theft story and generate some leads. It would be a huge help. We need something big, something positive to balance out the negativity in this region."

"All right. I'll see what I can do."

She got up and headed back to her desk.

Lena began sorting through her notes, tidbits of information she'd gleaned from research online about dog thefts, when her phone rang. She scooped it up and saw it was Aiden on the caller ID.

"Hey sweetheart. How's the battle going?" he asked.

"Busy," she replied. "How did it go this morning?"

Aiden had taken Ethan to his weekend self-defense class paid for by Noah.

"Brutal. Not exactly turn the other cheek but hey, he seemed to enjoy himself. Look, I was thinking I would cook dinner tonight. Figured I would show you what you are in store for long term," he said. He was trying, maybe a little too hard, to impress her.

"Ugh."

"You're working?"

"Something's come up. I..."

Lena heard him sigh. "We'll do it another time. That's not a problem. We only have the rest of our lives," he said.

"Right," she answered. If she was honest, she'd been having second thoughts about getting married. It wasn't him per se, or even the return of Noah to the region, she just wasn't sure she was ready to give that kind of commitment. Something about that marriage paper changed things.

Aiden was quick to change the topic. "Oh. I should mention something. On the way back we stopped at that ice cream parlor Ethan likes. Well, he saw a flyer on the wall for golden retriever pups for sale from some breeder in the area."

"He wants one, doesn't he?"

It wasn't a mystery. Since his time with Axel, Ethan had been biting at the bit to get his own dog. He'd brought it up several times in conversation but adding another member to the family only brought with it more responsibility and cost, and she knew Ethan didn't understand that, and after what she'd just heard from Maggie, she wasn't sure if she was going to be employed in the next few months.

"Can we, Mom?" she heard him shout in the background.

"Put him on."

"Be my guest," Aiden said, handing the phone over.

"Hey," Ethan said excitedly. "I saw a flyer today for dogs. They're really cheap. Can we get one?"

"You remember what I told you."

"I'll look after it."

"Famous last words," she said.

"I will."

"We'll see, Ethan," Lena replied. "These dogs, how much are they?" Ethan reeled off a number. It wasn't cheap but compared to some of the prices she'd seen for purebred dogs from reputable breeders, it was enticing. Then again, most of the reputable breeders didn't need to advertise in ice cream stores as they were usually registered with their breed associations and received enough buyers that way. "Do you have the number?"

"Yeah, I ripped one off."

She took out a pen and scribbled it down.

"Ethan. Go easy on Aiden. Okay? No more talk about getting a pup. Let me look into it."

"All right."

"Where's your sister?"

"On the phone."

"All right. I'll see you this evening."

After hanging up, Lena looked at the number. Something about the situation made her uneasy. She picked up the phone again and dialed it. Some woman with a harsh throaty voice answered.

Lena introduced herself and asked if they were a registered breeder.

"Yes."

"Can you give me any more information, references, or can I come and see the mother and father?"

"We don't do that."'

"Why not?"

"Look, are you interested in the dog or wasting our time?"

"I just wanted to see where the dogs are being kept and the parents."

"Like I said, we do things differently. If you are interested in seeing a dog, we can meet you and show you one or two." Lena thought for a moment and then agreed to meet them.

12

Monday, November 21, 4:20 p.m.

Every investigation was full of secrets and lies, the truth lay somewhere between.

It wasn't so much a matter of retracing her steps on the night she went missing as it was understanding the victim. In doing so they might learn what happened. Noah was acutely aware that he was probably only hearing half the story and parts were being purposely left out. The question was why?

Finding the women's shelter wasn't easy.

Katherine never told her husband where it was, only the name. There was good reasoning behind that, in the event that she might need to go there again. Most emergency shelters for women coming out of an abusive relationship operated that way.

It was for safety reasons.

The actual residence was only made known once a person

had been carefully vetted. They didn't want an ex-husband or controlling boyfriend to show up unannounced. For it to be an effective safe house, anonymity was crucial.

Still, Noah figured if Katherine had continued to go to work while staying at one, it couldn't have been too far away. There were only two in the county. A quick conversation with administration at each of them eventually yielded an address.

It was located up in Wilmington, New York, a quiet town twenty minutes northeast of High Peaks. It wasn't far from one of the State Police Satellite Offices, a location that seemingly had been picked in the event they needed to call for assistance.

The building was set back from the road with a manicured lawn, pristine landscaping and plenty of trees that provided privacy and a sense of calm. It was an historic, two-story brick building with an additional side building that resembled a small motel. The residence had a modern aesthetic, offering simple sleeping quarters and living spaces. Noah was struck by its humble exterior. The faded sign which read "Adirondack's Safe Haven," and the brick wall surrounding the property showed signs of wear and tear.

"My sister was in one of these places," Callie remarked.

"Because of an abusive relationship?"

"Not exactly. She was trying to get her life in order. It was a combination of substance abuse and depression. She felt like she didn't have anywhere to turn to. Had she reached out to me, I would have put her up." Callie picked at dust on her pants. "She lives out west now. California."

Noah stuck the gear into park. "Did it help?"

"Yeah. It gave her a way to rebuild her life, save money and eventually get a place. But unlike what they'll say, it doesn't help everyone. Only those who want to help themselves."

"Isn't that always the case," he said, pushing out of the Bronco.

Upon entering the building, they were greeted by the sound of bustling activity as volunteers and staff attended to the needs of the residents. They were directed to a small office in the rear of the main building where they were met by the shelter's director, Sandy Willis.

"Please," she said, welcoming them and offering them seats. The office was small and tidy but functional, with a desk, a computer and several filing cabinets lining the walls. There were a few posters reminding readers that despite their circumstances, they were strong and capable. Some showcased self-care tips, including suggestions like going for a walk in nature or taking a bubble bath. For those in survival mode, it was a welcome reminder to take care of themselves. Noah eyed one that had a woman standing on a mountaintop, arms outstretched toward the sky, and encouraged having dreams even in the darkest moments.

Sandy noticed him observing them. "We try to instill a sense of hope, empowerment, and encourage the women."

"Does it work?"

"It depends. Every person has a different story."

He took a seat.

"So how can I help?"

Noah took out a photo of Katherine and set it in front of her. "Do you recognize her?"

"I never forget a face." She nodded. "Katherine Evans. Nice woman. She was different from the rest. We get women from all backgrounds but rarely teachers or those who have money."

"When was the last time she was here?"

Sandy took a deep breath and let it out. "I would have to check my files but I believe it was a good year ago. For about three weeks."

"And so, she hasn't been back since?"

"No. Is she dead or missing?"

"That's a strange choice of words."

"Not really. Officer, there are only a few reasons why women don't return here. Either they've managed to get their life back on track and don't need us, or they've derailed. If it's the latter, we usually see them again, not the police. Those who show up here are looking for safety. I gather she never found it."

"We believe it was her body pulled from a lake not far from here."

"Believe?"

"We're still in the process of getting a positive ID."

"But you must be confident if you're here."

"Somewhat. The condition of her body makes it difficult to know."

"That was the woman in High Peaks, yes?"

"Yes, well. What can you tell us about why she came here?"

Sandy leaned forward, lacing her fingers together. "The same reason others tend to. They need help, they don't feel safe, they aren't mentally capable of dealing with whatever happened or is happening in their life."

"I understand but did she give specifics?"

"No. Family trouble. Work. She was vague. You have to understand, officer. For many that show up here, they're embarrassed, humiliated and skeptical about whether anyone will believe them. We provide a safe place for recovery. For some that's a few days, others a couple of weeks. Most usually can find a friend, family member or alternative living situation. This place isn't a permanent solution."

"So after she left here a year ago, did she go directly home?"

"I couldn't tell you for sure. From what I recall, she said she would be going to stay with a friend."

Noah nodded. "This friend. Would you have a name?"

"Nope."

"You would have had to take down personal information, contact numbers, family names and so on, yes?"

"We encourage that but it's not mandatory."

"What information did she give you?"

Sandy stared back at him, then turned toward her computer. Her fingers pecked the keyboard, she moved her mouse and clicked a few times. "There was an emergency number she left with us. It was only to be called if she didn't return on the days she worked."

"Is it family? A friend? Her husband?"

She shrugged. "Not sure. We don't phone unless we need to and she left here of her own accord."

"Could I have the number?"

"That would be breaking our privacy policy."

Noah tapped the photo of Katherine on her desk. "She's dead. Right now, we are doing everything we can to find out who did this. You can either make that easy or we can get it another way. I'd just appreciate you not drawing this out."

Sandy nodded and took a pad of sticky notes and scribbled on one.

Lena was apprehensive about meeting the woman in the grocery parking lot, especially after reading all the horror stories of those who had the misfortune of having their dogs stolen.

However, there was a good chance the seller was legit.

Not everyone wanted people coming to their home, especially if something went wrong with the dog after purchase or the buyers decided they no longer wanted it and figured they could request their money back. As someone who had sold and bought items on online marketplaces, she knew most sellers and buyers would meet at a local coffee store. It was public. It lessened the chances of anything weird happening.

On the phone the woman had told her to look for a blue GMC van that would be parked the furthest from the entrance. As Lena swung into the lot, she scanned the area and saw the van with tinted windows.

Lena pulled up her red Mazda and got out, nerves getting the best of her. The woman was sitting in the driver's seat, holding two small golden retriever puppies. They couldn't have been more than twenty weeks old.

The driver brought the window down, revealing a sleeve of tattoos, some bright and colorful, others dark and frightening. From a distance she looked exotic but as Lena got closer, she noticed the woman was a rough looking individual. Her hair was dull, uncombed, with strands of green like she wasn't sure if she was a teenager or a grown-up. She slouched in the driver's seat, wearing an old off-white cami undershirt that appeared several sizes too small for her. On top of that she had donned a heavy flannel shirt covered in dogs' hair that had a tear in the upper breast pocket. Her face was pockmarked, and crow's feet pulled at the corners of her eyes from years of hard living.

"You here to see the pups?"

"That's right," Lena replied, trying to hide her nervousness.

"We have a large selection to choose from. Once we get the clear by our vet, they're usually good to be picked up at twelve weeks. These are two older ones."

Lena's heart melted as the pups wriggled around on the woman's lap.

"Um, can you tell me a bit more about their living conditions and health?"

The woman's expression turned guarded. "They're all healthy and well cared for. We have a big farm with plenty of space for them to run around."

"And the mother and father — any health issues?"

"None."

It would have been easy to take her word and be overcome by the balls of fur. How many others had been suckered in with no idea of where they came from? Were they born on the farm or stolen from someone's home?

"Do you get them chipped?"

"That's something you'll have to do. We cover the first vet bill. Are you interested?" And there it was, getting down to business. Lena couldn't shake the feeling there was something off about the situation.

"So, it's not possible to see the mother and father?"

"It's too intrusive. Rest assured; they are in good hands. So?"

Lena handed back the bundle of joy to her. It pained her to think that the dogs might have belonged to someone else — perhaps the mother and father were stolen. Or was the business legit? There was no real way of telling.

"As much as I would like to say yes, I need some time to think about it. You think I can get back to you?"

"Sure. I can't guarantee we'll have any left. They move pretty fast. You got our number. Don't take too long."

As Lena moved back around the van, she reached into her bag and pulled out an Apple AirTag with a magnet on it. She placed it under the metal bumper and returned to her vehicle. She got in and waited until the van pulled out of the grocery lot. She wanted to make sure the coast was clear before she began to follow.

Using her phone, Lena brought up the Find My app and watched as the AirTag signal moved out of Saranac, heading north of the town.

In the back of her mind, she knew that the woman might just be a legitimate dog seller working a side gig for extra cash. It was becoming all too common. Folks snapping up dogs and trying to cash in by breeding them from home. It wasn't her place to discuss the right and wrong of it, as she knew there were many decent folks who were careful not to overbreed dogs and to give them long breaks. It was the other ones that concerned her.

Lena's Mazda headed north up Route 86, following the winding road toward Harristown. She glanced at her phone as the van moved along the road. Eventually it slowed and took a hard right and then stopped.

Five minutes later, she closed in on a large farmhouse set back from the road just off Wellsprings Road. She pulled to the side of the road, feeling a sense of unease. A sprawling field stretched before her, the long grass swaying gently in the breeze. Trees hedged in the farm, casting long shadows over the landscape.

Getting out, Lena locked the Mazda and climbed over a country-style fence, navigating her way through dense forest. Leaves crunched below her boots as she got closer. Nearer to the tree line, she had a good view of the farmhouse and noticed several outbuildings. They looked neglected with peeling paint and rusted metal roofs. Lena could hear the sound of barking coming from within.

She dug into her bag, took out her long-lens Canon camera and began snapping shots.

She had to get closer. It was the only way to be sure. She was well aware that she was trespassing. It wouldn't have been the first time. To nail a story, she had to go outside of the norm, bend the rules. In her mind as long as no one was hurt, she wasn't harming anyone.

About to duck out, she saw the woman come out of the house and return to her van. She collected the two puppies and carried them into the house. Lena could hear swearing coming from inside.

Not wasting any time, Lena hurried across the field up to one of the outbuildings. She eased the door open and peered in. There was no one there but from front to back it was filled with cages. Pups yapped hard, clawing at their cramped quarters, their eyes pleading for help. Lena began taking photos. She photographed the filthy conditions.

The smell was overpowering.

It stank of animal waste, soil and vegetation.

As she made her way around the property, Lena saw the extent of the operation. There were dozens of malnourished dogs. Each one looked terrified. She snapped a few more photos, capturing every detail.

"We're meant to get another delivery of dogs this evening," someone said.

Lena's eyes widened. She ducked behind a stack of old tires and wood, hidden out of view. Her heart skipped a beat as the door creaked opening and heavy footsteps followed.

"Magnus! How many times do I need to tell you? You have to lock the door."

"Sorry."

Peeking through a gap in the tires, she saw a middle-aged man. He had a weathered look from spending long hours outdoors in the sun, wind and rain. He wore overalls, a plaid shirt and a pair of yellowed work boots.

He looked disgusted. He hauled over a large bag of food, cut it wide and poured some into each cage with little regard to the dogs inside. When he was done, he dropped the bag, then kicked one of the cages. He mumbled something incoherently then she heard the threat. "Keep yapping and you won't see tomorrow."

Lena felt a surge of anger, but also a deep sense of fear. She was afraid he might walk to the back of the building and discover her.

Fortunately, he turned and walked out.

With enough photos taken, she filmed the rest on her phone and headed for the door. A quick shove with her shoulder on the door then dread set in.

It was locked.

13

Monday, November 21, 6:10 p.m.

The panic was unmistakable.

Noah was having a meal at Peak 46, going over what they had so far and waiting on a call from High Peaks Academy, when Tanya phoned. He let it go to voicemail but when she called a second time, he answered.

"Whatever it is, Tanya, it'll have to wait because—"

"Is he with you?" she asked, quickly cutting him off. There was an edge to her tone.

"What?"

"Ray."

"No. Why…?"

"I can't find him."

Tanya was known for making a mountain out of a molehill, it's what had led to the demise of her first marriage, at least according to Ray. Everything was an issue even if it wasn't.

"It's Ray. You know him."

"And I know he's not like this."

"Look, take a breath and calm down."

"Don't tell me to calm down. I'm worried. I can't find him."

Noah inhaled and let it out.

"Did you check his house?"

"What do you think?"

He raised his eyebrows and exchanged a glance with Callie who was feasting on fried potato skins. "What about the casino?"

"Already phoned there."

"Maybe he got called into work."

"Noah. I know his schedule."

He sighed. "It might be overtime or an emergency. Local PD is helping with the case of the woman pulled from the lake."

"That's not it. He phoned me last night. Drunk. A mess. Apologizing. Saying I deserved better. That he wished things could have been different. You know, the usual crap that he tries to pull to get me to come back. I hung up on his ass. Then when he didn't call back, I got worried and decided to swing by his place today."

"And?"

"His truck was outside, the curtains were drawn. I figured he was sleeping it off. But he didn't answer his phone. So, I went back around there this afternoon and his truck was gone and the door to the house was unlocked. He never leaves it unlocked, Noah. His phone and wallet were inside too." She paused. "I'm worried. I'm scared he's going to hurt himself."

"Tanya. Ray wouldn't do that."

"You don't know him like I do."

"He's my brother. I think I do."

"Yeah? Did he tell you he's in the hole?"

"What?"

"He owes a shitload of money. That's why I left the first time.

Somehow he managed to dig himself out of that mess, I think it was with the help of your father, but this time. Noah. Please, would you just look around and see if you can find him."

"You're sure he's not at work?"

"I dropped by. He's not there. No one's seen or heard from him."

"Are there any bars, motels, places he's gone to before?"

"I don't know."

"Great. That helps," he said in a low voice under his breath. "All right. All right. Leave it with me." He hung up and sat there for a second or two. Callie was chewing, studying him.

"What's happening?"

"Look, we're going to have to stick a pin in this. Do you think you can find out who that phone number belongs to and when the Academy calls back, let me know." He got up.

"Noah. Where are you going?"

"It's a family matter," he said, turning and heading for the door. This was one of the many reasons why he'd been hesitant to return, besides his father's insistence that he stay away. He knew he would be pulled back into the drama of it all. Outside a light rain was falling, making the night seem even more miserable than it was.

On his way to the Bronco, he placed a phone call to Maddie. It went straight to voicemail. He figured that Tanya would have called her and she had probably gone into mother mode, but just in case he left a message.

Getting in his vehicle, he contemplated calling his father but then he'd have to explain why he hadn't been in contact since he'd returned and that was the last thing he needed right now. It was easy to swing by the house and Casino and see if Ray had returned. Knowing him, he'd simply ignored Tanya's calls and hit the bar for the day, or an eighteen-hole round of golf had morphed into one too many drinks.

Ray had always been the most reliable in their family, answering his calls or at least getting back in touch within a couple of hours. As an officer, Ray knew all too well what worry could do. Despite Tanya's history, Noah couldn't help feel a knot form in his stomach, especially after the tragedy of Luke. It filled him with a sense of dread. Alicia had warned him that returning to High Peaks was not in his best interest but he figured that was just her.

On the way back through town, Noah tried calling Ray himself, but got no answer. He tried again, but the result was the same.

When Noah arrived at Ray's place, a two-story brick home in a quiet suburban neighborhood, he noted his truck was still not there. He got out, approached the door, twisted the knob and entered.

"Ray!"

A quick search of the house yielded no answers. Nothing was in disarray as if someone had ransacked the place. No note was to be found. Seeing his wallet wasn't a good sign, however, had he been drinking he might have forgotten to take it with him.

Drinking?

Shit. Had he gotten into his vehicle drunk and ended up in an accident? Noah phoned High Peaks Medical Center, followed by the one in Saranac.

It turned up nothing.

"Where the hell have you gone?" Noah exited the house and got back into his vehicle. Although Tanya said she'd phoned around, he called the casino and the department.

"You're saying you can't find him?" the sergeant on duty, Vern Rollings, asked.

Noah didn't want to make a big thing out of it, especially since it was probably something minor, a momentary lapse in judgment, too much to drink, or he'd overlooked the time, but he couldn't shake the feeling that something was wrong. The last thing he wanted to do was have other officers searching for him and wasting their time.

"I'm sure it's fine."

"Noah. If you don't have any luck, give us a call back."

"Will do."

Noah's pulse ticked upward as he drove the streets of the downtown, scanning every corner. Had something happened to him? Or worse, had he done something to himself? He didn't want to go there, to think he might be capable of that, but anything was possible. Questions raced through his mind as he drove, his eyes darting from side to side.

He dropped by the High Peaks Pub & Brewery which was now under new management. He received a few worried glances from the new owner, Bob Westman, a well-to-do guy who had decided to take it on despite its name having been dragged through the mud. "Sorry, we haven't seen him."

Out in the parking lot, he stared at his phone. It was the last call he wanted to make but he opted to do it. Strangely, Hugh picked up. "Hey, Dad."

"Well, isn't this something. Good to hear your voice."

His positive note caught Noah off guard but maybe that was because Hugh didn't know he was back.

"Is Ray with you?" Noah asked.

"No. Why would you ask that?"

"Look, I'm just going to put it out there, we can talk about it later, but I'm back in High Peaks. Permanently. At least for now. Ray's gone missing."

"Um. Hold on a second. You're back? Since when?"

"It doesn't matter. Look, have you seen or heard from him?"

"No. And why are you acting like it's a missing person case?"

"Tanya phoned me. Said she can't find him and..."

He laughed. "Oh, so she phones you and you drop everything to go scour the streets, is that it?"

"Did you get him out of debt?"

"What?"

"Debt. Was Ray in debt?"

"He borrowed some money from me but he's paying it back each month. Look, Noah, he'll probably show up. Tanya thinks the sky is falling every single damn day. I've told him countless times to leave her, but for whatever reason, he keeps going back. She's a troubled individual."

Noah thought that was fresh coming from him.

"Whatever. Listen, do you know any bars he frequents, places he might go?"

"Did you check to see if his bow was at home?"

"No."

"Well then, he's probably gone bow hunting. You don't need a wallet for that. He has a spot he frequents up in the McKenzie Mountain Wilderness. Check the Haystack Mountain Trailhead. If his truck's not there, I don't know. But, Noah..."

Noah hung up; he knew he was just going to get into it with him. Noah made a beeline for the trailhead, his mind focused only on the worst possible outcome. As the last rays of the sun began to set and streetlights flickered on, Noah's search continued. He drove out on Route 86 to Haystack Mountain Trailhead but the pull-off area was empty.

He did a U-turn in the road and headed back into town, calling his father back again. "Anywhere else?"

"Um. I'm not sure."

"Dad. Think."

"Well, there's Luke and your mother's grave, or one of the other trailheads heading up to Whiteface Mountain. He's been known to park there."

His father didn't have a clue. He was just throwing out ideas as they came to his mind. In some ways he was fortunate that Hugh could remember anything with all the talk of him having early Alzheimer's. He'd yet to see it but then again, he hadn't been around him long enough.

Somehow, Noah remained composed. Years of working in law enforcement had shown him that despite urgency and anxiety, a cool head prevailed. He couldn't let his emotions cloud his judgment or deter him.

After checking the cemetery, the search seemed fruitless. Noah drove out of High Peaks heading toward Whiteface Mountain. He scanned the trailhead parking for Connery Pond, Shadow Rock Pool, Owen Pond and Coopers Pond Trailhead.

Nothing.

He was going to try one more up near Wilmington Notch Campground when he passed High Falls Gorge parking lot and caught sight of his brother's black Ford truck.

Noah slammed on the brakes, fishtailing. He veered into the lot and brought the Bronco up beside the 4 x 4. The cab was empty. He got out and called out his name, but got no reply. The wind howled in his ears.

Fearing the worst, Noah hurried into the 22-acre park along a trail which gave access to the waterfalls. His heart pounded in his chest as the rush of water grew louder. With each step, his mind was filled with terrifying thoughts of what might have happened.

As he rounded the final bend of the trail, Noah reached the steel bridge that arched over one of four waterfalls cascading over rock into a deep crevice carved thousands of years earlier. It was one of the Adirondacks' most breathtaking year-round attractions, drawing in thousands each year.

Tonight, however, it was barren, empty, cold and dark.

"Ray!" he yelled, his eyes scanning the river.

His mind raced with possibilities of what might have

happened. Had he gone deep into the forest, seeking solitude to hunt? Was he injured and unable to respond, or worse — fallen into the crevice?

The sound of rushing water echoed through the park, reminding Noah of the dangerous beauty. Taking out a flashlight, he scanned his surroundings, moving along the trail, searching for any signs of life.

That's when his heart skipped a beat.

There, lying motionless against the rocks further downstream, he spotted a figure. He immediately recognized the brown leather jacket and the white insignia.

Without a second thought, Noah raced toward him, clambering down the rocks as quickly as he could. The water was icy cold and the rocks slick, but he pushed himself on, driven by the sight of his brother lying there.

"Ray!"

When he finally reached the water, he waded in. His toes numbed instantly in his boots. The current pulled at his knees, trying to drag him down. Noah grabbed Ray's jacket, flipped him over and placed two fingers on his neck.

There was a pulse. It was weak. But he was still alive.

Noah dragged him to dry land, heaving his body up the slippery slope until he could get him to a flat piece of land. There, with trembling hands, he began performing CPR. His chest compressions were quick and forceful as he fought to bring him back from the brink of death.

He had no way of knowing how long he'd been out here, only that he was in a bad state. "I'm not burying another. Don't you die on me," he implored.

Tears welled in his eyes.

The crash of water continued behind, a cool mist blew over him, chilling him to the bone. Yet now it was all at the back of his mind as Noah focused solely on the task of saving his brother.

"C'mon!"

For what felt like an eternity, Noah worked tirelessly to revive his brother, his arms aching and his heart breaking with each passing moment. And then, just as he was about to give up, Ray's chest suddenly rose and fell, and he spewed water.

Relief hit Noah as he moved him into the recovery position and watched life return.

Adrenaline dumped out of his system, leaving him numb and panting from tiredness as he tried to make sense of the situation. He pulled out his phone from his pocket and rose to place a call for emergency service.

"I need an ambulance," he began.

"Noah, hang up," Ray cried, waving him off.

Noah glanced back, his face contorting in confusion. "Hold on a second," he said to the dispatch as he put his hand over the phone. "I've got to get you to a hospital."

"Hang up!" he said, struggling for breath.

"Sir?" the dispatch asked.

Against his better judgment, Noah got back on the phone. "Sorry, um. Cancel that request." Getting off the phone, he stared at Ray. "How long have you been out here?"

"I don't know," he said, out of breath and coughing hard.

Noah removed his jacket and wrapped it around his shivering body. "You need a hospital. Hypothermia is setting in," he said, helping him to his feet, a task that wasn't easy. He curled an arm around him and had to use all his strength just to get him up.

"You take me to the hospital; they will put me on a 5150 hold. Then they'll take away my badge and..." He coughed hard.

"No. You fell in, they'll..."

"I'm not going."

"You don't know what you're talking about."

"I'm *not* going."

"Give me one reason why not?"

"Because I never fell in," he croaked out.

Noah glanced at his brother. He didn't need to explain.

Often those experiencing a mental health crisis could be involuntarily detained for 72 hours while they were evaluated to see if they were a danger to themselves or others.

Shivering hard, Noah carried Ray in a fireman's lift just to get him back to the Bronco as his legs were too numb and barely functioning.

He dumped him into the passenger side, took a blanket from the back and covered his body while he went and got his IFAK kit out. It was designed for high-stress emergency situations. Inside were survival items: a tourniquet, hemostatic gauze, adhesive bandages, trauma shears, chest seals among other things. He tore out the emergency blanket used to keep patients warm and prevent hypothermia. It was also known as a space blanket because of its highly reflective plastic and its ability to retain body heat and maintain temperature. Noah wrapped it around his body.

He got in the other side and fired up the engine, blasting the heat to warm his body.

"Ray, just let me take you to the hospital."

"No. You do that, I'll do it again. I swear."

Noah stared at him as heat pumped into the cab. "I can take you home."

"No, Tanya will return if she's not already there."

"Then dad's or Maddie's?"

"His place is out of the question. Somewhere else. It can't be family."

"Ray. C'mon. People are looking for you."

"Please. Noah."

Ray shivered hard.

Noah shook his head. "Damn you!" he said under his breath. He was sure his brother heard. He wanted to pepper him with questions. He wanted justification for the attempt. To understand why he didn't reach out. But there was none. He didn't smell of alcohol. He sure as hell knew Ray wasn't on drugs.

He understood falling into a dark place, he'd been there many a time himself, but this... Noah shook his head as he reversed and peeled away into the night, taking him to the only person who he knew would say nothing.

THE FAMILIAR SIGHT of dense forest along with the smell of pine needles and damp earth brought a degree of peace. Tucked away, not far from the clearing that had once held Alicia's cabin, was the abode nestled near the edge of the lake with the small dock stretching out into the water.

Noah eased his brother out and carried him toward the home. A small light outside the door illuminated the wrap-around porch and two Adirondack chairs. Noah knocked and after a few moments, the door opened to reveal Ed Baxter. The old-timer looked surprised, but then scoffed. His expression changed to concern upon seeing Noah holding his brother. "Do I look like a damn hospital?" he snapped.

"Sorry, Ed. He didn't give me much choice," he replied, unable to hide his own anger.

"I would ask if you're out of your damn mind but I think we established that months ago." He moved out of the way. "Bring him in."

Without saying another word, Ed ushered them deeper into the cabin.

The warmth of a roaring fire and the smell of woodsmoke washed over them.

Ed helped Noah lay his brother on the couch, then he shuffled away to gather a few blankets and towels.

"Get him out of those wet clothes," Ed said.

Ray's strength was all but gone. As Noah peeled the layers off, he could see the fear and exhaustion on his brother's face.

"I'm sorry, brother. I'm really sorry," Ray repeated.

Behind them the fire crackled, casting a warm glow throughout the room.

Noah stepped back as Ed took over, covering Ray then giving him some water. Ray's eyes closed; his shivering barely noticeable.

Noah watched from the fireplace, turning back every so often.

"You!" Ed jabbed a finger at him. "Outside. Now," he said in a demanding tone.

He followed him out the rear sliding doors, then closed them for privacy.

"What the hell is going on, Noah, and when did you return?"

"Two weeks ago."

"Two weeks? And only now you decide to show up. With another problem, I might add. I'm pretty sure the last time you were around, I ended up with a concussion and several days in a hospital."

Noah couldn't hide his amusement.

Ed wagged a finger near his nose. "I'm glad you find it funny. What happened? Did you two idiots decide to go skinny dipping? I mean, you, I could expect it from, but him. He's with local PD, right?"

He said it in a way to suggest that State investigators were out of their mind.

"Something like that." Noah let out a sigh and took a seat. "You think you've got a drink?"

"You don't drink."

"You're right, but at this rate I probably will again."

Ed observed him before taking a seat. "So?"

Noah sighed, running hands over his wet pants. "I pulled him out of the river at High Falls Gorge." He shook his head. "Fuck knows how long he was in there. I was going to take him to the hospital but he refused."

"Tough shit. You take him. I don't like the damn place any more than him but I know my limits."

"I'm with you on that but you don't know Ray. Hell, you don't know my family."

"Actually, I think I'm the only one who can say I do. And so far, I've begun to think you are all a little batshit crazy."

"Being a Sutherland will do that to you." He gave a pained smile before staring out across the lake toward the three islands. "They'll detain him on a 5150. He could lose his career."

"By the looks of him, he was ready to ditch it anyway. I gather he didn't slip?"

"No," he said again. "That's what makes this difficult."

"For you or for me?"

Noah took a seat in a wicker chair, feeling chilled to the bone. "Ed. Look. I appreciate this. I just need a place for him to get warm, somewhere he can put his head down for a day or two until we can work this out."

"And what happens if you don't? What happens if he decides to go take another dip in the lake, outside my house? What then?"

"He won't."

Ed grumbled. "You know, most people when they haven't seen someone for a long time, they usually show up with a gift, a six-pack of Buds, a bottle of wine. You show up with a drowned rat."

"I will make it up to you."

"I look forward to that," he said, eyeballing him.

Noah gazed across at the property where Alicia's cabin had burned down. The charred remains had been cleared away, nothing remained except the foundation. Ed followed his eyes. "Oh yeah. That. What a damn mess. I've been waiting on Alicia to tell me when they're going to rebuild or if she plans to sell the land."

"She is. To me. At least, she's looking into it."

"To you?"

"Yeah, that a problem?"

"Ugh. Why me, Lord, why me?" he asked, looking toward the dark sky.

"You don't want me as a neighbor?"

"I want you as a neighbor as much as I want another dose of hemorrhoids."

Noah chuckled as he rose and took out his phone. He stepped away to make a call to Tanya. "And it's good to see you again, my old friend."

"So what now?" Ed asked.

Noah brought the phone to his ear, waiting for Tanya to pick up. "Damage control."

14

Monday, November 21, 7:15 p.m.

There was no signal.

"You've got to be kidding me!" she said, holding up the phone and moving down the aisle while pups barked around her. There were a couple of dirty, cobweb-covered windows but they were higher up.

Trapped inside the outbuilding, Lena figured it would be easier to contact Noah and kill two birds with one stone. He would swoop in, arrest the farm owner and maybe even get charges of trespassing dismissed. She figured, under the circumstances, that the last thing they would care about was someone who had risked their life to gather evidence against an illegal breeder.

In that moment that's what she believed they were. Even if they were doing everything above board, the conditions the dogs were being kept in were far from ideal.

"C'mon. Not even one bar!"

As darkness enveloped the building, the temperature began to drop.

She shivered and decided to call 911. Regardless of shabby service or no plan or even a SIM card, phones were meant to go directly through to 911. It was required for all phones in America, except for some reason it wasn't working.

"This cannot be happening."

Nothing. She held the phone high.

It had to be the building or her location to the nearest tower. After multiple attempts from different locations in the building, she gave up and surveyed the darkened space. With evening in full swing, very little light from stars entered. The dogs were in complete darkness, afraid, cold, just like her. That only gave her more sympathy for their plight.

Using the flashlight feature on her phone, she shone it around trying to get a better feel of what her options were. She tried to remain calm and composed as she searched for a possible weakness in the walls or door. Nothing. The only thing that was dilapidated was the roof and the two windows that were high up. Even if she could reach them, there was no way she could squeeze out, they were too narrow.

She berated herself for even stepping foot on the farm.

In all the years she'd been a reporter, she'd been careful not to get too close to a story. Noah had warned her after seeing journalists wind up the target of those they were investigating. Still, if no one did anything about the individuals stealing pets, it would just fall between the cracks, overlooked, and become nothing more than a small article in a newspaper or a social media post that people would scroll by.

Lena returned to the steel door and pushed hard against it. It was like beating a dead horse. It wouldn't budge. She wanted to scream in frustration but that would only draw attention and that was the last thing she needed.

As she crossed to the stacked-up tires, an idea formed in her mind.

She'd seen the weathered roof from the outside, back when there was daylight. All that stood between her and freedom was weathered plywood and rotten shingles.

She coughed hard, placing a hand over her mouth.

The air was thick with the scent of wood and rust, and the only moonlight filtered through cracks in the roof.

Casting the flashlight beam around her prison, looking for a tool she could use to punch her way to freedom, she felt like a caged animal.

What to use? she thought.

Rusty old chains, hooks and a length of rope, frayed and worn from years of use, were hanging from the rafters. An old pulley system was mounted high up on the wall for hoisting heavy objects up and out of the barn. A tractor was gathering dust in the corner. Near the back, there was a trailer filled with hay and straw.

A crowbar or a tire iron would have been handy but there wasn't either.

Moving around the tractor, shining the light across it, she found a small toolbox near the front. She dug inside and brought out a flathead screwdriver. It wasn't much but it would have to do. She knew time was running out; if she didn't act fast, they'd either find her or she'd succumb to the cold.

Returning to the old tires stacked up in one corner, she began dragging them over to the wall where she could use them to climb. She stacked them as high as she could, using all her strength to push them into place and create a makeshift ladder.

With her heart pounding in her chest, Lena began.

The tires were unsteady and wobbled beneath her weight, but she kept going, pulling herself up rung by rung.

The roof was old and dilapidated, with patches of rusted

metal and holes that let in slivers of light. She pulled the screwdriver out of her pocket and began to dig at the edges of the plywood, breaking pieces of it away and prying up a section of rusty metal sheets. The metal creaked and groaned, but she kept going.

A large section broke away and she let it fall to the floor, revealing a space wide enough to get her head through but not the rest of her.

Keep at it, she told herself, digging the tool in and stabbing weathered wood to pieces until she could see more of the light from the stars.

Just as she was making real progress, and figured she'd be able to squeeze out of the hole, she heard voices from the ground below. Her heart raced with fear, she paused and listened, trying to make out what was being said.

As she strained to hear, the voices grew louder, and she realized they belonged to the owners of the farm. They'd heard her and were making their way over to the building.

Lena's hands shook as she pulled herself up onto the roof just as the main doors opened. She was at least twenty feet off the ground, so jumping down was out of the question. She figured she would find some other way down but under pressure that luxury was now gone.

"Patrick. Go around the outside. They're on the roof."

Frantically, Lena gazed down, searching for a way off. Pitching sideways on the sloping roof, she knew that one wrong step could mean death. She took a deep breath and made a split-second decision to head across the roof to the other side, hoping there might be a vehicle, hay, anything stacked against the side before...

It happened too fast.

A section of plywood gave way beneath her, and before she could react, she fell through the roof.

She screamed, plummeting down through the air, feeling her body collide with a cage before bouncing off onto the hard concrete floor. Pain exploded through her body and for a moment or two, she lay there, gasping for breath.

Even if she wanted to move, she couldn't.

Lena wasn't sure if she had broken her back, a rib or both. All she knew was pain wracked her body. As her vision blurred, she could just make out the faces of the farm owners as they loomed over her.

Over the next few minutes, she heard muffled voices as they talked about what to do with her. "Take her inside the house," a woman said. "We'll figure out what to do next. And if she has a phone, destroy it."

Lena felt a surge of fear and pain wash over her as someone lifted her and carried her over their shoulder towards the farmhouse. She felt the bitter wind on her skin. She couldn't have struggled even if she wanted to, the pain was too much.

Inside the home, Lena took in her new surroundings.

The farmhouse was dark and cluttered with piles of junk and debris littering the floors. As they passed a room on her right, she noticed it was dimly lit with worn furniture and peeling wallpaper that was stained with damage. If anyone lived here, they were disgusting individuals. A large dog bed sat in the corner, and she could see several older dogs of different breeds sharing it.

In a daze, her eyes roamed, soaking in every detail of the space.

A staircase led up to the second floor. To her left was a doorway that fed into an old country-style kitchen. She caught a glimpse of a sink piled high with dirty dishes and a worn-out refrigerator covered in fridge magnets.

She was set down on a sofa. The hearth of a fireplace on the opposite wall was filled with ashes and debris. A collection of old magazines and newspapers were stacked haphazardly on a coffee table beside a plate of food and an overfilled ashtray. Framed photographs of farm owners hung on the wall alongside a deer's head.

Despite the state of the farmhouse, there was a sense that someone called it home. Any warmth that might have come from that was overshadowed by the grim reality of her situation. She was trapped, and at the mercy of those who had no qualms about breaking the law.

"Little bitch."

"You know her?" the male asked.

"That's the same woman who wanted to see the dogs earlier today."

A door opened. "Teresa. I found this in the barn," a younger voice said.

All of the activity happening around her was just a blur. The world kept fading in and out, nothing more than a haze.

"I knew it," the burly woman said, looking at the camera then passing it to the older guy. "Seems we've got an animal activist. Is that what you are?" she asked, grabbing Lena by the shirt.

"Please. I need to see a doctor."

"See a doctor?" The woman laughed.

"No, she's right, Teresa. Maybe we should drop her off at the hospital. She doesn't look too good."

"And you're not too bright," she retorted, slapping him around the back of the head. "What do you think she's going to say to the cops?"

"I won't say anything," Lena muttered.

"Of course you won't, as you aren't going to speak to them."

"Teresa. A word over here," another male said. He was a stringy-looking fella with an angular face that was weathered and lined from years of working in the fields. His hair was greasy, with grey intermingled with dark brown. He reminded Lena of a rat with his slanted forehead and beady little eyes set deep within his skull. He was wearing a tattered denim jacket with frayed cuffs and a ripped collar. Underneath, a faded plaid shirt that had seen better days, a few buttons missing. His jeans were stained or covered in muck with one of the knees torn.

Lena strained to hear the conversation.

While they talked about her and the situation they found themselves in, she could tell that the one called Patrick wasn't going down for something Teresa wanted to do.

"You are as much in this as I am. If we let her leave now, we are screwed. Forget this little side business. Forget retiring. The only view you will see will be from behind bars," Teresa told him.

"We move the dogs. We've done it before," he said.

"Yeah, and you know how much that delayed things? No. Not this time. It's one woman. We stay the course. It's taken us this long to make connections. This place is prime pickings. No one is looking for missing dogs around here. Tourists, residents, this region is the armpit of Upstate New York, millions of acres of wilderness, plenty of mountains, more than enough space for dogs and people to vanish from sight."

Lena wanted to protest but among the many aches and pains, her head was starting to throb hard. She kept fading in and out of consciousness.

"You might be trigger-happy but not me. I say we put it to a vote with the others. We can destroy her phone and camera. Then she has no proof. It's her word against ours."

"She knows where we are, bonehead!"

"Fuck you, Teresa!"

"Hey, guys, chill."

"Don't tell me to chill. She's a problem," Teresa said. "One woman. That's all."

"One woman whose phone will be tracked here if we don't let her go. Haven't you ever watched any crime shows? They will ping that phone off the towers and triangulate on this place. Then try explaining that," Patrick said.

Teresa seemed overly confident. "That's simple. We sell dogs. We are a legal breeder. Just like anyone else. Just people don't know where we get our main dogs from or the high-priced ones that sell. The rest, they are just a litter. So, she came out to see me about a dog. I showed her, she couldn't make up her mind and left. You take the phone and dump it in a lake, off a cliff, I don't give a fuck. But anywhere but here."

Patrick laughed. "You must think cops are stupid. The last place she was seen was us. Even if they don't arrest us, they will stick a cop in an unmarked car outside the farm and watch us day and night. Then how are we going to conduct business? Huh? Yeah, just like I thought. Who's the bonehead now!"

Teresa lashed out, cracking him with a right hook and knocking him to the floor. He bounced up about to retaliate but the third guy intervened. "Stop. Enough. This isn't helping. You're both right and wrong. What's done is done."

The front door creaked open. "Hey Teresa."

"What is it, Magnus?"

"I think I found her vehicle. It's parked down the road, off to the side."

Teresa marched over to Lena and dug her grubby little fingers into her pockets, searching for keys. Lena couldn't have resisted even if she tried.

"Please, I work for the newspaper. People will be looking for me."

"What?" she asked, pulling out a set of jangling keys then tossing them to someone off to her left.

"The *Adirondack Daily Enterprise.*"

Teresa looked back at the others.

"Fuck!" Patrick said as he kicked the coffee table then plowed a fist into a photo frame on the wall, cracking it.

Teresa grinned. "So? You think that changes anything?"

"My ex works for State Police."

Lena tossed everything and anything she could at them, realizing that this wasn't going to end well if she didn't try. They would have to work fast and get rid of her. They had no intentions of keeping her around. Time was their enemy and as long as she was alive, they could go to jail.

15

Tuesday, November 22, 7:25 a.m.

The pressure was relentless.

The news that another person had gone missing arrived by way of a phone call to his mobile at after six fifty in the morning, waking Noah from his slumber.

"Yeah?" he mumbled, pawing at his eyes.

"We've got another," Callie replied.

Ana Silva had called the county sheriff's office late in the evening after her partner Laura had failed to return from her evening jog.

It was a common myth among the public that they had to wait twenty-four hours or discover something unusual before they could report a loved one missing. Having been involved in numerous searches, Noah was all too familiar with the problems that arose when a family took too long to call the police.

In this case, however, Ana had trusted her instincts, called it in and then gone out to search. She was the one to find her shoe near a trailhead not far from Laura's Ford Explorer. Fortunately, she had the good sense not to touch it.

Having slept at Ed's the night before, Noah had only a short drive to River Road, one of the many running routes used by joggers. The four-mile stretch ran along the Ausable River, offering breathtaking views of the High Peaks. North of the local airport and southeast of the town, it was a common spot for those training. It was also very remote with few homes nearby.

Noah sipped at the coffee Ed had handed him on the way out after reassuring him that his brother was in good hands.

If he took a turn for the worse, Ed had told Noah he would strong-arm Ray into his truck and take him to the hospital. Noah still wasn't convinced it was the best thing to do but his brother had been adamant — no hospital. So, he'd slept on the sofa across from him, his mind chewing over what Tanya had told him about Ray's debts. He would have that conversation when he was well enough, until then, he'd opted to give him space.

Morning offered positive signs. The color was back in his cheeks. He was sleeping so Noah didn't bother to wake him. Still, he wasn't out of the woods yet. The first forty-eight hours were critical. Any number of complications could arise from water exposure – infection, pneumonia, heart failure, it was all on the table.

"Meet me at the Connery Pond Whiteface Landing Trail-head," Callie said.

"I thought you said River Road?" Noah replied as he drove out.

"I'll explain when you get here."

He couldn't miss it, as it was the exit and entrance that led up to Ed's place.

~

Arriving that morning as the sun began to rise, Noah noted the presence of multiple cruisers. They'd already cordoned off the area. He swung the Bronco around and parked it alongside the others.

"Yes, just keep them back. I want that road blocked on both ends. The only ones that get through are those who live on that road," Callie said to another deputy before turning and crossing the trailhead lot.

She fell in step with him, pointing to an area close to a 2020 Green Explorer.

There were several yellow sandwich board markers placed to preserve spots where evidence had come to rest. "One of her sneakers was found there, her headphones a short distance away, over there. It looks as if she was dragged to a waiting vehicle."

Noah eyed the path through the gravel. "No dog?"

"Her partner says she doesn't own one. She was out for her evening run. Never missed a session. She'd just come off a four day stretch of ten hour shifts over at High Peaks Academy."

Noah turned abruptly.

"I know. A coincidence or targeted?" Callie said, nodding. "Seems she works in their infirmary as a nurse. We assume she knew Katherine."

"And her partner?" Noah asked.

"Oh. Um. Ana Silva. Forty-six. They've been seeing each other for just under a year. Ana works for city hall. She doesn't live with her but she's a resident of High Peaks. She was cooking dinner at her house when Laura stepped out to squeeze in the evening run."

"What time was that?"

"Just after six."

He nodded. "So, it would have been dark out."

"And with next to no traffic out here, and homes spread far apart..."

"No one saw anything." He sighed.

"Actually, we have a couple of witnesses. Not to her being dragged and shoved into a vehicle but a couple walking their dog witnessed a suspicious SUV driving back and forth up this road, they aren't exactly sure but the husband said he thought it looked like a blue Kia Sportage. An older model."

"Could he identify if the driver was male or female?"

"Nope."

Noah swept back his jacket and rested his hand on his service weapon. He glanced off toward River Road. "So, the connection with River Road?"

Callie brought out her phone and pulled up a social media website. "This is Laura's Facebook page." She scrolled up through several of the posts. She had posted all of her runs online showing the route she took. "Laura put out an invite to other friends a few months ago, stating that she usually parks here and then walks over to the mouth of River Road and runs the full stretch down to Cascade Road and then back again. It's about eight miles round trip."

"So, others knew the route and routine."

"And these posts online are marked public. Meaning anyone could have seen the announcement."

He shook his head. Social media was making it easier to connect and even easier for stalkers and crazies to hone in on the vulnerable. "All right, so there was no post for last night. Where's her phone?" he said, glancing around the gravel.

"That's the thing. We haven't found it yet. The corded headset must have been yanked out of the cellphone when she was jumped and dragged. At least that's the going theory. I've called for search and rescue to assist this morning."

"If she's out here."

"Right. But it's where we begin."

Noah dropped to a crouch, touching the gravel. "The tire tracks could have been useful if they weren't driven over multiple times," he said, glancing at the police cruisers.

"And they could have belonged to any number of locals and tourists before or after. Public place and all," Callie said.

He nodded.

Mistakes were made all too often in cases. Police and neighbors unknowingly could destroy evidence. "So where did you dash off to last night?" Callie asked.

"Ah, just some matters related to family."

"Problems?

"It's personal."

He didn't want to get into it with her or tarnish Ray's reputation. Whatever he was going through, it wasn't his place to air his dirty laundry. Likewise, he would have expected nothing less from him. "By the way, any luck with that phone number from the shelter?" Noah asked.

"Yeah, it came back to a private company called the Sawyer Group owned by a journalist. Nate Sawyer."

"Nate Sawyer?"

"You know him?"

The name rang a bell. That's when he remembered the newspaper article from Katherine's home. "I think so. What about High Peaks Academy? What did they tell you about Charlie?"

"There was only one Charlie who was seeing Katherine for counseling. A Charlie Delaney."

"Is he still at the school?"

"Yeah."

"All right. Let's see what we can find this morning, and hope to God that Laura is still alive."

Within two hours the trailhead popular for jogging was packed with experienced SAR professionals, equipped with advanced technology and trained in all forms of search and rescue, along with county deputies and anxious trusted volunteers.

They were given a quick briefing on the situation and how to conduct the search. Then they were divided into teams and provided with maps of the area, along with radios to communicate with the other team leaders. They would be working on both sides of the road and spaced 14 to 20 feet apart as they performed a grid pattern search. They were to alert the others if they found anything of significance: clothing, footprints, personal belongings even if it couldn't be confirmed as Laura's.

The search was conducted with meticulous care and every effort was made to cover as much ground as possible. The upside was the weather was in their favor. A bright blue sky stretched overhead. It was cold but nothing that would deter them from continuing.

The teams worked tirelessly, combing the terrain and calling out for Laura.

High above, two drones were brought in along with a helicopter using FLIR technology to get a better lay of the land.

As the morning wore on, the search became increasingly desperate. The voices of searchers echoed through the forest. "Laura!"

Despite their efforts, there was still no sign of her.

"High Peaks Academy isn't far from here," Noah hollered.

"Less than a few miles down the road," Callie said as she brushed aside tree branches and gazed down into the thick underbrush.

Noah couldn't help but wonder about the connection between Katherine and Laura besides their employer. His thoughts were distracted, circling between searching, Nicholas

Evans, Charlie Delany, Nate Sawyer and Ana Silva, when his radio crackled.

One of the teams had made a breakthrough. They had found a cellphone that matched the description of Laura's provided by Ana. With renewed energy, and feeling as if they were heading in the right direction, the searchers pushed on, surveying the area close to where her phone was found discarded in a ditch.

It was the beginning of the end.

Several hours passed before they found what none of them really wanted to find. It took Noah a good 20 minutes to wade through the thick underbrush to reach the location. It was set far back from the road, about three miles from the trailhead where her sneaker had been found.

Laura was dangling from a tree, fully clothed, a rope of similar color and design to the one tied around Katherine was looped over her head.

Below her dangling feet, a small log kicked to one side.

There was no suicide note. Nothing to indicate she'd willingly done this. As several deputies took photos, others secured the scene. Noah's gaze drifted through the tree line toward the historic property of High Peaks Academy.

His mind wandered.

Two victims found a few miles from each other, one in water, the other hanging from a tree. Both made to look as if they'd committed suicide, yet on closer inspection, it was much more.

"Noah."

His mind was lost, making connections, thinking about times, days, the way each one met her end. "Noah!" Callie said again, clicking fingers in front of his face. He turned back in time to see deputies cutting Laura down. Searchers were turned away, thanked, and told not to speak to media or anyone until an official statement was made by the county sheriff's office.

"What?" he replied.

"This place will be swarming with media and oddballs in the next hour. You know how it goes. We need to get the coroner out here."

"Yeah, best of luck with that."

He turned his attention to Laura. It didn't matter how many times he saw the dead, it didn't get any easier. As they set her down, he noticed her blonde hair was matted in blood. Noah got closer, gloving up. "Roll her over," he said. He used a pen to lift some of the hair to get a better look. There at the back of her head was a deep laceration. Was it from being dragged or cracked on the back of the skull? He looked up, entertaining for a second the idea that she'd had some kind of manic episode. In his years, he'd seen it all. Those who had attempted suicide and failed, then tried again and succeeded.

He scanned the ground and noticed droplets of blood leading away to a jagged rock. "Bag that," he said.

Noah stood below the branch Laura had been dangling from. He glanced down, noticing more blood. Although his mind wanted to go to murder, as everything was pointing to that, he couldn't help but rule out what this attempted to look like.

"Seems someone cracked her over the back of the head with the rock," Noah said.

"Then why hang her?" she asked

"To make it look like suicide. I figure she put up a fight," he replied.

He stepped back and looked up at the knot around the tree. It was a similar knot to those used on Katherine. He'd have to break the branch and slide it off to get a better look.

Noah looked back at Laura. Her one foot was bare. There were grazes on the bottom but not on the heel as if to indicate she'd been dragged. Her other one still had on a sneaker and sock.

"The ankle sock?" Callie said, observing him. "It's inside the other sneaker back at the trailhead."

He rose and looked back at the branch.

"What is it?"

"I'm thinking." He pointed to her foot. "She was walked out here. The grazes could indicate that."

"So she was conscious?"

"Conscious, maybe. At least for a while. Perhaps she came to and tried to make a run for it while whoever was setting this up... or..."

"You think she could have done this to herself?" Callie gazed down. "But what about the laceration on the back of the head?"

"I don't know, Callie. Again, it's just a theory. We have to explore all possibilities. Maybe the first attempt failed. The rope came away from the branch and she landed hard hitting the back of her head."

"But why would she take her life?"

He looked at her. "Could be any number of reasons. Guilt maybe? And, if so, did she play a hand in Katherine's death? Or was she targeted? We need to speak with Rector Hawthorne again."

As he was speaking, his train of thought was interrupted by singing. He glanced past Callie. She turned and the two of them watched as the coroner of the region came sauntering into view. His love of metal music was obvious from the faded black T-shirt emblazoned with Slayer under his brown suit jacket. It looked as if it had been fished out of a thrift store bargain bin. Oscar Westborough had shoulder-length curly black hair, dark jeans and was sporting a pair of red Doc Martens.

Noah's brow furrowed, he was a stark contrast to the serious and somber atmosphere. He arrived wearing earphones, bopping his head from side to side, cigarette in the corner of his mouth with a very devil-may-care attitude.

"Thank God it's not the summer, right? Mosquitos love to eat me more than my lady does," he said, grinning. "Oscar Westborough, but you can call me Ozzy."

"I wonder why," Noah muttered.

Ozzy dropped to a crouch, humming to whatever tune was playing in his ear. He took out his cigarette and blew smoke. "Well, she's dead. That's for sure."

Noah rolled his eyes.

What was this, amateur hour?

He took a tablet out of his backpack and began tapping. "Well, we better get her back to the hospital. I expect Dr. Adelaide Chambers will be just rearing to get her grubby hands on this one."

"Laura Summers."

"What's that?"

"That's her name," Noah said.

"Well, you would know. I just examine the bodies, pronounce death, you know, usual run-of-the-mill stuff."

"How long you been a coroner?" Noah asked.

Ozzy took one last drag on his cigarette and dropped the butt. "A couple of years."

Noah looked at Callie. It was hard to hide his disdain for the kid. "There are four coroners in this region, and they sent you?"

"Three actually. One quit two weeks ago, realized he didn't have the stomach for it. Five years." He laughed. "You'd think he would have figured that out by now."

"And the other two?"

"Oh, well, you'd be hard pressed to reach them, they like to play hard to get," he said, cracking a joke to which Noah didn't smile.

Ozzy picked up on it almost immediately, especially after Noah reached down and picked up the cigarette butt.

Ozzy coughed, clearing his throat. "Anyway, we should get this moving."

Noah placed the cigarette butt in Ozzy's top jacket pocket, patted it to make it clear that's where it belonged, not at a crime scene, then Noah walked past him. "You do that."

"Where you going?" Callie asked.

"To pay a visit to Nate Sawyer," Noah replied over his shoulder.

"You want me to come?"

He turned, answering her as he walked backwards. "No. Have Laura's phone dusted for prints, get Rishi on it to see what we can extract, and then get a list of all licensed blue Kia Sportage's in the area. Canvass the neighborhood for video footage and check with local PD and State to see if there have been any reports of stolen vehicles in the last month matching that model." He walked on, then stopped. "Oh," he waved a finger at the ground. "Bag the rope. Check for prints, hair, you know the routine."

16

Tuesday, November 22, 12:15 p.m.

What on earth was the stranger doing?

It was only as he got closer that Noah recognized it was no stranger. Detective Angus McKenzie had his back turned and was resting his foot on top of the Bronco's rear bumper, pumping it as if testing the suspension.

The vehicle groaned.

After working his way out of the collective group back to his vehicle, Noah was surprised to see the peculiar Scotsman. He had a phone up to his ear and was talking loud enough to scare a flock of birds out of the trees. They soared overhead, squawking as Noah cleared his throat.

McKenzie turned, eyeing him. "Aye. I'll tell him. I will do."

He hung up.

"You mind," Noah said, gesturing to his muddy boot on the bumper.

He removed it, sniffing hard. “Shabby ride. State not able to swing you a cruiser?”

“I prefer this,” Noah replied, moving around him to get in. He had his hand on the handle when McKenzie let loose.

“Well, if I’m going to be with you, we should probably discuss rules. One being who drives.”

“Excuse me?”

“I prefer to drive. Nothing against you but with retirement around the corner the last thing I need is my life cut short by a heavy-footed Yank. I’m not going out that way.”

“Um. Back up the train.” Noah released his hand from the driver’s side, closing the door. “You must have your wires crossed; Thorne is assisting.”

“Not now she isn’t. I mean. Let me rephrase that. Not in the capacity you think.” He winked at him as if suggesting his relationship with Thorne was more than copacetic. McKenzie strode around to the driver’s side completely convinced he was getting in.

Noah pulled out his phone and stood in front of the driver’s door, blocking access.

“If you’re looking to run it by Rivera, forget it,” McKenzie added. “That’s who I was just speaking to on the phone. She was the one that green-lit this little shindig. Now, I’ll admit, it’s not my first choice but I can’t argue with the powers that be.”

“But you said you were snowed under with work.”

“I am. Trust me, lad, if I had my way, I would be anywhere but here. But with another body on our hands, and no nearer to solving it, between you and I, Rivera doesn’t want this going sideways. Hence, the need for me.” He held out his hands. “Keys.”

“You’re not driving my vehicle.”

“Aye, I am, lad.”

“Oh, hell no.”

McKenzie jabbed a finger in the air. "Now let's not start off on the wrong foot."

"I'm not your lad." Unconvinced by the crap spewing from his mouth, Noah leaned back against the Bronco and made the call, keeping a close eye on him. Rivera answered almost as if she knew what he was about to ask.

"It was my decision, Noah," she said.

"I have Callie."

"Of course you do, but now you have McKenzie."

"I appreciate that but we can handle it."

"I have no doubts. I am just tripling our efforts in light of the recent discovery. The sooner we have answers, the better. The mayor and media are all over this. Rumors of a serial killer in our midst are already being tossed around. That kind of talk, well, it gets everyone a little antsy."

"I understand, but—"

"Let's not forget, Noah. State is working with us and local PD, not the other way around this time. With all due respect, this isn't the murder of your brother, and so, I want the best working on this."

"And that's McKenzie?"

The Scotsman looked over at him through narrowed eyes as he tried to eavesdrop on the conversation. He already had an unlit cigarette in his mouth.

"I should remind you that Thorne isn't a detective. Maybe one day, but for now, she's just one of our deputies."

"And a damn fine one at that," Noah shot back.

"I don't dispute that but McKenzie brings two decades' worth of experience from the big city."

"City policing is very different."

"It doesn't take away his experience, Noah. Now I've made my decision. Run with it or I'll call State and have them assign someone else."

"Understood." He hung up.

"So?" McKenzie said in his brash tone.

Noah turned and got in the driver's side before he had a chance to argue. "She's cleared you to work with me... but not to drive. Something to do with your eyes aren't what they used to be."

"What?"

"They dropped you off here, yes?"

"Aye."

"Exactly. Read between the lines. Sucks, but hey, don't shoot the messenger." He slammed the door closed and through his open window thumbed over his shoulder. "Get in. You're riding shotgun."

Noah stifled a laugh as McKenzie mumbled a few choice words and skirted around the rear to the passenger side.

~

THE SAWYER GROUP operated out of a warehouse just off Old Military Road. It was located just across from High Peaks Self Storage. It stood out, abandoned and forgotten. The outer walls, once painted in a bright shade of blue, had faded to a dull grey over the years.

Reaching it was a headache in and of itself, not only because McKenzie wanted to be brought up to speed, but because a section of the roadway had been closed off for repaving in the months prior and still hadn't been opened, causing a detour through the town and traffic headaches.

"And you say this lad is a journalist?" McKenzie stifled a laugh. "What does he write about — the homeless?" He chuckled and glanced at Noah who said nothing. After parking, they got out and headed over to a large steel gate that blocked off the entrance and required a code for entry. There were two cameras angled down. The owners of the establishment certainly looked as if they were taking security seriously. A large sign on the gate read: WARNING: KEEP OUT! GUARD DOGS ON PATROL.

Beyond the gate, Noah could see activity. The property was used by multiple businesses, none of which were related to each other. The sound of machinery could be heard coming from an auto repair shop — sanders in operation and the steady clang of wrenches and steel. Several doors down were an out-of-business printing company, beside that a clothing manufacturer, and finally a coffee roastery that also didn't look as if it was open. If the Sawyer Group was operating out of one of the offices, he couldn't see a sign.

Noah reached out of the driver's side window and hit the button. The speakers squawked. "Can I help you?"

"Here to speak with Nate Sawyer."

There was no answer.

Noah gave it a second or two before he pressed the button again. This time no one answered. McKenzie's impatience bubbled up to the surface. He got out. "Aye, let me handle this." He went over to the gate and gave it a shake to see if it was open. The clatter brought an angry Rottweiler out from underneath a stack of metal on a stand.

It came barreling toward the gate, barking furiously.

"Ah, shut your noise!" McKenzie said.

"McKenzie. Get in. They've probably gone to get him."

McKenzie returned. Noah tried the buzzer again. "Hello? Mr. Sawyer. I'm an investigator from State. We need to speak with you. Could you pull the dog back and open the gate?"

He released the button and waited. Then the same voice from earlier came back on the line. "You got a badge?"

Noah took it out and waved it toward the angled cameras.

"Can't see it," the voice replied.

He stretched it out a little further.

"All right," the voice said.

There was a short pause before the door to one of the offices opened farther down and a large African American stepped out. He was sporting a blue shirt with the top button undone, a pair of black slacks and highly polished shoes. He let out a whistle and the dog retreated into the office. The guy disappeared back out of view and then the gate groaned open. He reappeared a moment later, standing in the doorway.

Noah drove through and parked off to the right of the building. He got out and was about to approach when the guy hollered, "That's close enough. Whatever you need to say, you can do it from there."

"You Nate Sawyer?"

"I am."

Noah looked off to his left then back at him. "Sir, it's probably best we go inside."

"Why did you look toward the gate?" Nate asked, looking a little skittish.

"Can't be too careful. Look, we're here about Katherine Evans."

Nate squinted. "Zeus. Sic 'em!"

"What?" McKenzie blurted.

In an instant, the dog shot out of the office, darting toward them. McKenzie bolted back to the Bronco. Noah reached for his service weapon, intent on scaring the dog off. But the dog was too quick. Before he managed to withdraw it, the beast was on him, knocking him to the ground and latching on to his forearm. Fortunately, he was wearing a thick jacket, otherwise the dog's jaws would have made quick work of a suit. Still, Noah writhed in agony as it yanked at his arm, tearing through the jacket. He had every right to shoot the dog but it had a hold of his gun arm.

"McKenzie!" Noah shouted.

If there was ever a time he wished he had Axel, it was now. He loved dogs but the merciless beast was rag dolling him. Out the corner of his eye he saw Nate sprint for a nearby truck.

Crack.

A round boomed.

Now he knew what McKenzie had gone for. The shotgun between the seats. The dog yelped, let go and streaked away back into the safety of the office.

"I didn't say shoot the damn thing," Noah yelled as he scrambled to his feet and ran toward Nate's truck, hoping to stop him before he could swing out of the property. The truck was too fast. Nate floored it but not before Noah latched on to the back of the tailgate. His feet dragged behind him as it tore out of the gate, bounced over the curb and headed north to what would become Route 86.

Noah had only once seen this happen in his career, and it was back when he was a regular state trooper. The officer he trained under had stopped an unlicensed vehicle. He was in the process of getting the driver out when the vehicle tore away. The officer had half of his body through the driver's side, trying to get at the keys. Eventually the driver shook him off and they ended up catching the guy one state over.

His partner had ended up in the hospital for a couple of days with a broken arm, and multiple scratches and bruises. He was lucky.

Noah figured he might not be.

"Shut off the vehicle!" Noah yelled but his voice was lost in the roar of the engine. Was Sawyer even aware that he was dragging him? Releasing his grip seemed the most logical thing to do, but at the speed he was going, having his skull bounce off the asphalt might have been game over. Instead, Noah hung on for dear life, his boots trailing behind him as he tried to pull himself up while the truck slowed to take the T-junction off Old Military Road and 86. By a stroke of luck or fate, as the truck turned, Noah managed to get a forearm over the tailgate, keeping his body high up on the back.

An engine roared behind them.

Noah cast a glance over his shoulder to see his Bronco driven by McKenzie closing in on them. Wind blew grit up in his face, making him squint as Sawyer tried to shake him off the tailgate. But that wasn't happening.

One thing Sawyer had underestimated was McKenzie.

The Scotsman quickly closed the gap.

Still, unable to get his feet up, Noah glanced back at McKenzie who was dangerously close to the back bumper. Had Sawyer slammed the brakes on, Noah would have been sandwiched between the two of them.

Noah figured if McKenzie brought the Bronco close enough, he could bring his boots up onto the front bumper and use that to push himself over the tailgate into the bed of the truck. It was a feat that might have been easier had Sawyer not been zigzagging all over the road to prevent McKenzie from trying a pit maneuver.

The situation only got worse by the second. With the wind whistling in his ears, he couldn't tell McKenzie to back off. If he lost his grip now, he would go under the Bronco.

Noah could already feel his hands slipping as he desperately tried to maintain his grip. Then, as if McKenzie could read his lips or realized by Noah's frequent glances back what he had in mind, he closed the gap, bringing the Bronco in really tight, almost to the point of pinning him. Noah slapped the worst thoughts from his mind as he used every ounce of strength to lift his boots onto the front bumper of the Bronco directly behind him. It wasn't easy as Sawyer could see in his rearview mirror and was trying to put distance between the two vehicles.

Still, McKenzie stayed close, allowing Noah to finally lift his boots up onto the bumper. As soon as they touched, he pushed off and went over into the bed of the truck. His body thumped hard against the metal, causing Sawyer to glance back. Battered, bruised and more pissed off than before, Noah clambered towards the front of the truck. As soon as he was behind the rear window, he pulled his service weapon and tapped the window. "Pull over. Now!"

He might have had every reason to squeeze the trigger and end Sawyer's life but he didn't. Reality came rushing in as Sawyer eased off the gas and slowed the truck, bringing the vehicle to a stop at the edge of the road.

Gravel crunched below the tires. Grit swirled in the air.

In an instant, McKenzie swerved the Bronco up beside it to block off any attempts by Sawyer to change his mind.

With a gun raised, Noah cried out commands.

"Driver. Turn off the truck. Take the keys out and put them on the roof."

The engine died. A cautious hand extended out the driver's side and placed the keys on the top. Noah scooped them up and got out of the back of the truck. His body ached. His muscles felt as if they'd been stretched far beyond what they should. His arm felt like it was on fire, and he could feel trickles of warm blood running down to his hand.

"Get out with your hands up!"

"You good, Sutherland?" McKenzie hollered while keeping his service weapon trained on Sawyer.

"Never better," he said sarcastically.

"Like I said, you should have let me drive."

Noah scoffed, shaking his head. Within seconds, Noah dragged Sawyer to the ground and put a knee into his shoulder blade and began to read him his Miranda rights.

CHAPTER 17

SEVENTEEN

Tuesday, November 22, 2:40 p.m.

Noah was in no mood for Sawyer's lies but since cuffing him and hauling him back to the Adirondack County Sheriff's Office, that's all that was coming from his mouth.

"My lawyer is going to have a field day with you all. I've done nothing wrong except protect myself from you lunatics. What did you expect? You show up in an unmarked police vehicle. Neither of you are in uniform. You flash some bogus badge. You could have been making it all up."

"Aye, you must think we're fools," McKenzie said. "Setting a vicious dog on a law enforcement officer. My partner is having his arm sewn back together as we speak. If he doesn't pull through, you might as well slap on some lipstick and prepare to sing for your supper as you are going to be getting really friendly with your cellmate. You are in a whole world of trouble, lad."

Noah shook his head. He was standing outside the interview room, peering through a one-way window as McKenzie delivered his good cop, bad cop act. To be fair, he was pretty good at it, switching from hard-nosed to — we're here to help you routine. The strange part was someone else was meant to be performing one of the roles. No, McKenzie figured he could handle both.

"He called you partner?" Callie asked, her eyebrow shooting up. "That's new."

"His words, not mine."

"So will you pull through?" she said, her lip curling up.

Noah shook his head. "He loves to exaggerate."

"How is it?" she asked, glancing at Noah's bandaged arm.

He felt a surge of pain go from his forearm up to his neck. Adrenaline had been pumping through his body so hard that he didn't realize the dog had punctured his jacket and torn into his arm. It was only when he felt blood trickle off the tips of his fingers did he assess the damage. Fortunately, the leather had taken the brunt of it and the wounds were shallow. Still, the pain was hard to ignore. He'd have to swing by the hospital on the way back home that evening to get a tetanus shot. The last thing he wanted was to have bacteria enter his body. For now, he'd tossed back some Advil and bandaged it up.

"Oh, it's just dandy," he muttered, turning his arm and wincing. "Well, we should get in there and bring some order to this before Angus starts delivering his William Wallace speech."

"Well, here you go," Callie said, handing him a folder with new information she'd uncovered. The two of them entered the interview room. Nate Sawyer was on one side of the table, while McKenzie was inched up close to him.

As soon as the door opened, McKenzie glanced at Noah. "Ah, look at that, Lazarus rose from the dead. Seems it's your lucky day, laddy." He patted Sawyer on the arm as he turned toward Noah and Callie. Callie leaned against the wall, there to observe while Noah took a seat. He slapped the folder down in front of him.

Sawyer leaned forward, appearing all contrite. "Listen, I'm sorry about your arm. Like I told your partner. I didn't know you were cops. Had I known, I wouldn't have fled."

"Right, because you thought we were out to get you for...?"

"Anything."

"Because that's your usual response when people show up to speak to you."

Sawyer scowled. "Why do you think I'm operating out of a warehouse with steel fencing and a guard dog? You have to understand, in my line of work where I'm looking to expose secrets and lies, I have all manner of people gunning to take me down. You aren't going to charge me for what happened today, are you?"

"Well, that depends on your answers." Noah flipped open the folder. "Nate Sawyer, thirty-eight years of age. Not married, no kids, resident of High Peaks, formerly of Saranac Lake and before that you were based out of Syracuse. Freelance journalist. Previously worked for the *Adirondack Daily Enterprise* until you were fired for sexual harassment."

"That's bullshit. In fact, I'm taking them to court for unfairly dismissing me. My lawyer thinks we have a good case. A real slam-dunk."

"Sure you do. That was two years ago."

"Takes time to get the wheels in motion. You all should know that." His gaze bounced between them.

Noah continued reading. "So, you're willing to chat with us without your attorney present, is that right?"

"That depends on your questions today," he said in a cheeky manner as if mirroring Noah's previous response. Noah could tell he was going to be a handful.

"Well, as Detective McKenzie said. You've been read your

rights. If you wish to have an attorney present, you should tell us now."

"And if do?"

"Then this conversation is over."

He eyeballed the others in the room and shrugged. "Like I said, I have nothing to hide. Shoot."

Noah nodded. "Okay then. Where were you last night?"

"Why?"

"Answer the question."

"Balls deep in my secretary."

McKenzie took a step forward. "Aye, that would imply you have balls."

Sawyer cowered back in his seat as if McKenzie was going to strike him. "I was piecing together information that would help my case against the newspaper."

"From what time until?"

"Um. I picked up a chicken burger and fries at roughly five from a local restaurant and headed back to the warehouse and worked until roughly eleven that evening."

"And yet your lawyer said you had a slam-dunk case against them. Sounds as if they had all the information they needed already."

"I was working other angles."

"Can anyone else verify this?"

"For sure."

"We'll need names," McKenzie said. "And numbers."

Sawyer nodded as he fidgeted in his seat, looking even more nervous than before. Noah thumbed his way through the material Callie had gathered. She had done her due diligence. He took out a piece of paper from the folder that had a colored snapshot of an SUV grabbed from online, one that fit the profile of the vehicle seen that night. "You own an all-wheel-drive blue Kia Sportage, don't you?"

"Well —"

Noah continued. "You purchased it at a dealership in Saranac Lake last year for twenty thousand dollars, paid with a certified check from Wells Fargo." Noah took back the piece of paper that had a copy of the check. "The limited-edition model, right?"

Sawyer leaned back in his seat, regarding them with a smirk. "Hold on a second. You put me through hell this morning and dragged me in here because of my vehicle?"

"Answer the question," McKenzie said in a firm tone.

Sawyer chuckled. "For a second there I thought you had something serious on me." He breathed out a sigh of relief. "So did you find it?"

Noah stared back at him.

"Well, I reported it stolen to the High Peaks Police Department last night. Please tell me it hasn't been wrecked?"

Noah glanced at McKenzie.

"Convenient," McKenzie muttered.

Sawyer scowled at him but continued. "You want to tell me what this is all about?"

"A vehicle matching the description of yours was seen multiple times at a murder site last night."

"A murder?"

"Laura Summers. You know her?" Noah asked.

He sat there for a second, studying Noah. "Sure, I know her. I mean not well but I've met and talked to her."

"When was the last time?"

"Maybe a month ago."

"What was it in regards to?"

"A journalistic investigation of the Academy. Katherine Evans reached out to me after reading an article related to my dismissal from the newspaper. She figured we had something in common. We met. Talked. I said I would consider it and after some serious thought, I decided I might be of service. There's nothing worse than seeing good people get unfairly released from a job because the powers that be want to cover their ass."

"Aye, you'd know all about that," McKenzie said.

"Screw you. You asked. I'm telling you what I know."

"So why did Katherine have your phone number on file at the shelter from a year ago?" Noah asked. Sawyer got this confused look. So far, the media hadn't run any story about the identity of the woman pulled from the lake but it was clear that the cogs of Sawyer's mind began to form a picture.

"We were friends."

"How friendly?"

"Look, what is this about?"

They just looked at him and then the penny must have dropped. Sawyer's jaw widened. "Oh, my God. He really did it."

"Did what? Who?"

"Katherine was the woman pulled from the lake, wasn't she?" He hung his head and shook it slowly. "She said that if anything happened to her, that it would be her husband, Nicholas. The two of them weren't getting along well." He sighed. "Look, all I know is that she had to step down from her job. Well, was forced to step down or suffer humiliation and potential career ruin. Nicholas didn't like that. He didn't believe her story and that's why she wanted me to look into it, to clear her name."

"Concerning what?"

"The reason why she was forced to step down."

"Which was??"

"The Academy was trying to say that she was sexually involved with the teens she was counseling. You know, taking the angle that has been seen with other female teachers across this country. Now sure, there have been some that have overstepped the line but not Katherine. I never got that impression.

No, there was something more to this. That's why she hired me. To help. To dig. To uncover the truth." He shook his head and offered back a genuine look of surprise. "And now Laura? And my vehicle? Oh, yes, I can see how this is trying to be spun."

Noah thought back to what Nicholas Evans had said when asked why the parents of students hadn't filed a complaint with the local PD. *"High Peaks Academy is a prestigious school. They wouldn't want that kind of heat. No. She was told to step down to avoid bringing the school's name into disrepute."*

Could they have covered it up?

"Would you know who might have wanted to steal your vehicle?"

He laughed. "Despite the obvious. Nicholas. Someone from the Academy. Take your pick. There are any number of people that would love to see me go down in flames."

"Why?"

"Envy. Hatred. Greed. Pick one. The newspaper, government officials, I've exposed handfuls of assholes over the years. In my line of work it comes with the territory. Don't believe me? Look at all the journalists who have mysteriously ended up dead when they were investigating corruption."

"So, you're a popular guy," McKenzie said.

"No. Unpopular but for all the right reasons," he replied.

"Did you know Katherine was pregnant?" Noah asked, coming straight out with it. He wanted to gauge his reaction or lack thereof. The smile disappeared from Sawyer's face, as if someone had stolen a breath. He leaned back and got this expression that could have been read any number of ways.

"She was pregnant?"

Noah nodded.

"Listen, where were you on Friday the eighteenth of November?"

"That's simple. I worked all day then had a meeting in the evening."

"With who?"

"Alexander Hawthorne."

"Would he recall that?"

"I sure as hell think so. I was about to write one hell of a piece on that place."

Noah stared at him, trying to see a break in his demeanor. There was none. He rose from his seat. "You want some coffee or a cigarette?"

Sawyer nodded slowly. Noah figured it would be a good time to confer with the others. He gestured with a nod of the head to the door and the three of them stepped out. They went back into the room that gave them a clear view of Sawyer. His head hung low, he was rubbing his hands and muttering to himself.

"You think he could be the daddy?" Callie asked.

"We'll soon know once they get the DNA of the fetus."

McKenzie put his foot up on a chair and leaned forward, eyeballing Sawyer through the window. "Only if there is a match. I hardly think he is going to give us consensual DNA without a warrant or court order."

"Hence the reason for a cup of coffee and a smoke," Noah said. They would use surreptitious DNA, otherwise known as cast-off DNA, which came from a tissue, a cup, or another used object.

"Do you think he could have murdered Katherine over the baby and then taken out Laura because Katherine had told her?" Callie asked.

McKenzie balked. "Steady on, lass, you're jumping to a lot of conclusions there. Murdering someone over a baby? You saw the look on his face. He had no bloody idea that she was pregnant."

"Or he wanted it to appear that way," Noah added, not taking his eyes off Sawyer.

"Aye, you could be right. Yeah, I think the bastard is playing us," McKenzie said, staring through the glass. "Seen these types before. All irate one minute and then giving an Oscar performance sob story the next. He fancies himself as some Morgan Freeman. If he keeps this up, the only damn award he'll be getting is my foot up his ass."

Noah stifled a chuckle. "Check with local PD to confirm the report of a stolen vehicle."

McKenzie was quick to offer a rebuttal to Sawyer's answer. "Doesn't mean he wasn't involved. He could have murdered the jogger, dumped his vehicle in some remote place where he had already parked his truck, and then driven over to High Peaks Police Department and reported the SUV missing."

"Possibly but that's where the names of those who can verify his alibi will come into play. Maybe you can handle that," Noah said, patting McKenzie on the arm.

"No need, Callie will do it, won't you, love?"

"Well... I ..."

"That's a good lass, and while you're at it, get me a cup of coffee. I think this is going to be a long ass day. Oh, and don't get me one from that shite machine in the break room. I'm taking a hammer to that bastard later. No, nip down to the local café. I take a large with two cream and three sugar. And snag me one of those strawberry scones. Fucking love those." He lifted a hand, all theatrical. "You know the ones with the icing on the top. And what'll you have, Noah?" he asked, turning to him.

Callie looked at a loss for words.

Noah waved her off and shook his head, to indicate to ignore him. Callie looked utterly perplexed as she strode away. Once she was gone, Noah piped up. "You want coffee, pal, get it yourself. That's not what she's here for."

"Aye, I see, so she only does favors for you. I get it. You cheeky wee lad."

"McKenzie. I don't know how you ran things down in the Big Apple but up here, you're liable to find yourself with a black eye if you keep rattling off at the mouth like that."

McKenzie scoffed, squaring off to him. "Aye, you and whose army?"

Before Noah could reply, Callie returned looking out of sorts. "Noah. Is your phone off?"

"Yeah, while we were in the interview."

"Your daughter Mia is on line two. She sounds pretty worried."

He nodded, hurrying to the nearest phone in the office. He took a seat on the edge of the table and scooped up the handset. "Mia?"

"Dad. I've been trying to get hold of you all morning."

"Sorry. I..." He took out his phone and turned it back on to see a whack of text messages and missed calls from Mia, Ethan and Aiden. "I had my phone off."

"It's mom. She never came home last night."

"What?" He stood up, his body tensing. With the two women dead, and talk of a serial killer on the loose, his mind began to think the worst.

CHAPTER 18

Tuesday, November 22, 3:25 p.m.

A bright afternoon sunshine bathed Ray's face as he awoke. The world came spinning back into view like a kaleidoscope of images through his slitted eyes. He groaned, pawing at his face to dust out the cobwebs of sleep. The aroma of coffee attacked his senses as did the continual sound of metal clinking. His mind was in a hazy fog as his eyes slowly fluttered open and he tried to piece together what he was looking at.

It was an overwhelming sight.

Above him, an intricately painted ceiling displayed a tapestry of vibrant colors and lifelike figures inside panels. He lay there still feeling groggy and took it all in, utterly perplexed. He was lying on a sofa inside a cabin and yet the imagery above looked more geared toward a church. As Ray looked up, he saw a multitude of figures and scenes. It was familiar but for some reason he couldn't quite place where from.

"Quite something, isn't it," a voice said off to his right. "It took Michelangelo five years to paint 343 figures on the ceiling of the Sistine Chapel. It took me all of an hour to wallpaper that print on mine. Sometimes I just lay on that sofa, wondering how on earth he managed to do that without a crook in his neck. It's beyond me. I put that up two months ago and I'm still feeling pain in mine." The stranger ran a hand around the back of his neck. "But hey, it was worth it. It's a beauty, right?"

"Yeah. A real beauty." Ray rubbed his eyes again. The colors were so vivid and figures so real that he almost felt like he could reach out and touch them. He started to recognize some of the scenes from the fresco. There were nine main panels, each depicting a different scene from the book of Genesis, starting with the creation of the world and ending in the account of Noah's ark.

"By the way, I'm Ed."

"Ray."

"I know."

His gaze honed in on the most famous of them all which showed the creation of Adam. It was an iconic scene, one of God depicted as a muscular bearded man stretching out his hand to touch the hand of a reclining Adam. The fingers of the two almost touched, symbolizing the very moment when God breathed life into Adam and gave him the spark of divinity.

"From the first time I laid eyes on it, I knew I had to have it in my home," Ed said. "A masterpiece of Renaissance art that tells the story of humanity's creation and fall from grace. And oh, how we have fallen. Of course, we don't like to think that we have. Not us. No. But we have."

"That's great," Ray muttered, still trying to crawl his way back to the land of the living. Vague fleeting memories of the previous evening flickered through his mind. Dark thoughts that at the time he felt could only be solved by removing himself.

"You know, I often wonder, is humanity the fallen angels? You know — the ones who at one time were angels but pissed off the big fella so much that he gave them their marching orders. Of course, we couldn't entertain that thought. It's so much easier to think that we are separate from the horrors of this world, as we quickly align ourselves with the good. And yet what we have done right?" He paused. "Makes you wonder, doesn't it?"

"What?"

"Are we the light denying our darkness and trying to find our way back?"

His words were too much for Ray. His head was pounding from an intense hangover from all the alcohol he'd consumed prior to his leap into the gorge, most of which he could barely remember. "Do you have an Advil?"

"Hang tight. I have something better."

Ray glanced off and saw the blurry looking old man shuffling over to a cabinet as he continued to talk. His gaze bounced to a modest kitchen, well equipped with everything that was needed to whip up a hearty meal. The countertops were thick durable wood, and there were all manner of pots, pans and utensils hanging over an island which was surrounded by mismatched chairs. "So, who do you owe money to?" Glasses clinked. He heard the slosh of liquid.

"What?" Ray replied.

"Money. Debts. Loan sharks. If life isn't working, it usually boils down to money," he said as he returned holding a glass full of red liquid. "Get that down you. A Bloody Mary. Always does the job." He stuck it under his nose and Ray felt his gag reflex kick in. He turned his head away, groaning.

"I'll pass."

"Don't be silly. Get it down you. You'll feel as right as rain in twenty minutes."

"Thanks, but no."

"Suit yourself." The old-timer chugged it back in one gulp and returned to his seat.

Ray glanced around the cabin. The rustic wooden walls were adorned with hunting trophies and antique pieces, including an old bear trap and a pair of mounted antlers. The floor was a polished hardwood, covered in a soft, plush rug that was the image of the American flag. The guy's choice of décor was eclectic to say the least.

The leather sofa and two armchairs were arranged around a stone fireplace. Further down the hall he could see into a study where there were bookshelves filled to the brim with what he could only imagine was classic literature, adventure novels and survival guides. There was a large, weathered map of the region hanging above a computer desk.

"Where's my brother?" Ray asked.

"At work, I believe," Ed said, returning the glass to the cabinet. "Besides the hangover, how are you feeling?"

"Like a steamroller went over me."

"I expect so. You know the problem with your generation?"

He groaned, rubbing his eyes. "No. But I expect you're going to tell me," Ray said as he swung his legs off the edge of the sofa and the world turned on its axis bringing the old-timer into view.

"Too soft. Too self-centered. Always looking for someone to stroke your head and tell you it's going to be okay. Well maybe it's not. Maybe you won't get that caramel latte with whipped cream when you order it. Maybe life doesn't hand out gold stars for using your damn brain cells. And maybe you'll have to deal with the consequences of your own choices. Too bad. You see in my day, if we came home with our legs attached to our ass, it was a good fucking day. We didn't have time for the bullshit you all get wrapped up in. So come on. Whose pooch did you screw?"

"None of your damn business."

"Au contraire, mon frere. The moment your brother dragged your ass in here, it became my business. You see, since I've been associated with you Sutherlands, I've learned fast that your clan are like a bad dream. I've been threatened, beaten over the head, and if that wasn't bad enough, I've had to endure listening to you snore for the past sixteen hours. Now if trouble is going to show up at my door, I'd like to know one good reason why I shouldn't hand over your ass to them on a platter."

"I'm a cop."

"Obviously not a smart one."

Ray glared at him. He didn't have the strength to argue. "You think I could get some coffee and Advil?"

Ed eyed him through a suspicious gaze. "You're in luck. I poured one only ten minutes ago. Or is that considered not fresh enough?" He was being sarcastic.

"That will do fine."

"I'm glad because I wasn't going to make any more." He got up and went into the kitchen. Ray ran a hand over his face and staggered to his feet.

"Um. Where's the bathroom?"

"Down the hall. But if you're taking a piss, use the seat. And by that, I mean, sit your ass down. I don't want to be wiping up drops from the floor."

Ray gave a half-hearted salute and went to relieve himself.

He passed the master bedroom. It was simple but odd with a king-size bed covered in a camouflage bedspread. There was a bedside table that held a small lamp and a few books related to foraging, different kinds of mushrooms and surviving the end times.

Ray shook his head and wandered into the bathroom. It was small but functional, with a rustic sink and mirror, a clawfoot tub that looked as if it had seen better days, and a separate shower. The walls were wooden planks and there was a small window which offered a view of the surrounding yard and forest.

On the wall was a framed motto: "The only easy day was yesterday."

He returned a moment later to find a mug of coffee, a bottle of Advil, some cream and a bowl of sugar on the table. He sank into his seat under Ed's watchful eye. He tossed two pills back and swallowed before drinking some black coffee.

He kept glancing up at Ed. He knew the old fart wouldn't back down unless he told him.

"The casino. Okay? That's who I owe," Ray blurted out.

"How much?"

He was hesitant to say. It was embarrassing.

"C'mon. Spit it out."

"Four G's."

"Four thousand?"

"Add two more zeros to that."

"Four hundred thousand?"

"Give or take."

There was silence for a minute or two.

Ed blew out his cheeks. "Ah, I can respect someone owing money to try and get by in life. A loan for a business, a mortgage, a college course, hell, even a car, but gambling?"

"Go ahead. Say it."

"Oh, I'll say it because I'm sure your family won't. That takes some high-level stupidity. Have you never heard the saying the house always wins?"

Ray yawned and took another sip of his coffee, letting him ramble.

Ed continued. "Of course you have. But that's not it, is it?"

Ray met his gaze, his brow furrowed.

"I mean, sure, many a man has killed himself over debt, but

you, a cop, a Sutherland who cares more about the reputation of their name? What else did you fuck up?"

Ray groaned again, squinting at him. "You know, I've had one hell of a night. I'd appreciate it if we didn't do this right now."

"And I'd appreciate you cutting the bullshit. And don't tell me it's your missus. We might be the bane of the female species, and likewise, but no Sutherland is going to toss himself into a gorge over a woman. If that was the case, you would have done it when she divorced your ass years ago." He paused. "Oh yes, Noah told me. So...?"

Ray set his cup down and eyed him. It was like the old-timer could see right through him. He looked up at the Sistine Chapel painting. He knew more about it than Ed realized.

"Do you know that Michelangelo never wanted to paint the Sistine Chapel?" Ray looked back at Ed. "Yeah, he was already busy working on a marble tomb for three years when he received the commission." He paused for a moment and reflected upon the copy of the masterpiece above him. "He accepted, despite the fact that he told others he felt he was more of a sculptor than a painter and had no experience with frescos. You know why he agreed? Most will say it was because he was commissioned by the pope to paint portraits of the twelve apostles and that he felt it was an honor to work for him. That's what they would have you believe. It sounds so much more palatable than the truth. It's all bullshit. They leave out the part about the letter he wrote to his friend, where he told him that Pope Julius II forced him to do it. Apparently, Pope Julius was in the habit of beating him with a stick and had also fired him at one point. I believe his words were 'he could paint anything around the apostles and that he wouldn't hurt Michelangelo.'"

Ray looked at him as he continued. "Sometimes we are forced to do things we don't want to."

Ray dipped his chin.

"What have you done?" Ed asked.

Ray shook his head then met his gaze. "Fallen from grace."

Ed looked as if he was going to pepper him with more questions when gravel crunched beneath tires. He got up and went over to the window and looked out. "Did your brother tell anyone else you were coming here?"

Ray got this distant look in his eyes, then he got up and staggered over to see. Outside, a large black SUV pulled up in front of the cabin. Three tall, barrel-chested men got out, gazing around.

"Friends of yours?" Ed asked.

"Let me go speak to them."

Ray made his way toward the front door. Before he reached it, Ed brushed past him holding a pump-action shotgun. "I swear you Sutherlands will be the death of me," he said.

"This is my problem, old man."

"Like I told you. It was until you stepped foot inside here. Now stay inside." With that said, Ed went out, Mossberg 500 raised and racked to get their attention. "I can tell you three assholes aren't Mormons and you sure as hell can't read otherwise you would have seen the big ass No Trespassing sign on your way in, so I can't wait to hear the reason why you are on my property," Ed said.

A fourth man stepped out from the rear, wearing a long wool business trench coat. He had a black sweater below that, black pants and black shoes. He removed a pair of sunglasses. He was native in appearance.

"Ed. It's all right," Ray said, appearing at his side and placing a hand on the rifle to lower it.

The fourth man spoke up. "Mr. Ironwood wants to see you."

Ray nodded. He glanced at Ed then back at them. "I just need to get my coat." He went back inside. Ed backed up and closed the door behind them.

"Those the men you owe money to?" Ed asked.

Ray picked up his jacket that was still damp. "Tell Noah I've gone to the casino and that if he doesn't hear from me, I'm sorry."

"People don't send out that kind of force unless they're expecting resistance. They are trespassing on my property, Ray. I am within legal right to send them heaven bound. Let me handle this."

Ray scoffed. "Ed. I'm a police officer. They haven't shown deadly force. And if I thought this could be resolved another way, don't you think I would have made a phone call by now? No. I appreciate what you've done," he said, patting him on the arm. "But sometimes," he looked up at the Sistine Chapel painting, "the painter has to go and speak to those who paid his wages."

Ray exited the cabin and got into the back of the SUV. He looked at Ed through the darkly tinted windows. Ed was already on the phone and it didn't take a stretch of the imagination to guess to who.

CHAPTER 19

Tuesday, November 22, 4:05 p.m.

The investigation had roadblocks every step of the way.

As Callie approached his desk, McKenzie tossed an antacid tablet into his mouth. He lifted a finger to tell her to wait while he gulped down water then tossed the paper cone into the trash. He grimaced; eyes tightly shut before he let out a loud belch. "Sonofabitch." He glanced at his watch. "Not even halfway through the day. That's the fourth one. You suffer from acid reflux, Thorne?" he asked, slumping down in his seat.

"Can't say I do."

"What's your secret?"

"Simple. Don't drink so much coffee."

McKenzie gave her an incredulous expression as if dumbfounded by her response. "Next you'll be telling me to give up alcohol." He sniffed hard and glanced up at her. She shrugged. "Oh please." He waved her off. "What you got there?"

Callie tapped a folder on the edge of her leg. "Is Noah still around?"

"No. He had to leave urgently. Didn't say why. I don't expect he'll be back for the rest of the day, so it looks like it's just you and I, princess."

"Well, it seems that Nate Sawyer's alibi about the SUV checks out. He filed a stolen report the same night with High Peaks PD. Made a big fuss about it. Even said he would sue them if they sat on it." She handed over a printed report.

McKenzie took it and scanned the sheet. "That sounds like our lad," he said. "One glance at him and you can tell he thinks the world owes him something. So, what about the names he gave?"

Callie looked back down at her folder.

"Eight employees at the warehouse that evening, two of whom work for him doing research, six others in the adjacent businesses, were there until eight. They spoke with him after he returned from picking up his meal that night at around ten minutes past five. The restaurant has him on video paying for it a little before that at five o'clock. He was at work the rest of the night except for a window of about twenty minutes after six when he went back out to the local liquor store to get some beer."

"And?"

"And what?" she replied.

"Did you verify it, because that's in line with the timing of our jogger?"

"Of course. CCTV has his truck arriving outside the liquor store and him going in," she said, handing him a photo taken from the footage. He noted the time stamp.

"He entered at six twenty-five. That's a little more than twenty minutes."

"Five minutes. Give or take."

McKenzie pulled up Google Maps. "Station Street Wine and Liquor is no more than five minutes away from the warehouse and you say he was gone for at least twenty minutes, where did he go between six and the time he arrived at the liquor store? He's then seen arriving back at work at six-thirty."

"You think he was involved?" Callie asked.

"I don't jump to conclusions, honey, I explore scenarios. Everything is on the table until it's not."

Callie shook her head. "It's just under ten minutes to go from Old Military Road to Connery Pond Trailhead. That would only give him a ten-minute window to kill Laura and hang her in the woods and then he still has to drive back to the liquor store. No. He would need more time."

McKenzie sniffed hard. "You ever heard of a thing called speeding? Last I heard, it reduces time."

"Don't be a prick."

He chuckled.

She continued. "Someone who is under pressure and worried about being seen would need more time. Far more than thirty minutes."

"Possibly. If he was the only one involved."

"And what about motive?"

"In this day and age, does anyone really need a motive? We are living in a weird world. Who knows? Maybe Laura rejected his advances. He does have a history of sexual harassment."

"Alleged."

"Sure. Alleged," he replied.

She rolled her eyes.

McKenzie eyed her as Callie collected up the paperwork and placed it back in the folder. "You have aspirations to become a detective, don't you, Thorne?"

"I never said that," Callie replied, still busy stuffing the paperwork back into the folder.

"Didn't need to. After assisting Noah with Luke's murder. That must have put a feather in your cap, you know — put the idea in your head that you can do this, right?"

She didn't reply.

"Let me give you a reality check. You know, princess, back when I was in the Big Apple, I encountered all types who wanted this position. Take a guess at how many quit or returned to a different position?"

"Like you?" she asked, getting a sense that he was trying to dissuade her.

He smiled. "I'm just saying that it takes a very particular person to do this job. Only the brightest minds can weather the storm, see through the bullshit and handle the frustration of the revolving door of justice."

"Well then I guess I'm fortunate to be learning from the best," she said, cocking her head.

He wagged his finger at her and winked. "See, now you're catching on."

"Oh, I was referring to Noah," she replied as she turned. She couldn't hide her amusement as she walked away with a smile.

"Well, you're not with him right now, princess, you're with me, so don't get cheeky." He got up from his desk and thumbed over his shoulder. "Let's go."

"Where?"

"To speak with Hawthorne about Sawyer's alibi for the night of Katherine's death and see what else we can find out that got overlooked."

"Shouldn't we wait for Noah to get back?"

"Justice doesn't wait for anyone."

CHAPTER 20

Tuesday, November 22, 4:10 p.m.

Fear masked their expressions.

Ethan, Mia and Aiden were waiting for him on the porch step as the Bronco got closer. Noah had hoped, moving back to Adirondack County, that he'd be able to shield his kids from the worst of life, but it was a naïve thought. Being proactive, he'd already tried calling Lena. That got no answer. He hated to jump the gun but with all that had happened with the other women, he couldn't leave anything to chance. He'd already phoned around to the hospitals, and alerted county deputies and local PD to be on the lookout for her vehicle. Had a murder investigation not been underway, he might have taken it in his stride, and considered it a momentary lapse of judgment on Lena's part.

But this wasn't like her.

On the way over from High Peaks to Saranac, Noah had contacted the *Adirondack Daily Enterprise* to speak to Maggie, only to be told she wasn't in. If there was any reason for Lena to vanish without contact, he figured it would have to be related to work, as there was no way on earth, she would have done it purposely. It had been a point of contention early in their marriage when Noah didn't inform her that he would be late. She wouldn't have put the kids through that kind of worry.

His phone rang as his vehicle arrived in the driveway. Noah tapped accept.

"Noah? Sorry, I was out at a meeting."

"Maggie, was Lena in today?"

"Not sure. One of the guys at the paper called me."

"Have you spoken with her?"

"No. What is the matter?"

"She hasn't been seen since yesterday."

He brought his window down, and Mia and Ethan came running up. He lifted a finger to let them know he was on the phone.

"I saw her just after noon yesterday then she dashed out," Maggie said.

"Did she say where she was going?"

"No, but then she never really does. That girl is like a tornado. Always on the move."

"Maggie. What was she working on?"

"Uh. I asked her to look into the dogs being stolen from owners."

"Anyone specific?"

"No. I just asked her to find the story. You know…" she paused. "Noah, you are worrying me."

"Listen, can you have someone check her computer, find out if she told anyone in the office where she was going?"

"I'm on my way there now. I'll see what I can dig up and get back to you."

Noah hung up and took a breath before pushing out of the

Bronco into the arms of his kids. There were no tears yet but the worry was evident. "It's all right. I'm sure we'll find her." He looked over the top of their heads at Aiden who didn't seem as convinced.

"Give me and Aiden a moment," he said. Mia nodded, and she and Ethan went back into the house. He waited until the door groaned shut before Noah asked.

"Why didn't you call me last night?"

"Because it wasn't anything out of the usual."

"So, she usually doesn't come home?"

"No. I mean, sometimes she rolls in late and..."

"And?"

"Well, then when she didn't come back, I thought it was about us."

"You?"

Aiden glanced off toward the house. He sighed. "Lena has been having second thoughts about us getting married. She said she's not sure if she wants to go through with it, that it felt a little rushed." He shook his head. "I asked her if it was because of you."

"Me?"

"Returning to the area."

"How would that change anything?"

He shrugged. "It shouldn't have but I got a sense it did. The past two weeks she's been different. Distant, you could say. I mean you're an investigator. If everything is good then suddenly it's not, more often than not, something's changed." He paused. "The only change is you."

Noah's gaze drifted away. "In the last two years, Aiden. Has she ever not come home?"

"No."

"Then we treat it for what it is," he said, making his way toward the house.

"Which is?"

"She's gone missing. I've checked the hospitals. No sign of her. So, unless she's had an accident and..." His mind went back to the two dead women and how their deaths were made to look like suicides.

"And?" Aiden asked.

"This isn't like her. Regardless of you or me, one thing Lena would never do is leave her kids worrying about her." Noah went into the house. Mia and Ethan were upstairs. The TV was on in the living room. The volume low. Local news. It was a tactic Mia had used to keep her brother calm when there had been tension at home. The two of them would retreat to a room, close the door and allow Noah and Lena to hash it out.

"Mia!" Noah yelled. She appeared at the top of the stairs. "Just to be clear, mom never texted you or Ethan to say where she was going?"

"No."

He turned to Aiden. "What about friends, family?"

"Already called them. No one has seen or heard from her."

"What did Doug or Jack have to say?"

"They're out there looking for her as we speak, which is where I think we need to be," Aiden said, collecting his coat as there was a cool breeze blowing in across the county. With evenings getting darker and sunset around 4:30 p.m., the chances of finding her by driving the streets were slim to none. "I'm taking out my car, probably best we have as many of us out there as possible," Aiden said.

"Sure... keep me updated."

"I gave her a number for a dog," Ethan said.

Noah turned abruptly and looked up the staircase. "What?"

"Mom. When I spoke to her yesterday on the phone."

"Why didn't you tell us?" Mia asked angrily.

"I... I just thought of it now."

"Ethan. What number?" Noah asked with urgency in his tone.

"It was on a flyer," Aiden said with his hand on the door handle to go out. "They're posted around town. Ethan saw one. I put him on the phone with Lena. He's been asking for a dog for a while. But I didn't hear him give her that, otherwise I would have told you."

"The number. Did you keep it?"

"No, I tossed it. But I can show you where the flyer is," Ethan said, hurrying down the stairs.

"All right. Let's go," Noah said, clapping his hands together. His kids wanted to go with him which allowed Aiden to follow, after which he would take them home. It was clear he was as worried as the rest of them. Although Noah didn't want to go there in his mind, he couldn't help but ask his kids once they were in the car.

"Mia. Have you noticed any changes in Aiden?"

"None."

"And mom?" he asked, reversing out.

"A little. Nothing that stands out. I heard them arguing the other night. Mostly mom saying that she was having second thoughts. Aiden said it was normal to have cold feet and to second-guess since she was married before."

"He never touched her, did he?"

"No. He's not like that, Dad."

The Bronco sped through the streets, curling around the winding road back into town until they reached the ice cream parlor. Ethan was out the door before he even put it in park. He rushed into the store just as they were getting ready to close up for the evening. "It's right up..." Ethan stopped, his gaze zigzagging a board on the wall. "It was here. It was right here."

"Are you sure?"

Aiden appeared behind them. "It was there. He's right."

Noah turned to one of two youngsters who were manning the store that evening. "The flyer for dogs. Where's it gone?"

They shrugged.

"Maybe someone took it if it was the last one," Aiden added.

Noah had seen those types of flyers selling goods over the years. Someone would take an 8 x 11 sheet of paper, print a photo of whatever item they were looking to sell on it, add their advertisement and price, cut ten or twenty times at the bottom and write a phone number on each strip so those interested could rip off the number. Mia checked the trash. It was full of half-eaten ice creams and wet napkins.

"Nothing," she said.

"Do you know the people who put up the flyer?" Noah asked.

A teenager behind the counter replied, "No. Anyone can leave an ad there. It changes from day to day."

Noah looked around the room and noticed two small cameras. "Those working?"

"Yeah."

"How long do you keep a recording?"

"A week."

"When was it last wiped?"

"On Sunday."

They would need a warrant to obtain the footage. "Make sure you don't wipe the footage. We might need it," he said, taking out his badge and showing them. The two youngsters looked nervous but nodded. Heading back out, Noah looked up the road, running a hand around the back of his neck, trying to think.

"I can take the kids home if you need to go," Aiden said before Noah cut him off.

"Mia. Long shot but are you and mom still sharing location through your iPhones?"

Mia's eyes widened as she reached into her pocket, understanding what he meant. "Shoot, why didn't I think of that?"

"Hold on. What? Why would she do that?" Aiden asked.

"Parental worry," Mia said. "She wouldn't let me disable it because of trust issues."

"No, she cares," Noah corrected her. "And I should remind you, I had to do the same."

"Yes. You were the reason behind it," Mia said, thumbing her phone.

"Until you were," Noah replied, his lip curling.

"Sorry. I'm a little behind the curve here. What?" Aiden asked.

Noah explained. "If you lose an Apple device – iPhone, iPad, Apple Watch – Apple gives users a way to view its last known location even if the battery is dead, or the phone is turned off, as long as Find My and Location Sharing is enabled."

"You can track movement too, but only if the battery has life," Mia said, swiping the screen on her iPhone. She groaned. "Why didn't I think of this?"

"When did you last use it?" Noah asked, recalling it was a long time ago they'd set it up.

"A year ago."

"Mom was still sharing her location?"

"That was the agreement," Mia replied.

Mia tapped the green icon to view a live map. At the bottom she clicked the icon for People. Mia handed the phone to him. He squinted and pinched the screen to get a better view of the location. Noah turned back to his vehicle but not before pointing. "Aiden, take them back to the house."

"I'm coming with you, Dad," Mia said.

"No, you're not. You stay with Aiden."

"That's my phone."

"And you will get it back."

"We want to know where mom is."

"And you will. Please. Just go with Aiden."

"You sure you don't want me to come with you?" Aiden asked.

He shook his head and got back into his vehicle.

The evening was thick with fear and the crispness of fall as his Bronco raced through the winding roads of the Adirondacks. Noah's heart pounded in his chest as he clutched the steering wheel, his knuckles turning white with anxiety. His mind raced with questions. Lena's disappearance was already unnerving enough, but the remote last known location was a red flag that only elevated his worry.

As the engine roared, the forest loomed on either side, dark and dense; the only light came from the beams of his headlights. He couldn't help but fear the worst — was she still alive, hurt or lost, or had something more dreadful happened?

After all he'd been through with Luke, he couldn't allow his thoughts to creep into the worst-case scenario and yet trying to keep his mind at bay was like holding back the ocean from the shore.

The last-known location was indicating Split Rock Falls, a place that was part of the Bouquet River and tucked out of view of the roadway. There were multiple waterfalls that drained into a natural pool at the base. In the summer months many locals could be found there swimming and cliff jumping into the ravine. It was twenty miles southeast of High Peaks, a fifty-minute drive on a good day.

What made it worse was that it was just off Route 9, the road that intersected with Route 73, the same place Luke's body had been found, in the foothills of the Giant Mountain Wilderness.

As he got closer, Noah's eyes darted back and forth between the phone and scanning the trees for any sign of her.

There was no Mazda abandoned at the side of the road.

Panic set in as he eased off the gas, swerved off to the edge and got out. In the eerie silence of the forest, every creak of a branch sounded like a gunshot. He hurried to the edge of the slope, staying behind the steel barrier that was strung along the side of the road in sections. Noah called out her name, his voice echoing through the trees. With the phone in hand, he could see he was almost upon her.

Had someone just tossed the phone out as they passed by?

He took out a flashlight and inspected the road, searching for skid marks, anything that might indicate she had left the road.

That's when he saw it.

It wasn't on the ground but there was a collection of branches, snapped, pushed back toward the falls. As he got closer, the rushing water grew louder and more intense. The sound of it drowned out all the other noises, its roar almost like a low rumble that increased as he got closer.

He followed the wide gap in the trees, and a trail of broken branches leading deeper into the darkness. Then his heart dropped into his stomach as he saw the wrecked Mazda partially submerged in water. His mind raced as he tried to think of a way to get down the treacherous forty-five feet that went over a double drop with additional separate eight-foot ledges downstream.

It was precarious even in the day but now far more dangerous.

Noah got on the phone to County to call for police backup and an ambulance. Not wasting any time, unable to just stand there wondering what the outcome would be, he took a deep breath, stared into the abyss and started to make his descent, pitching sideways down the slope. He lost his footing a few times and small rocks tumbled out beneath his feet.

Adrenaline coursed through his veins as he carefully made

his way toward the unknown. He slipped, landing hard and sliding a good ten feet before he managed to catch a branch and slow his descent. Out of breath, he took a second or two then continued until he made it to the bottom and worked his way through the water to the vehicle.

All the while, he kept saying, "Don't let her be in there, don't let her be in there."

The cold water numbed his fingers as he lowered himself down and shone the light through the back window that was barely above the surface.

His stomach sank.

His fears were confirmed when he saw Lena's lifeless body in the driver's seat.

Panic set in as he used a rock to smash the driver's side window, his mind tumbled with questions. How long had she been in? How did she end up there? Had she been alive after the crash? Why hadn't she called him?

Utterly crushed, he reached in, cut the belt around her and pulled her out, dragging her limp body to the riverbank. Though he could tell she was gone, that didn't stop him from foolishly trying to perform life-saving CPR even as the sound of sirens in the distance reached his ears.

He wasn't sure why he continued to pump her chest.

"Come on. Come on. Don't you do this. Don't you leave!"

His words echoed even as the rescue team arrived, their faces solemn with the knowledge that deep down it was too late. Lena was gone.

"Noah. Noah," one of them said.

He backed away, numb, cold, and in shock.

As the team took over and he sat on a boulder with an emergency blanket wrapped around him, his heart was broken and full of endless questions.

CHAPTER 21

Tuesday, November 22, 4:55 p.m.

Extracting truth was an art form, at least according to McKenzie.

On the journey up to the Academy, he'd wanted to make it clear that he was to do the talking and her job was to observe, evaluate and take notes. Nothing had changed. It was the same old boys' club mentality she'd experienced the moment she put the uniform on. It was as if they were intimidated but not enough to have her stay behind. Oh, she saw it for what it was — a power trip — a stand back and watch how it's done kind of deal.

"It's a fine balancing act, Thorne. We often only get one shot before these idiots' lawyer up. No offense but I've been at this so long, I know how to read a room long before they even open their traps. So, leave the talking to me."

She blew out her cheeks. "You got it."

In some ways, she was glad to take a backseat. At least if he dug himself a hole, she wouldn't be the one on the hook.

The tension in the room could be cut with a knife from the moment they entered. However, it was different this time. It was clear that Rector Hawthorne had his guard up as there were other faculty members in attendance.

Hawthorne stepped forward. "Alexander Hawthorne. Please, take a seat."

"Thank you," McKenzie said, extending his hand and shaking Hawthorne's. "Detective Angus McKenzie, I'm the lead investigator for Adirondack County Sheriff's Office." He turned and with a gesture of the hand pointed to Callie. "This is Deputy Callie Thorne."

"Yes, we've had the pleasure of meeting already," he said, shaking her hand.

"You have?" McKenzie's gaze darted between them. "Ah, well, she is just here to observe." Of course, he had to throw it out there. A slight jab to make it clear to others that he was at the helm.

"Mr. Sutherland not with you?"

"I'm afraid he was called away. An urgent matter," McKenzie replied.

Hawthorne nodded then turned to the three others who were present. "This is our residential director, Helen Anderson, and Dalton Mathers is our expedition leader, and of course, last but not least, Erin Spencer is our current counselor. I've asked them to join us."

Erin squinted and shook Callie's hand. "You wouldn't happen to be related to an Abigail Thorne, would you?"

"That's my mother."

Erin took a seat. "What a small world. I had the honor of listening to one of her talks when I was studying at Harvard. A true pioneer."

"Really?" Callie replied.

Erin turned to Hawthorne who looked intrigued. "The deputy's mother is Abigail Thorne, a psychologist and professor of Psychology and Computer Science at Harvard."

"Was," Callie was quick to correct her. "She passed on two years ago."

"I'm sorry to hear that. I admired the work that she did. It was very influential." Erin turned to Hawthorne to clarify. "Abigail developed a unique approach to rational analysis and cognitive science and was heavily involved in ACT, which stands for Adaptive Control of Thoughts. She had a lot of interesting insights into planning, solving and response stages as well as breaking down problems into more manageable components." She looked back at Callie. "I expect what you learned from your mother will be an asset to the Sheriff's Office."

"I hope so," Callie replied.

"You're lucky to have her," Erin said to McKenzie.

McKenzie cut her a sideways glance, an eyebrow rising. "Seems so."

Hawthorne fidgeted in his chair, smiling politely but it was clear he wanted to get down to business. "So how can we help?"

McKenzie glanced around. He stood up and perused the room under their watchful eye, picking up items as if he was there to make some formal inspection before he turned toward them. "You ever heard the saying, kill two birds with one stone?" He paused. "I never really understood the phrase. I mean, sure, the idea behind it is to achieve two things by doing a single action. But really. Why would you ever want to kill birds in the first place? And if you did, could you really do it with one single action?" He smiled.

"It's a metaphor," Hawthorne said, chuckling.

"Well of course it is." McKenzie joined him before losing his smile. "Still, two birds together, so close. You know — something that brings them so closely together and yet offers enough reason for both to die. Katherine Evans and Laura Summers for instance. What are the odds of that?"

Hawthorne exhaled loudly. "Our nurse. Yes. We heard." He paused for a second. "Her partner, Ana Silva, notified us."

"Well, that saves us a lot of time. I mean, I hate having to give the death notification. It never gets easy," he said sarcastically. Callie glanced at the others to gauge their reaction. Either he knew what he was doing or once again he was being an ass.

Hawthorne remained stoic.

"It's a real tragedy. That's what it is. A definite blow for the Academy."

"Oh, I'd say it affects more people than the Academy."

"Well, of course, that's what I meant. It's just... because she worked here."

"As did Katherine Evans. Who I'm glad to see you managed to find a replacement for," he said, eyeing Erin Spencer.

"It's been six months since Katherine stepped down," Hawthorne added.

McKenzie snorted. "Stepped down. Interesting choice of words. Incidentally, I wouldn't mind seeing Katherine's office."

"Erin would be glad to show you. Is that all?"

McKenzie smirked at Callie before looking back at Hawthorne. "No. That won't be all," he said before blazing into his line of questioning. "Friday, November eighteenth, the night Katherine's body was found in the lake, journalist Nate Sawyer said he had a meeting with you. How did that go?"

"It didn't. Once I learned what his end game was, I canceled."

"What was it in regards to?"

Hawthorne glared. "Outlandish lies."

"Those lies wouldn't by any chance be the reason why Katherine was forced to resign?"

"Detective, no one forced Katherine to resign."

"Oh, that's right. She... stepped down. My bad. Look, I'm really not one for doing the dance. So, how about we cut the crap and get straight to the point. You see, we know she didn't willingly step down. There was a reason that gave her no other choice. And if I am correct..." He turned to Callie. She flipped the pages in her notebook and then handed it to him. He took out a pair of glasses and donned them. "... you told Investigator Sutherland we would need to ask her. Is that right?"

Hawthorne shrugged. "If I said that. Yes. It wasn't my place to speak on her behalf."

"Of course," he chuckled. "Conveniently. We can't do that now. However, we did confer with two individuals close to Katherine. Nicholas Evans, her husband, and Nate Sawyer who told us a very different story. One in which she was told in no uncertain terms that if she didn't leave of her own volition, she'd never get a job in counseling again. Sound right to you?"

"Like I said. Misconstrued. Lies."

"Okay, let's deep dive into those alleged lies." He flipped the pages a few more times. "Ah, here we are. Accusations. According to Katherine's husband, there were several accusations that had been brought to your attention. Rumors, some might say of a sexual nature. Students saying that Katherine was interfering with them. How am I doing?"

Hawthorne cleared his throat and glanced at his colleagues. "Correct."

"You gave Katherine the option to either leave or face the consequences of what could not only land her in jail but would most certainly destroy her career and the reputation of High Peaks Academy."

"I gave her an option. Correct."

McKenzie stared back at him, waiting for more. "If there is

anything you feel I might be overlooking or have misunderstood. Now would be a good time to clarify."

"Sure," he replied, looking directly back at him with a smile but not offering anything further.

McKenzie continued.

"How long did Katherine work here?"

"Six years."

"And in any of that time, did anyone ever spread rumors about her before the recent accusations?"

"No."

"Well then that seems a little like jumping the gun, wouldn't you say so, Alexander? I mean, is the Academy in the habit of letting staff members go over unproved rumors?"

"We had a strong reason to believe they were true."

"Okay, then if that was the case, why wasn't a report filed with the police?"

"After Katherine willingly stepped down, we felt as if the issue had been resolved."

"Resolved?" He cleared his throat and offered back a surprised expression. "You hear rumors that one of your teachers is interfering with your students and you decide to brush it under the rug?"

Hawthorne moved uncomfortably in his seat. He pulled at his collar. "The matter was handled."

"That's good to know. Except what did the parents have to say about that?"

Hawthorne laced his fingers together and leaned forward in his chair, placing them on top of his desk. "They were rumors."

"Aye but rumors you felt were strong enough to believe. That was what you said, right?"

"I did, Mr. McKenzie."

"Detective."

Hawthorne glared at him. "Detective McKenzie. Please. You

have to understand. High Peaks Academy was established back in the 1950s. As a state-approved organization, we've been around a long time. We've seen it all. Most parents send their troubled teens to our private school as a last-ditch effort with the hope of not only educating them but ensuring changes in behavior, empowering them to become leaders, and ultimately guiding them to make that transition back into their home communities with a different worldview. We take that very seriously."

"But not seriously enough to tell the parents their child was interfered with?"

"Like I said. They were rumors. I made a judgment call on those rumors."

"Based on what? From everything we've been able to dig up about Katherine, she had an exemplary track record of counseling without one report of conduct unbecoming."

"Based on who the rumors came from," Hawthorne shot back.

"Ah. I see. And who might that be?"

"That is confidential."

"Mr. Hawthorne. We have two dead women on our hands who both worked for High Peaks Academy. One who felt so angered that she had been unjustly kicked out of a position that she requested a journalist to assist her in investigating your Academy. Don't insult my intelligence. Who provided the rumor?"

He glanced at the other two and looked at him. "Laura Summers."

His eyebrows shot up and he couldn't hold back a stifled laugh. "Oh, now isn't that ironic. Certainly, brings new meaning to kill two birds with one stone. And who told her?"

"Like I said, it's confidential."

"Give me a name."

"I couldn't even if I wanted to. She made an agreement not to mention their names unless it was requested."

"And of course, their names weren't requested because Katherine stepped down."

"Exactly." Hawthorne took a deep breath. "Whatever was told or shown to Laura, was done in complete confidentiality. However, it was enough for her to believe them. She came to me. I then called Katherine into my office."

"Did Katherine contest it?"

"She didn't admit to it if that's what you're asking."

"Did you tell Katherine that it was Laura who told you?"

"No. And there was no need to. She agreed to leave. You have to understand, Laura had been a nurse with us for over ten years. She wasn't in the business of making up stories and especially not against Katherine, a fellow faculty member."

McKenzie nodded. "Well. All right. That about clears that up. I would like to see Katherine's office if that's okay."

Hawthorne nodded. "Erin, would you do the honors?"

"Certainly."

The two of them rose and were about to head for the door when Callie chimed in. "Just a second. I have a question."

"No, you don't," McKenzie said.

"Yes, I do," Callie said.

"Deputy."

Callie ignored him. "Mr. Hawthorne. A year ago, Katherine went through a split with her husband. A period of time when she went into a shelter. Nicholas said it was related to a loss in the family, stress at work and her relationship. Do you recall that?"

McKenzie sighed and took a seat.

"I do. I was the one who spoke with Nicholas."

"There we are! He recalls speaking with him. Time to leave," he said, rising again. Callie remained stoic, her gaze never breaking from Hawthorne.

"What was the stress at work she was dealing with?"

He shrugged. "I would have to look over her records of what she was handling back then. As you might appreciate, our environment here is very dynamic. Students graduate every year. New ones arrive."

"Like Charlie Delaney?"

She noticed Hawthorne exchange a glance with Erin.

"He is one of our students. Yes."

"And someone that Katherine was working with, correct?"

Hawthorne nodded, a smile forming. "That's right."

"You see, I did a little digging." She reached into a black zipper folder and pulled out a report. As she said that, she heard McKenzie sigh. "It came to my attention that there was a police report filed by State Trooper Samantha Torres back in September last year of four teenagers that were charged with third-degree assault. It was classed as a misdemeanor, after a fight broke out here at the Academy." She got up and placed it on his desk so he could see. "Troopers arrived here in the late afternoon after a sixteen-year-old boy was transported to Adirondack Medical Center in Saranac Lake. The victim had sustained multiple wounds, scrapes, and bruises around the back, face and head after being kicked and punched. Students Adam Tomlin, Joshua Whelan, Ricky Patel and Benjamin Kim were charged with misdemeanor assault and released with appearance tickets for Adirondack County Family Court. When asked for a statement, you said it was unfortunate that your students' behavior had become so disruptive, however, there were no significant injuries, all students would receive counseling, and that the matter would be handled."

"And it was."

"That victim of that assault was Charlie Delaney," she

replied. "Your residential counselor at the time was Katherine Evans. No motive was offered by the school."

"What can I say? We deal with troubled youth. Emphasis on troubled."

"Would any of that trouble involve hazing?"

He scoffed. "I was referring to the problems they bring."

"Well, it's just that a month after that event, the Adirondack Central Supervisory Union sent out a memo that gave an updated procedure on the prevention of harassment, hazing and bullying of students. It outlined what constituted as such, and detailed how students might report what they believe to be a hazing, harassment or bullying by promptly reporting the conduct to a designated school employee. In addition, it outlined clear guidelines for any school employee who witnesses conduct or reasonably believes conduct might constitute as a hazing, harassment or bullying and what measures they would have to take to stop and prevent a recurrence and who to report it to."

Hawthorne sighed, looking frustrated. "I'm familiar with it. The memo also from my recollection outlined how to deal with false complaints."

"Is that what Charlie Delaney's claim was?"

"I wouldn't know. He met with Katherine and no report was filed."

Callie stifled a laugh, nodding slowly. "Or maybe she didn't get a chance to file it."

"I'm sorry, what are you alluding to?"

"She's not. I think our time here is over," McKenzie said, rising for the third time to his feet, this time taking her arm. "Let's go, deputy."

Unmoved, Callie continued. "What I am trying to say is that I think Katherine was dealing with the aftermath of what was being deemed a hazing. So. Was it a hazing gone wrong or something more?"

"Deputy. Mr. Hawthorne has answered the questions we came to ask."

"Not yet."

McKenzie got really close and whispered, "What did we agree?"

Callie ignored him and continued. "Mr. Hawthorne?"

He took a deep breath. "I don't recall you being this outspoken when you were here with Mr. Sutherland. Maybe you only take orders from those who you respect." He glanced at McKenzie. "You've got your work cut out for you, detective."

Callie pressed him further. "Mr. Hawthorne. Was it a hazing? And if that hazing was covered up, what else has been covered up here?"

Hawthorne ignored her, continuing on as if she wasn't even speaking. "But that's the thing about High Peaks Academy. We've yet to run into that kind of work. Since the 1950s, we've yet to have a woman as rector. In other places, sure. Here? Not yet."

"Answer the question," Callie said.

"Careful, deputy. While you are here, you are a guest, and as such, I would ask you to extend the same respect and courtesy that we have to you. Don't force me to call a lawyer." He narrowed his gaze. "You want to know if hazing still occurs and how we deal with them? Fine. I strongly ensure that order is maintained here as does my staff. We follow whatever governing rule is over us and guidelines given. If we didn't, we wouldn't have been around for sixty-two years. We've yet to have one official complaint. But let me be clear. Unlike other boarding schools, we are dealing with the most troubled youth that this nation has, and maybe that comes with a little friction... what is the term?" he asked, turning to Helen but she never got to answer before he continued. "Iron refines iron. That's it." He stabbed a finger at her. "So, if a few of the youth happen to rub shoulders with one another to work out a few differences and neither I nor my staff witnesses it, then so be it. It comes with the territory and those we work with but it does not affect our success rate one iota. And that's all that matters to those who pay to have their children here. You want to come here and make statements like that idiot Nate Sawyer — that the Academy is covering up things to save face — go ahead. But you won't get far. There is nothing you can say or accuse us of that we or our lawyers haven't heard before, but believe me, Deputy Thorne — you are going to need more than accusations, assumptions and a scrappy old police report to prove it. Good day."

He handed back the paper.

McKenzie took it and gave Callie a stern look. That was enough.

As they walked toward the door, McKenzie looked back. "Mr. Hawthorne. One last thing. We are going to need a list of the names of students that Katherine counseled in the past two years and a copy of any and all reports that she did file. You do have those, yes?"

"I'm sure we can accommodate that. Erin will assist you."

"Much appreciated."

They turned to leave.

"Just one last thing," Hawthorne said.

They glanced back. "Yes?"

"For the future, it's Rector Hawthorne." He smiled, doing exactly what McKenzie had done to him.

CHAPTER 22

Tuesday, November 22, 5:30 p.m.

The darkness felt suffocating.

A silence had fallen over the Adirondacks except for the sound of an 18-wheeler tow truck that was using a rotator to haul the crumpled Mazda out of the gorge. Pulsating red and blue lights from police cars cast an eerie glow over the rocks and trees surrounding the crash site.

Noah stood at the edge of the road; his gaze fixed on Lena's vehicle. The tow truck whined as it slowly pulled the Mazda up the steep embankment. A state patrol deputy and other law enforcement from the county stood nearby talking. Noah couldn't hear the conversation. His mind was elsewhere, circling between what he would tell Mia and Ethan to replaying the events of the night over in his head.

While the empty SUV was lifted onto the flatbed of the tow truck, his thoughts returned to the EMTs who had only ten minutes ago emerged through the forest, carrying Lena's body on a stretcher. Noah had watched numbly as they loaded her into the back of the ambulance and drove away to the hospital for the medical examiner to determine the cause of death. Noah couldn't fathom that she was gone. It seemed unthinkable. Like a nightmare he couldn't wake from.

He'd been standing there for what felt like hours, waiting for the tow truck driver to lower the Mazda. Finally, with the SUV on the flatbed, Noah approached, his heart racing to see if there was anything inside out of the ordinary.

As he explained to the driver that he needed to look inside, Savannah Legacy, his supervisor from State Police Troop B, arrived.

"Noah," she said softly. He glanced back. She shook her head. "I am so sorry. I just got word that it was Lena. Listen, go be with your kids. We'll take care of everything from here."

Still in shock, Noah glanced back at Lena's vehicle. "I can't, not yet," he replied. "I need to see inside. I need to know what happened."

Savannah looked at him sympathetically. "Noah, please. Let us handle the investigation. You need to be with your family."

"And I will but..." Before she could stop him, he climbed up onto the flatbed truck and made his way to the driver's side. Gloved up, he opened the door. An overflow of river water poured out, covering his boots. Shining a light inside, he noted there was nothing jammed against the accelerator. The amber glow of the flashlight illuminated the seat and then the gear stick.

"Noah," Savannah said.

He turned. "It's in neutral, Savannah."

He didn't need to explain what that could mean. "Make sure you get forensics to brush for prints. No mistakes on this one. Have them use cyanoacrylate and dust with a black powder." Degradation of prints played a role, but submerged prints now could be detected up to six weeks, although usually after ten days, it got harder. Still, because prints were made by the oil from the ridges of skin, there was a chance they still existed. A lot of factors came into play: the surface of material and its porosity, time submerged, the type of water source, whether it was fresh or salt water, and the reagents used in recovery.

He hopped down, his clothes still damp from the river.

"She didn't kill herself. Don't let them go there."

"Come on, I'll give you a ride back to town."

"No, that's my vehicle over there."

She placed a hand on his shoulder. "You're in no state to drive."

"I'm not going to harm myself, Savannah, if that's what you're thinking."

"As a friend, not as your supervisor, let me take you home. I'll have one of the troopers follow in your vehicle."

Noah gritted his teeth; his emotions were all over the place. One moment tearing up, the next feeling intense anger. Had it been anyone else, he might have dug his heels in, but a long history with Savannah had taught him that she always had his best interests at heart.

Minutes later, riding back in a Suburban, he was already beginning to switch from processing the tragedy for himself to what it now meant for Ethan and Mia. He'd need to bring the kids home with him, but to where? For the past two weeks he'd been between homes, feeling more like a vagabond than an anchor. At that moment what they needed was surety, safety, someone who would be there to guide them through the storm as in minutes, the rug of life would be pulled out from underneath them.

It was quiet on the journey back.

He glanced in his side mirror to see his vehicle behind them, driven by a trooper.

Noah asked Savannah to take him to Saranac Lake instead of Gretchen's. The kids needed to know. He could have made a phone call to Aiden but these things were better done in person. It was one death notification he thought he would never have to give.

"Whatever you need. Just ask."

"I appreciate that," he said in a low voice.

"Take as much time off as you need."

"Time off?"

She glanced at him, her hands clutching the wheel tightly as she navigated the dark, winding roads. "Yes, Noah. You'll be taking time off."

"I'm in the middle of an investigation."

"You were. I'm assigning Ellis."

"The hell you're not."

"I'm going to let that one slide because of what's happened. But friend or not, I'm still your supervisor, and the decisions I make are for what is best for this county, the bureau and you. This is..."'

"Oh, cut the bull, Savannah. We have two dead women on our hands, and some psycho out there trying to make it look like suicide. Now Lena. Who knows if it's related?"

"Until we process that vehicle and the M.E. does an autopsy, we can't be certain what we are dealing with."

"The gearstick was in neutral."

"It could have shifted out of drive when it landed."

"How many times have you seen that?" he asked. She didn't reply so he continued. "She didn't kill herself."

"I didn't say she did."

"If anything, that suggests someone put the vehicle in motion and pushed it in."

The tension was building and he was regretting accepting her offer of a ride. Now he realized why. She wanted to have this conversation, to have him in a place where he couldn't just walk away. She knew him too well.

"How did you find her?" she asked.

"Apple Phone. Her last known location."

"Do we know where she was before that?"

"I don't know. Ethan said he gave her a number for some pups that were being sold in town. I expect if we pull her phone records, we can triangulate on her phone and determine where she was before where we found her."

"I'll get on that. You think it's related?"

"Maggie wanted her to look into a dog kidnapping ring that's been operating in the area."

"Katherine Evans. Didn't you say that her dog was scooped up by Thomas Green?"

"That's right. But he has a history of dropping off dogs at the shelter."

"First impressions of him?"

"A little slow. Harmless."

"The kind of person that most wouldn't bat an eye at if he was pulled in for taking dogs?" she asked.

Noah looked at her. He could tell where she was going with it.

"He was straight with us. There's nothing that ties him to any ring."

"For now."

They drove on until Savannah pulled up to Lena's house. Noah had a sense of dread settling heavy in his chest. The thought of telling Ethan and Mia that their mother was no longer alive made it almost hard to breathe. He'd given death notifications all his career but, in that moment, he didn't know how to do it, how to say it, or how to prepare them for the pain that would follow.

The Suburban idled.

Noah saw movement behind the curtain. Aiden appeared at the window, looking out.

Savannah stared. "You want me to come in and tell them?"

"No, I need to do it." He got out. "Thanks for the ride."

"Remember what I said."

Noah held on to the door, looking at her. "Don't force me out of this one, please. Of all the ones you could. Give me this."

She sighed. "Noah."

"I've never asked anything of you."

Savannah groaned. "I should have never told you about this position."

He closed the door, knowing that Savannah would wrestle with her decision but ultimately, their history together and her confidence in him would override what she considered was best.

Noah took a deep breath as he walked up to the door. He hadn't made it within five feet when it opened. Ethan answered the door. He looked at his father quizzically before glancing around him. "Is mom driving your vehicle?"

That was answered when the trooper got out and brought the keys to Noah before leaving with Savannah. "Dad, what's going on?" Ethan asked.

"Let's go inside."

Ethan looked beside himself, confused, already emotional.

Mia on the other hand was sitting in the living room with Aiden. Poised, as if almost expecting bad news. One glance at Aiden, and his chin dropped.

Noah struggled to find the words but eventually they came out.

"Ethan. Mia. Mom isn't coming home. She's no longer with us," he said, forcing the words out, his voice barely above a whisper. "There was..." He trailed off, he wanted to say an accident as if it would have somehow been more acceptable, but he couldn't. He didn't know. He could only speculate but that's all it would be. Before he could continue, Ethan's face crumpled, tears streamed down his cheeks. Mia, the oldest of the two, sat frozen in shock, her eyes wide and unblinking.

Noah reached for his son to hold him tight but he sprinted away, up the stairs, leaving only the echo of his hard sobbing behind.

How Mia managed to hold in her emotion was a mystery, but everyone handled bad news differently. Some buckled and broke, unleashing a river of tears, and for others it came later, in the quiet of night, muffled by a pillow. Mia stood up. "I'll go see him," she said, putting on a brave face that no sixteen-year-old should have to wear.

Once she was gone, Noah turned to Aiden who was seated, his hands clasped together. A few tears streaked his cheeks. "What happened?"

"We don't know yet. Her vehicle was in the gorge."

Aiden looked up at him. "She hated water."

"I know."

Aiden got up and went over to a cabinet and took out a bottle of Jack Daniel's. "You don't drink, do you?" he asked, about to pour himself one.

"I haven't for a long time, but pour me one." In that moment, he didn't care. He wanted to have something, anything to latch on to, to block out the pain. Aiden returned with two fingers of the golden liquid in a glass. Noah swirled it around, staring at it. It had been several years since his last drop. There was a second of hesitation as newly formed habits implored him to not drink, to set it down and walk away, but instead he knocked it back, feeling the familiar burn in his throat.

In a sad way it felt like coming home, a returning to a familiar friend even if that friend had almost destroyed him. Many would fault him and cast judgment, but at that moment, he didn't give two fucks.

Aiden piped up with tears in his eyes, "You know, before I went into the ministry, I considered becoming a cop. Realized fast I didn't have the stomach for it. Death. I know about that. Comforting people. Leading a funeral. But seeing it close up and personal, to witness what one person might have done to another, or to themselves. I wasn't made for that."

"No one is," Noah said.

"Will you be taking them with you?" Aiden asked.

Noah set the glass down. "Of course."

"I love those kids," Aiden said. "Lena and I were considering having one of our own. I guess that's..." He trailed off, shaking his head. "If you need any help with them. Time to yourself. Or work-related. My door will always be open. That won't ever change."

"It'll change," Noah said. "Change is the only thing that remains."

With that said, he got up and made his way over to the stairs. He was about to call up to the kids when Aiden spoke again.

"Hey, uh, Noah, it's late. Maybe just tonight they should stay here. You too. It's Lena's place after all."

"She was renting this, right?"

"Correct."

There was an awkwardness between them. Noah nodded. "Sure. I'll figure something out tomorrow."

He strode back into the living room.

"I'll go get some blankets and a pillow," Aiden said and disappeared up the stairs.

Noah approached a series of photo frames on the mantel above the fireplace. He picked up one, a snapshot of better times. Lena was in the middle, hugging Mia and Ethan. Several tears rolled down his cheek. As he set it down, he took out his phone to check for messages. To avoid getting distracted, he'd set it to airplane mode.

There were multiple missed messages from Ed.

Aiden returned with the blankets and set them down as Noah made a call to Ed. He picked up. "About damn time. I've been trying to get hold of you all night."

"Is everything okay?" Noah asked.

"Would I be ringing you if it was? Of course, it's not. That damn brother of yours is gone," Ed said.

"What?"

"Four assholes showed up here in a blacked-out SUV this afternoon. They said Mr. Ironwood wanted to see him. He went with them. Told me to tell you that he's gone to the casino, and that he's sorry."

"Sorry? What? Ed. What else did he say?"

"That was all. I mean I asked if these were the fools he owed the four hundred thousand to, but he never gave me a clear answer. Just said something cryptic along the lines of 'The painter has to go and speak to those who paid his wages.'"

"Four hundred thousand?"

"He never told you?"

"No."

"Seems your brother has landed himself in a bad situation."

"All right. Thanks, Ed."

"Hold up. Where are you? I called State and County but they wouldn't tell me a damn thing."

"I'll bring you up to speed later. I have to go."

He hung up and stood there clutching the phone.

"Everything okay?" Aiden asked.

"No. Nothing is okay but I should have expected that coming back here." He walked outside to have some privacy and call the one person he knew could potentially get Ray out of whatever shit he'd gotten himself into. Now it was starting to make sense. His frequent visits to the casino, Tanya leaving him, the suicide attempt. He'd always thought Ray was the steady one in the family, but it couldn't be further from the truth.

"Noah, I heard the news," Maddie said.

"From who?"

"Savannah."

Noah figured; Savannah had gone behind his back with the intention of getting his sister to speak to him.

"Maddie. I need you to do me a favor."

CHAPTER 23

Wednesday, November 23, 7:05 a.m.

A bright sun peeked above the horizon, revealing the black smoke.

Within the hour of the 911 call, Thorne and McKenzie arrived at the wooded area just ten minutes south of High Peaks. It was just off one of the main trailheads leading to Mount Van Hoevenberg. They pulled up to the scene to find a burnt-out SUV that matched the description of the one belonging to Nate Sawyer.

A short distance away, at the mouth of the trailhead, Callie exited her cruiser to the sight of the vehicle still smoldering. The air was thick with the smell of burnt rubber and gasoline. There were already two deputies on scene along with the fire department, who had made short work of the blaze before it could spread.

They were just in the process of rolling up hoses.

"Well, that adds credence to his story of it being stolen as he's still being held until he sees a judge," Callie said.

"Unless he had a propane tank set with timers," McKenzie added.

"You've been watching too many movies," Callie retorted.

"Oh trust me, princess, assholes who want to get away with things, do all manner of shit to keep you looking in the wrong direction."

"Call came in the early hours of the morning from a farmer. He said he was out feeding his livestock when he saw the flames through the trees," said Ansel Carlton, the fire chief. "Accelerant was used."

"Propane?" McKenzie asked.

"No. Gasoline."

"Whoever lit it made sure to douse the vehicle good," Callie added, holding a handkerchief up to her mouth and nose and skirting around it to get a better look at the steel bones. The flames had chewed their way through the inside and devoured the paint, leaving little behind.

"Plates had been removed and were in the back of the SUV. I fished them out. Whoever tossed them in there obviously wasn't smart. The paint's gone but the embossed letters and numbers are as clear as day. It's a perfect match."

"And no one saw who walked away?" Callie asked.

"Nope," Ansel said.

"Vehicle tracks?"

"If they used one, it must have been parked by the road or they set off on foot through the forest."

"Footprints?" McKenzie asked.

"Nothing found so far."

Glancing across the wreckage, Callie noticed a figure approaching in the distance, coffee in hand. It was Noah.

"What's he doing here?" McKenzie asked.

"Your guess is as good as mine," she said. "Give us a moment."

Both of them had been told late last night about Lena. It was devastating news. She couldn't even fathom the amount of pain it would put his family through. They'd already suffered so much loss as it was.

As Noah got closer, Callie noticed his eyes were bloodshot and his face pale. He looked as if he hadn't slept at all. "Is it Sawyer's?" Noah asked, his voice barely above a mutter.

She exchanged a glance of concern with McKenzie before looking back and answering. "Seems so. Plates are a match. Noah, what are you doing here?"

"Same thing as you are. Investigating."

He went to walk around her and she took him by the arm.

He shucked her with a stern look. "Let me do my job, Callie."

"That's what worries me. Can you? Should you even be here?"

Noah nodded; his eyes fixed on the burnt-out SUV. "I had to see it for myself. I can't stay at home. I have to do something."

"What about your kids?"

"I dropped them off at my aunt's."

"You should be with them."

"And do what? Huh? Stare at a wall? How is that going to change anything? I can't change the way they feel. I can't soften the blow anymore. Or take away their grief. But I can try and find the asshole who took her life. That I can do."

Callie understood. She'd seen cops like Noah before, the ones who threw themselves into their work to distract from their personal lives. She didn't blame him for being there, but she figured it was best for his kids if he wasn't.

There was a short pause.

"Let me guess, no one saw them drop it off?" he asked.

"Nope. A farmer spotted the smoke," McKenzie replied, walking away.

Callie added, "Sawyer told me that this was a second vehicle that he kept at home in his driveway. I already had a deputy canvass the area for footage. So far nothing. It's like they just stole it up from underneath his nose, committed a crime and..."

"Them?" he asked.

"Him, her, them. Who knows how many we are dealing with right now." She narrowed her gaze.

"What did you get up to yesterday?" Noah asked.

"Where do I start? Yesterday we got confirmation on the dental records. So, we have a positive on Katherine. We also found out that DNA from Sawyer's cup is a match to Katherine's fetus. It's his kid. That's not even the half of it all. Sawyer's alibi checks out for the night of Laura's death, barring twenty-five minutes when he went to a liquor store, but even if he was speeding, I can't see him being able to kill Laura, stash his vehicle here, hike it back to his truck and return all within that short window. However, someone is lying."

"About?"

"Well, we visited the Academy."

"Without me?" Noah asked.

"McKenzie would have gone alone had I refused to go with him."

"And?" he asked, still eyeing the charred remains.

Callie shifted her weight from one foot to the next. "Seems as though Sawyer's alibi for the night Katherine was found is a crock of crap. That meeting he said he had was canceled according to Hawthorne, which means Sawyer doesn't have an alibi for the night Katherine died."

"Or Hawthorne's lying," Noah added.

"That's possible. If Katherine told Sawyer about the baby and he decided he wanted her to have an abortion and she didn't, it's possible that he lost it and killed her. And maybe Laura knew."

"And so, you think that's the connection with the school nurse?"

"Well, that's the interesting part. According to staff members, they were close friends but something about it doesn't add up. When we told Hawthorne what Nicholas had shared about Katherine being forced out of her job due to rumors of interfering with students, he didn't deny it. In his words, he gave her an option to leave before it went any further than a rumor. The thing is, he can't verify who the rumors came from because they were shared in confidence with Laura."

"Who's dead."

"Exactly. You'd think she would have gone to Katherine directly?"

"We'll never know if she did," he said, staring at the wreckage.

"Anyway, apparently, Laura held back the names of those Katherine supposedly interfered with from Hawthorne, at least that's what he wants us to think. And because Katherine never dug her heels in when confronted, the rector felt there was no need to go any further. The matter was dropped."

"Because he wanted to protect the Academy."

"You got it. Parents never learned about the interference. They dealt with the issue inhouse. The alleged victims obviously were persuaded not to say anything out of fear of tainting their educational record or they chose not to say anything to their parents out of embarrassment. Who knows? Either way, the matter was quashed with Katherine's exit."

Noah shook his head. "So where does that leave us?"

"I managed to dig up an incident report from State Police of an arrest made at the Academy a year prior to Katherine's death.

Four teenagers assaulted another in what is considered a hazing gone wrong. The victim was Charlie Delaney."

"That's the kid Nicholas mentioned Katherine was seeing before she left."

She nodded.

"You dug that up?"

"Devil's in the details, right?"

He smiled. "So?"

"We think that the hazing was related to the stress Katherine was going through when she left her marriage the first time, as it was around then that Charlie started seeing her for counseling. Before we left yesterday, Erin Spencer, the new residential counselor, gave us a list of names and dates for students that Katherine met with over the past year one-on-one."

"Any record of what they talked about?"

"Sealed. We'd need a warrant. Client confidentiality."

"There are limits to that."

"Yes, but without knowing what was shared, and Katherine not being alive and Charlie no longer continuing therapy with Erin, they have no justified reason to share those records. And also, it depends if Katherine even took notes. According to Erin, she was told by Hawthorne that Katherine wasn't in the habit of keeping good records. Apparently, it wasn't her style."

"Convenient if you want to keep something buried."

"I agree. For all we know, by the time she was hired they destroyed what records Katherine had, especially if the contents could have brought the Academy into disrepute."

Callie glanced over to McKenzie who was squatting and staring at a chunk of metal. He was an oddball if she'd ever met one but she couldn't deny he'd had a way of drawing out information from Hawthorne.

She looked back at Noah. "Anyway, among those names there are only two that stand out that she saw on an ongoing basis. One was an eighteen-year-old girl, Isabella Perez who graduated last year, and the other was Charlie who is still a student at the Academy."

"The timing of her graduation?"

"A week before the assault."

"Well, let's speak to Isabella Perez. Do we have an address for her?"

CHAPTER 24

Wednesday, November 23, 9:25 a.m.

Before leaving for the Perez home, they'd returned to County to ask Nate Sawyer why he lied about the meeting with Hawthorne. The answer would have to wait as an urgent call came in while they were on route from Savannah, offering a lead that could be tied to all three women.

"You're sure that's the location?" Noah asked, bringing it up on Google Maps to get a bird's-eye view before half a dozen squad cars, a forensics van and State would descend upon it.

"The phone company confirmed it. This is the last location of Lena and the woman she called before heading to Split Rock Falls," Savannah said.

"We got a name?"

"Teresa Barkley. Previous felon. Has a rap sheet as long as your arm. Warrant is already out for her arrest. Marshals have had her in their crosshair for the past fourteen months. Almost got her in Chicago, eight months ago. Seems she decided to settle down here."

THE ADIRONDACK MOUNTAINS were silent and still as a convoy of police vehicles rumbled down the winding dirt road towards an old farmhouse nestled in the woods. Noah's jaw clenched; his mind full of anger. He could feel his heart pounding against his chest as the Bronco bumped over the uneven path.

No sirens wailed, filling the air with an eerie sense of foreboding. They had finally tracked down where Lena had been prior to her demise. Had she died here? Or had they waited until she was out at the gorge?

As they got closer to the dilapidated farmhouse, his heart sank.

He eased off the gas, killed the engine and got out, service weapon at the ready. He felt a surge of rage as he made his way forward.

Like a wave, deputies moved in on the farmhouse and outbuildings, and orders were bellowed.

There was no sign of anyone.

No one rushed out to flee or meet them spewing lies. It was early but not for farm life. His eyes scanned the tree line, the outbuildings, the farm equipment and a barn which was full of bales of hay stacked high into the rafters.

There was a slew of empty cages and dog crap.

Near that was a shed for cows with milking equipment and a large tank for storing liquid. A pigpen was nearby with a group of contented hogs snuffling around in the mud.

The earthy aroma of hay and manure mixed with soil was overpowering.

"What have we got?" he asked as he approached the large

farmhouse with a wraparound porch and a faded red roof. The paint was peeling everywhere. The overall appearance was one of age and disrepair. The windows were large and open, letting in light but not enough fresh air to clear the musty stank inside.

"It's empty," a deputy said, passing Noah on the way in.

Deputies cleared the rooms, checking for any sign of Teresa and those responsible. But all that was found was empty space and the remnants of life lived. It looked as if they had abandoned the house in a hurry, with furniture overturned and personal items scattered about. Cops rummaged through drawers and closets, but found nothing.

Then as he was about to leave, Noah noticed a glint of metal on the floor in the living room. Among all the trash, he might not have given it a passing glance if it wasn't for the gold band attached to it. He'd recognize that anywhere. He'd bought it in High Peaks. It was Lena's. Noah's heart sank at the realization. He figured she must have torn it off to leave behind a clue, to let him know that not only had she been there but that she'd never really put her relationship with him behind her.

As he bent down and picked it up, he muttered, "That's why you had cold feet."

Noah felt an ache in his chest. It was a bittersweet moment, knowing that she had thought of him in her final moments, but also that he was too late to help her.

"What you got there?" McKenzie asked.

He dangled the necklace and ring. "It belonged to Lena."

He expected the Scotsman to crack a joke, whip out a smart-ass remark but he didn't. Even he knew where to draw the line. Noah pocketed the necklace and was about to leave when Callie called out. "Noah."

He cast a glance over his shoulder. She held up a photo frame. He squinted and strolled toward her. "Seems Nate Sawyer isn't the only one that's been lying."

The photo was of three people out on a fishing boat. One of them was holding up a giant catfish, the other a fishing rod. Thomas Green was among the group, all smiles and celebratory. "Sonofabitch! Savannah was right."

He charged out of the house with the photo but not before smashing it against the door frame and pulling out the picture.

"I'll go with you," Callie said. "Hold up."

"I guess I'll just stay here and see what I can find," McKenzie muttered. Noah dashed back to his Bronco and jumped behind the wheel. With a screech of tires, he careened onto the dirt road leading back to the town.

The speedometer crept higher as Noah navigated the treacherous turns and bends, each one causing the vehicle to sway dangerously from side to side. Callie clung to the side of the door, telling him to slow down, but Noah was too furious to listen.

The Bronco hurtled down the road, and Noah felt his blood boil. He could feel the tension in his muscles as he gripped the wheel tight, white-knuckling it in frustration.

Finally, they screeched into the parking lot of the Sheriff's Office, and Noah jumped out, his heart racing.

"He's not going anywhere, Noah."

"Damn sure about that."

He burst into the building, demanding to have Thomas pulled from his jail cell. The correction officer in charge was taken aback at the request, certainly hesitant as he tried to make sense of the whirlwind before him. Following in his shadow, Callie was able to bring clarity to the situation while Noah paced, trying to calm himself.

They waited in a small interview room for an officer to collect the suspect.

The room was brightly lit, with a single fluorescent light flickering above them. The walls were a dull beige, and the only furniture was a small metal table and two chairs. The atmosphere was thick with tension, and Noah could feel his impatience mounting with every passing second.

He glanced up at the clock.

It took close to fifteen minutes before Thomas appeared.

Finally, the door opened and the correction officer escorted the suspect in. Thomas looked disheveled and tired, his orange jumpsuit a stark contrast to the drab walls of the room. He eyeballed them both before slumping down on a chair across from Noah. Callie stayed off to one side of the room.

"Am I getting out?" he asked.

Noah wasted no time getting started.

"Is there anything about your statement you want to change?"

He frowned, his gaze bouncing between them, confusion spreading. "I told you everything."

"Everything?"

Thomas shrugged. "Am I missing something here?"

"I don't know. You tell me?"

"I was straightforward with you all."

Noah dipped his chin and snorted, then lifted his eyes. "Thomas, you've been lying to us. About the dogs. About your involvement with them. Haven't you?"

Thomas looked confused. "I'm lost. What?"

His anxiety only seemed to intensify. He struggled to keep eye contact with them, as his gaze flickered away whenever they bounced it back to him.

Noah looked at Callie before he sighed, his patience wearing thin. "Don't play dumb. Okay? I'm giving you a chance here. So, tell us about the farm."

His voice was barely above a whisper, and it trembled with fear. "What farm?"

"We know you're involved in the selling of dogs or at least

associated with those who do it. Does the name Teresa Barkley ring a bell?"

Thomas' demeanor didn't change. He shook his head. "I have no idea what you're talking about."

Noah could feel his frustration building.

In a split second, he shoved the table out of the way, grabbed Thomas by the collar and pushed him back against the wall. "Don't fucking lie to me. People are dead! We have evidence that you know Teresa." He took the photo and shook it in front of his face. "Does this bring back any memories?"

"Noah," Callie said, trying to pull him back, but he shook her off, his eyes fixed on Thomas.

Thomas' gaze flickered down to the photo in Noah's hand, and he hesitated for a moment before finally admitting it. "I don't know her well," he said. "I was introduced to her that day by my cousin Jethro. They said they had a surefire way to make money. There was zero risk involved and it was all aboveboard."

"And?" Noah asked.

Thomas hesitated for a second before speaking again, stuttering as he did. "I M-met them a few years ago," he said. "My cousin took me out fishing, and we G-got talking. They seemed like grounded people, so we H-hung out a few times after that. You know, had a couple of beers. But I didn't really know them."

"Did you know they were going to harm people?"

"What? No, I swear I didn't," Thomas said. "Did they?"

"Don't fucking bullshit, man." His anger spilled over.

"I'm not. My job was simple. To go around and C-collect strays. Dogs that were off leash. I was to bring them back. The ones they wanted to keep they did, the others I C-could take to the shelter. They paid me. That was it."

"What about the golden retriever?"

"I was supposed to see them the next day to show them that

one. I couldn't bring M-myself to part with the dog so I was going to keep him."

There was a moment of silence.

"So, you have visited the farm?"

"Yeah. I was only ever allowed in the house. They didn't want me in the outbuildings. I was told everything was aboveboard. That they were D-doing a good thing, breeding and raising dogs and selling them to folks in town. I saw the flyers. I just..."

"Forgot that part? Right. Why didn't you tell us?"

"You never asked."

"Damn you, Thomas!" he shouted in his face. Callie tugged at Noah's arm. He stepped back, gripping the photo. "A woman is dead because of you. If I find out that you or they were connected to the other two, I swear, I fucking swear, I will...!" he said through gritted teeth, coming at him, but Callie got between them. Noah shook a finger at him, his anger boiling over.

Thomas stood there, his shoulders hunched and his eyes darting nervously between them. What little confidence he had was replaced by a tense and scared demeanor. His hands were clenched tightly in front of him, and his fingers fidgeted as he waited for what might come next.

"Look, I understand," Thomas said.

"You understand?" Noah threw the words back at him.

"I'm sorry that I didn't tell you about my connection to the others. I didn't think it was relevant."

"Relevant? Relevant? We asked you straight up if you were stealing dogs and you said you were collecting strays."

"I was."

"Yeah, you just left out the part about selling them. So, tell me, you never took any dogs out of someone's backyard?"

"Never."

"Did they?"

"I wasn't the only collector."

"Oh. Is that the title they gave you? You piece of shit!" Noah gritted his teeth, one hand balled tight. It was taking everything in him to restrain himself.

Thomas' face was pale and drawn, with a sheen of sweat glistening on his forehead. His eyes were wide and darted between them, as if searching for an exit. He bit down on his lower lip nervously, and his breath came in shallow and quick gasps.

Seeing the need to dial it back, Callie turned toward him. "Okay. Okay. Look. It's relevant now. That's all that matters. You need to tell us everything you know about Teresa Barkley and the others."

Thomas nodded. "I will," he said.

"Beginning with where they can be found," Noah said.

CHAPTER 25

Wednesday, November 23, 11:15 a.m.

Hours, minutes, seconds, it all came down to a matter of timing.

Although Thomas had offered up multiple locations for a so-called "trap house" where drug users, dealers and criminals on the run could hide out, they'd been able to verify fast that the place wasn't being used to harbor the assholes. They were smarter than that. It was the reason they were able to stay one step ahead.

Instead, the most concrete tip came simply by way of Thomas' cousin, who gave them what they wanted. Dogs.

As no one knew Thomas was in jail, Noah figured the best way to catch a mouse was to put out some bait.

Noah had Thomas call his cousin Jethro Ford to set up a time to meet. He said he'd obtained two French bulldogs, a Labrador retriever and a poodle, but that he'd swung by the farm and no one was there.

From there it was just a matter of following him.

As the U.S. Marshals had been chasing leads and tracking down every possible clue to the whereabouts of Teresa Barkley, it was only fitting they would take the lead. More often than not marshals would conduct raids at dawn as it gave them the element of surprise when apprehending criminals who might be armed and ready to resist arrest.

Safety was a huge factor. Daylight hours posed a greater risk because it was easier for targets to see them approaching. Of course, who could forget the one organization that cops hated almost as much as criminals — the media. Drawing the attention of media occurred far more in the hours they were active than at dawn, and with all the heat that the case had already drawn, the fear was Teresa would leave the county or state, if she hadn't already.

"I hope you are right about this," Rivera said as she picked up the phone to call the marshals and make the arrangements. While she did that, Noah stepped out to take a call from his sister.

"How did it go?" he asked, holding a finger up to his ear.

The office that morning was buzzing with activity, deputies coming and going, phones ringing off the hook and radios crackling. Murmuring voices talked about the case, from the raid on the farm through to what was now being put in motion. The sound of footsteps echoed, along with the occasional shout or whistle from a supervisor trying to get someone's attention.

"Noah, he got himself in a whole world of trouble. If I hadn't shown up when I did, who knows what would have happened."

"Did they accept it?"

"Of course. They want it by the end of today. Except it's going to cost an extra $50,000."

"Seriously?"

"It's interest."

"And if not?"

"You do the math. They're too smart to say anything in front of an attorney and legally they have grounds to collect. How they do that without taking a pound of flesh is what concerns me. I didn't get the impression that they were the type to put this kind of debt into collections, at least not the ones that phone you day and night or try to garnish wages." She paused. "Have you told dad?"

"Are you kidding? He would fly off the handle. Besides, Ray already hit him up for money. He's already paying him back."

"Which makes trying to pay this—"

"Impossible," Noah said. He ran a hand around the back of his neck. Callie and McKenzie were observing him from across the room. "Look, is he safe?"

"Define safe?"

"Maddie."

"He will be but you need to sign off. I've sent a copy over to your email. Digitally sign it. Send it back. The transfer needs to go through today."

"Fuck them. They can't hold him."

She went quiet.

"Maddie."

He heard her draw a breath. "The Ruger being held to the back of his head would say different."

"What?"

"Just sign it, Noah. I get a sense they've done this before and they know how to cover their tracks."

Thoughts of what Alicia had told him about the region, the bad element that had moved in, came to mind. It was true but how deep did it go?

"Put Ironwood on the phone."

Noah heard Maddie say, "He wants to speak to you." There was a muffled sound, followed by a sudden shift in background noise. It was clear that Maddie had just passed the phone to someone else.

He strained to hear the conversation as a new voice came into focus.

"Mr. Sutherland. I have to admit, I never expected you to step up to the plate. That's very generous."

"Look, asshole. You touch them and I will burn everything you have to the ground."

Ironwood chuckled. "I don't doubt it. The reputation of your family precedes you. Except that was from a different era. A time when the Sutherlands were in a unique position. Hugh was different. A reasonable man. He understood business and how things must operate. That's changed. Ray? Well, let's just say that our employer was more than reasonable with him. He chose the wrong option."

"So, you want to take a life for $400,000?"

"Is that what he said he owed?" Ironwood laughed. "I should have expected that. Oh, you have a lot to learn about your brother. You have been gone a long time, Noah. Still, your sister strikes me as a smart woman. She's confident that this can be cleared up today. It can be cleared up today, yes?"

"What's to stop me from raiding your casino right now and arresting you?"

He replied confidently. "Nothing. By all means if you think that's the way to handle this, do so. But have a conversation with your father first and see what happened to those who tried in the past."

Noah's brow furrowed in confusion.

"If it's paid, this is over and they walk?"

"You have my word."

"So operating outside of the law is what I can expect from you?"

Ironwood snorted. "Your father knew where to draw the thin blue line. Do you?"

The thin blue line represented the police as a line that kept society from descending into violent chaos. He'd never regarded it as something that could be moved but an immovable wall that chaos bashed up against. He couldn't help but wonder how different Hugh was from the previous sheriff.

"I look forward to receiving that payment," Ironwood said before hanging up. Noah stood there with one hand balled tightly, his jaw clenched. It wasn't just the nerve of this man but it was what he hadn't been told by Hugh that disturbed him. He checked his phone and found the email from Maddie. He digitally signed it and returned it, then stepped out of the office to make a call to have the funds from his bank sent over.

Whatever hope he had of purchasing the land from Alicia and building a home was gone.

"Noah. Hey!"

He cast a glance over his shoulder to see Callie gesturing for him to gear up.

"We're a go."

From one thing to the next. Life in the Adirondacks was giving him whiplash. It was a far cry from what he had to deal with in Peekskill. Now he was beginning to regret returning. Still, if there was one thing that mattered more than anything right now, it was nailing the bastards who had taken Lena's life.

WITH THE CONFIRMATION of the whereabouts of Teresa Barkley, the marshals immediately began preparing for the raid. They gathered their equipment, briefed the team on the plan and coordinated with local, county, and state law enforcement to ensure the safety of the surrounding community.

Despite the theory that Teresa and her pals had left the county, that wasn't the case. They'd simply gone east to Elizabethtown.

McKenzie was already there, huddled behind a garage near the apartment block along with a slew of county deputies. Marshals were down the road, ready to move in. Over the comms he heard McKenzie as he eyed them approaching at a crouch.

"You know you can't get good partners anymore," McKenzie said.

"I'm not your partner," Noah replied.

"And just when I thought we were warming up to each other."

"Glad you could join us," a deputy said, jogging toward them.

They'd brought Thomas Green with them. Originally they were going to get dogs from a local breeder, but with the danger involved, no breeder would let them take their animals. Instead, Thomas was wired and was to meet his cousin at the door and arrange for them to collect the dogs from his van. Drawing them out, away from the house, would make it safer for everyone. There was no telling what kind of arsenal they had inside.

"I still think it's a crazy move to send him in," McKenzie said.

"Marshals cleared it," Noah replied. "Stoltz, Palmer, take Davis around the rear. McKenzie is backing me."

"Backing you? You must have not gotten the memo. You're watching my six."

"Not today, pal," Noah replied. "You're at the side window by the bushes. Avery thinks you're too trigger-happy."

He clenched his hand. "Sonofabitch."

Callie grinned, knowing that Noah had made that up.

"All right. Get into position. Let's roll," Noah said over the comms.

Thomas Green looked as nervous as hell as he tucked in his shirt and strolled toward the lower apartment door. "Can you hear me?" he muttered.

"Loud and clear," Noah replied.

His heart must have been pounding in his chest as Thomas made his approach. He'd been chosen as bait to lure them out, and a large part of the success of the operation depended on him. While McKenzie had every right to be suspicious and nervous about him, they'd made it clear that if he cooperated, it would all be taken into consideration by the judge to ensure a lighter sentence. Noah watched Thomas wipe his sweaty palms on his pants and took a deep breath as he knocked on the door.

As seconds rolled by, Noah wondered if those inside had seen anyone or been tipped off. What if they saw through his ruse and decided to stay inside? He could feel a bead of sweat trickling down his back. He reached up and wiped his forehead with the back of his hand.

Finally, there was movement behind the curtains. He held his breath as the door cracked open, and a pair of suspicious eyes peered out at him.

"Yeah?"

"Jethro there?" Thomas asked.

"Jethro!" he heard another man say over the mic.

A straggly looking individual with shaggy sun-bleached hair that fell across his forehead came to the door. His style was casual and laid-back with a white T-shirt, jeans and flip flops.

"Where are the dogs?" he asked.

Thomas leaned forward and told them he couldn't find a close parking spot and the dogs were in the van. Law enforcement could hear every word just in case he decided to tip his cousin off. "Just tell her to grab them. I want to go."

Jethro looked over his shoulder. "Teresa. They're here. He wants a hand bringing them in." Another beat. Voices in the background. His cousin continued, "I know. I told him but there are no parking spaces close enough."

Cursing came from the back of the apartment before she came to the door.

"You know I don't pay you to make me do this," she said.

"I went to the farm but there was no one there," Thomas replied.

"Change of plans. Right. Let's go."

She and several others exited the apartment, following Thomas just as planned.

What happened next, occurred lightning fast.

As Thomas led them past the blacked-out van, marshals were waiting. Doors opened. Commands were shouted. Out of hiding, multiple local officers and deputies moved in, guns raised.

Teresa made a break for it but only got ten feet before she was tackled to the ground. Noah headed into the apartment behind a slew of marshals.

"Get on the floor! Drop it!"

It was loud and violent as a few chose to go out the hard way, opening fire. One of them unloaded a 12-gauge twice. The noise was deafening in the confined space. The first round took out an officer, the second round, took a shark-sized bite from the doorframe near Noah. He dropped to one knee and squeezed off two rounds, taking down the assailant before unloading on another.

Two in the chest. One in the head. The tweaker dropped hard.

A deputy broke in through the back door. Stoltz and Palmer charged in. Shots were fired, punching holes in plaster and peppering the walls.

Suddenly out of nowhere a freight train hit him. A naked woman covered in tattoos body slammed him headfirst into the wall. She tripped, landing hard. She was all nails, screams and spit. Noah grabbed her by the hair and slammed her nose into the floor, bursting it wide as he tried to get a knee on her shoulder. All the while shots were still being fired from further back in the apartment.

He caught a glimpse of Stoltz ducking as someone swung at him with a baseball bat. Like rats coming out of the woodworks, drug users emerged in a chaotic meth-driven state of violence.

"Palmer!" Noah shouted for help as he wrestled with the woman who was like a pig in mud. Palmer turned to assist but not before the bat wielding lunatic managed to strike Stoltz in the knee. Stoltz fired upward, sending a round through the user's skull.

A window exploded. Noah never saw it but he heard it. He figured some of them decided to escape that way. It wouldn't work, the place was surrounded.

"Would you stop resisting?!"

For a woman that couldn't have weighed more than one ten wet, she was putting up one hell of a fight. Most were like that when fueled by drugs. They were demon-eyed and pumped up on God knows what. Whatever was flowing through her veins, it was doing wonders as the fight never ceased.

"Stay put, you mad bitch!" Callie landed hard beside him to assist, taking over as he rushed forward to deal with another freight train who fancied himself as an MMA fighter as he was working the body of an officer with knees and elbows. Noah took out his baton, snapped it to get it to extend, then struck his knee with a bone cracking thud. He followed up with another strike to his back, causing him to crumple.

There had to be at least twenty crazies inside. As soon as they dealt with one, another came into view, white-knuckled and wide-eyed.

In the hallway, the next lunatic was packing an AR-15. He swung it towards Callie. She glanced up, her eyes wide, but before the asshole could squeeze off a deadly round, a bullet struck him in the temple.

Callie turned to see Noah's gun hand outstretched.

She mouthed the word thanks.

More marshals charged in and within minutes the chaotic scene was under control.

"Hey, hold up!" Noah said, jogging over to a marshal who was just about to tuck Teresa into the back of a van. "I want a moment with her."

"Who the fuck are you?" Teresa asked.

"Best of luck," the marshal said, stepping away.

Noah reached into his pocket and took out his wallet. He'd taken a photo from Lena's home of her and the kids. He held it up, demanding answers. "Remember her?"

"Fuck you."

Noah slammed her back against the van so hard, others looked over. "Look again!"

With venom in her eyes and spit on her lips, she glanced at it. "And?"

"Why did you kill her?"

"Kill her? What the hell are you talking about?"

"We tracked her to your farm."

"Well give yourself a fucking medal. We never touched her."

"What?"

"She was at our farm. Yeah. Nosing around. But once we found out she worked for the paper and that her ex was a cop — guessing that's you — we let her go! We put her back in her vehicle and sent her on her way. My mistake. Fucking bitch cost me thousands but we didn't kill her. I wanted to. I wish I had now."

Noah gritted his teeth; it was taking every ounce of restraint to hold back his emotion. "What about Katherine Evans and Laura Summers?"

"Who the fuck are they?"

He stared back at her, unsure if she was being genuine with her response.

"Look, we've done nothing wrong. Sold a few dogs. Whatever, man. We'll be out before the end of the day."

Noah motioned to the marshal.

"I wouldn't hold your breath to that," he replied as he walked away, his mind in turmoil and confusion.

CHAPTER 26

Wednesday, November 23, 12:30 p.m.

The caffeine was doing little to touch the tension headache.

Noah sat hunched over, devouring the remains of a ham sandwich, his eyes scanning timelines, dates, and occasionally looking up at the mugshots and names of suspects. His brow furrowed. He leaned back, trying to piece together the puzzle based on what evidence they'd collected so far, possible motives and opportunity. He took another sip of coffee; the dark bitter taste jolted his mind back into focus.

Callie barged into the room, holding a piece of paper that had an address scrawled across it. "I found her, Noah," she said, her eyes soaking in the sight of names on the mounted screens. "The girl from the Academy, Isabella, she's in Plattsburgh, an hour away."

Noah sat up straight, a flicker of hope igniting in his chest. They had been following every lead they could find, and this one seemed promising. Still, he couldn't quite make sense of what was before him.

"Did you hear me?" she asked.

"I heard you, Thorne." He pointed at the screen. "Katherine's husband, Nicholas Evans, could have been involved in both murders. He never reported her missing and there is the history of her feeling unsafe. Thomas Green was in jail when the second murder occurred and if he and Teresa are to be believed, they didn't even know the two women. The only connection they have is to Lena and they are adamant she left that farm alive. Then we have journalist Nate Sawyer, he was out at the time of both murders but swears he was in a meeting with Rector Hawthorne on the Friday when Katherine was found, even though Hawthorne denies it and says the meeting was canceled. As for the second murder, Sawyer didn't have enough time to kill Laura Summers, change vehicles and return. Based on surveillance, he had a twenty-minute window, tops. And he was inside when Lena was found dead and when his SUV was found on fire."

"So, what are you thinking?" she asked, standing by him and staring.

"I mean, on the surface Hawthorne or someone from the Academy had every reason to silence them. Katherine was trying to stir the waters with Sawyer's help. Laura was caught in the middle of that."

"And Lena?"

"I don't know. Sawyer worked for the paper. According to Maggie, Lena had taken his job. Maybe, she did some digging after it was confirmed to be Katherine and started nosing around." He brought a hand up to his mouth, feeling a wave of emotion.

"Hey. If this is too hard, I can get someone else to go out with me. It's just that it's out of our jurisdiction but not yours."

He exhaled hard. “I told her so many times to stay clear of stories that were dangerous but...” he took a deep breath. “Lena never listened. She moved to the beat of her own drum.” He reached into his pocket and took out the necklace with her wedding band on it. “You know, the day I bought this, I thought it wouldn’t fit her. It did. First time. What are the odds of that?”

“She kept it?”

“Wore it around her neck. Never told me.” He looked at her. “Look, what is McKenzie doing?”

“Forensics have gone to Nicholas’ home. You know, to run UV lights over the place. See if Katherine was killed there. McKenzie is following up with the bank and plans to speak with Nicholas again and pin down his alibi by canvassing the neighborhood.”

“He didn’t want to go with us?”

“McKenzie wants to do the least amount of work. Driving an hour to see a young girl who’s no longer at the Academy, is a waste of time in his mind.”

“And you?”

She shrugged. “Before Charlie, Isabella was frequently seeing Katherine.”

“Why not just phone her?” Noah asked.

“She isn’t picking up. I got hold of her parents. Told me she works at a gentleman’s club. She cut off communication from them last year.”

“A graduate of the prestigious High Peaks Academy and she’s working there?”

“Seems so.”

Twenty minutes later, as the Bronco wound its way up the highway through the Adirondacks, the sound of the engine was the dominant force. The rumble of the motor echoed off the trees, growing louder and more insistent as it snaked through the mountains. The vibrations thrummed, making the whole vehicle shake.

"You really should get this in for a service."

"It's new."

"Even more reason," she said as they navigated through the wild and rugged landscape. "How are you doing?"

"What?"

"How are you doing?" she asked.

"Staying focused on this keeps my mind from it. My worry is my kids."

"You really should take time off."

"Savannah said the same thing."

"If not for you, Noah, do it for them."

"That's the thing. I wouldn't know what to do with myself. The last real vacation I took, found me here dealing with Luke's murder. It's like even when I try to take time, some shit happens and pulls me away. And, me. I know how to deal with loss, regret and pain, I just bury myself in my work and ignore it. But them. Those kids. I don't even know where to begin to help them."

"Just being there is a start. Trust me, they don't expect more than that."

"What worries me the most," he stared blankly out the window, "is that I'm going to let them down. I feel like I'm becoming like my father every day and I hate it. I used to wonder why he spent so much time away from us working, but I get it now. This is the easy part. This we know what to do. But that... back home... Lena was always good at that."

"Well, now you get to learn, right?"

The air filtering in grew cooler and the smells of pine and woodsmoke were left behind as they got closer to the city.

The Crimson Lounge was nestled in the heart of downtown Plattsburgh, located inside a historic building that had been beautifully restored. The premises were situated on a bustling street, flanked by other restaurants and cafes. However, unlike the rest, the Crimson Lounge stood out with its deep red brick, which contrasted with the more muted colors of the surrounding buildings.

It wasn't a flea-ridden strip joint that might have attracted middle-aged drunks looking to get their jollies. It was clear that it catered to a higher-class clientele, those with deep pockets and hefty trust funds.

Noah took a narrow alley down the side of the building to make it into the lot at the back.

The entrance was discreet, a small hand-engraved wooden door that could have easily been missed if you weren't searching for it. The front of the building was very different, however, with crimson accents on its awnings, signage and window frames. It almost resembled a lawyer's office, or maybe that was the façade they wanted to convey. Sharing buildings had become the norm. It made sense, especially if most of the clientele came from the business district.

"You ever been in one of these?"

"Only for work."

"I expect that's what they all say," she said as she got out.

The door was adorned with a brass handle and a small gold plaque that read "The Crimson Lounge" in elegant script. Two tall lamps were on either side, casting a warm amber light on the sidewalk, as the tall building blocked out what little light made it into the alley.

They were met by light music as Noah pushed through the door.

Inside the vestibule, there was an immediate sense of sophistication, exclusivity and discretion, inviting those who stepped inside to experience what lay within.

"May I help you?" a strikingly beautiful woman asked, greeting them both with confidence. Her attire was impeccably tailored, with a fitted blazer and knee-length skirt that accentuated her curves in all the right ways. Her dark black hair was sleek, a modern bob, and her makeup subtle yet eye-catching. She stood tall and poised, with a regal bearing that commanded the attention of the wealthiest of men.

Noah took out his badge. “State Police, Noah Sutherland. We’re here to see an Isabella Perez.”

“Not in trouble, is she?”

“Not at all.”

The woman looked as if she expected them to clarify, maybe fill her in on the finer details, but after a beat, she took a step back, smiled and told them to follow. Callie glanced at Noah, her eyebrows raising as they ventured deeper into the establishment. The light was dim along the hallway, casting a warm glow on the plush furnishings and creating an intimate atmosphere. The air was filled with the sound of jazz music, played softly by a live band in a corner of the room.

The lounge was divided into various areas, each one had its own vibe. In another corner was a well-stocked bar, bottles lit up by lights, all tended to by a skilled mixologist who crafted artisanal cocktails with precision and care. The bar was surrounded by tall stools covered in leather. Well-dressed men sat, drank and chatted with astonishingly attractive women.

Unlike a strip joint, which might see men thirsting over untouchable women who looked as if the life had been sucked out of them, this had a stage where gorgeous performers took turns entertaining the crowd. Some sang standard songs or performed burlesque dances, while others slid down poles in high-end lingerie and high heels. Each one captivated the audience with her talent or curves.

Throughout the lounge, there were plush armchairs and sofas, arranged in intimate groupings for patrons to sit and converse. The furnishings were upholstered in rich red fabrics with ornate details that added a sense of luxury and elegance.

They passed walls adorned with art ranging from classic oil paintings to modern abstract pieces, all in an attempt to create an atmosphere of cultured refinement. At the far back was another bar set into a library filled with leather-bound books on history, philosophy, art and literature. Noah felt as if he was transported to another era, to a time when refinement was valued above all things.

"Wait here," the woman said after leading them into a VIP back room where there were several seats, a table with an array of wine and a large mirror on the wall. No doubt, it was one-way and being used by security to protect the women.

"Quite the place," Callie said. "I bet forensics would have a field day in here with a UV light."

That got a chuckle out of him.

"In here?" they heard a woman say before the door opened.

Before them was a Hispanic American woman. Like all the women they had seen so far, there was a sophistication to her, a subtle sexuality that wasn't cheap to buy, from the gold dress that accentuated her athletic build to the bold statement jewelry. She had olive skin, dark hair and dark eyes with a slightly round face and high cheekbones. Her lips were full and coated with a light lipstick. Her brows, thick and defined.

"Isabella Perez?"

"That's right," she said.

Noah showed his badge. "Noah Sutherland, State Police investigator. This is Callie Thorne from the Adirondack Sheriff's Office."

Her eyes bulged, darting between them. For a moment, he thought she might bolt. She didn't. "Did my parents call?"

"No. We were just hoping to have a moment of your time. To talk about Katherine Evans."

She sighed, reaching into her purse and taking out a gold case. She popped it open and took out a long white cigarette. "Do you mind?"

"Go ahead."

She lit it and took a seat.

"Katherine Evans. That's a name I haven't heard in a while."

"You studied at High Peaks Academy."

"I did."

"You graduated with honors."

"I graduated with more than that," she said, blowing smoke out the corner of her mouth.

"Forgive me if this sounds a little judgmental but..."

"Why do I work here?" she asked before he could say it.

He nodded.

"That's the million-dollar question, isn't it? I sometimes ask myself that at night until I look in my bank account or remember the past. Some might say I have daddy issues; others might think it was where I was always destined to be. I figured if I was going to get fucked, I might as well do it on my terms and get well compensated for it. At least here the men treat you with a degree of respect. Nothing less is tolerated."

Noah nodded.

Callie, eager to get answers to questions, chimed in. Noah didn't need to let her. She had as much right to ask as he did. He valued her approach. Had she not found that old police report, McKenzie might have walked out of there with little to go on.

"We have you listed as having seen Katherine on a fairly frequent basis. Far more than the other students. You mind sharing what that was about?"

She smiled and took a hard pull. "Client confidentiality means very little to cops."

"It does when we have a dead woman."

"Excuse me?"

"Katherine is dead."

Isabella froze, her eyes drifting down to the floor before she took a hard pull on her cigarette. "How?"

"She was pulled from a lake."

Isabella looked at a loss for words. She finished her cigarette and reached in for another. As she did, Noah noticed a small silver snub-nose.

"That yours?" Noah asked.

"I have a permit."

"Why?"

"I work here."

"You said they treat you with respect."

"And they do. This is for those who forget. It's not loaded," she said. As she went to take it out and show them, Noah placed a hand on his service weapon.

"Probably best you don't do that," he said.

"I'm not dangerous. It's never been fired."

"May I?" Callie asked, before snapping on latex gloves and checking the gun. She wasn't lying. It was empty. She handed it back.

"Why don't you keep it loaded?" Callie asked.

"Scared of guns," she said, placing it back inside.

Callie stifled a laugh.

"So?" Noah asked, prompting her to continue.

"I saw Katherine for anxiety, night terrors and just for someone to talk to because no one else would listen."

"About?"

She took a deep breath and took out another cigarette, lighting the end and blowing out a plume of smoke. "You wouldn't believe me if I told you."

"Why not?"

"Because no one did back then." She met their gaze.

"Try us," Noah said, taking a seat across from her. Isabella ran a hand over her face. They could tell she was trying to summon the courage or words to describe it. Maybe a little of both.

"It was a year before I graduated. The Academy is co-educational. Of course, girls' dormitories are a good distance from the boys. Occasionally, unbeknownst to the faculty, there would be invites to secret parties, you know, so girls and boys could mingle and do what most teenagers do. Drink, smoke, party. I attended a few. There were never too many that showed up, as having too many people know would have just been a giveaway. Besides, you couldn't trust everyone to keep their mouth shut. When you heard about them, it was often through word of mouth. Sometimes it was from a friend of mine, or one of the guys in the hallways." She took another hard pull on her cigarette. "I... I got an invite. It was a Friday night. The time was late as it always was but this was later than usual."

"Like?"

"Usually it was around ten, but this was closer to midnight." She paused for a second as if to try and recollect or compose herself. "We were all meant to meet at the place they did the laundry. It was far back on the property, mostly used by staff. Someone who worked there would leave the door unlocked. Anyway, I showed up and there was a group of guys there. I recognized them all. I began to drink. They said a few of the other girls were going to be running late. I'd seen it before. I didn't think anything of it. I mean, you have to understand. I drank and smoked with these guys before." She stopped and Callie placed a hand on her. It was something Noah appreciated about having her there. She made people relax.

"I don't really know how it started. I think they spiked my drink. I remember portions of it. Waking up each time with someone new on top of me. Laughter. Jeering. They cheered each other on. Took photos."

"How many were there?"

"Five. One of them didn't get involved. At least that I can remember." She closed her eyes. "When I finally came to, they were gone. I scooped up my clothes, got dressed and headed back to my dorm. It was close to five in the morning."

"How did you know one of them wasn't involved?"

"Because each time I woke up I could see him standing by the doorway. He was the lookout."

"Was his name Charlie Delaney?" Noah asked.

She lifted her eyes and met his, then nodded.

Noah glanced at Callie. She was taking notes.

"Anyway, a few days later I ended up getting herpes. I didn't even know what it was at the time. I just know I was achy, had the chills and was in pain. After I went to see the nurse in the infirmary, she said there was nothing wrong. That maybe I just had a cold or needed more rest."

"You didn't tell her what happened?"

"I was embarrassed. No. I didn't even know this was related to it. I ended up seeing my own physician but it was treated like nothing more than bacterial vaginosis or a yeast infection. I was given creams and medication but it never improved. I ended up getting worse. I went back to the infirmary. This time she said it was herpes. I was given a medication. I guess it had developed further. She never told my parents or even the head of the school. It just didn't make sense. I mean, I wasn't able to leave the campus without written consent so the nurse would have known that I contracted it there from a student or faculty member. Like any other student I just carried on but how do you carry on after something like that? After being treated, I confided in Katherine. I thought she would be a lifeline. At first I told her in confidence. I didn't want her telling anyone. Then she eventually convinced me that I needed to tell my parents and that's when they came up to the school. Katherine said she would be there to acknowledge that she'd been told it too."

"So what happened?" Noah asked.

"I don't know. I was no longer allowed to see Katherine. They said they would be doing their own internal investigation. You'd think that would include talking to me directly."

"You're saying the rector never spoke with you?"

"Nope. You have to remember I didn't have long left before I graduated. Maybe they thought they would sit on it and eventually it would go away because I would. From what I could tell they had spoken to other students about me. Maybe they didn't use my name but they alluded to behavior that was not allowed. Not just with those that were involved but others. Those guys knew. One thing I know is that they eventually came to a conclusion that the encounter between me and those boys was consensual."

"No one from law enforcement was notified?"

"I would need my parents for that."

"And what of them?"

"My parents were outraged. But not even that helped. They went up to the school and spoke with the rector, Alexander Hawthorne. I thought that would be it. That finally it would be resolved and I would be believed." She shook her head. "What I came to understand was when they returned, they had been convinced that I had consented to it, that I was known to sell weed on the campus, and that the evening in question I had not been black-out drunk at the time according to the boys and was capable of consenting to sex. The school painted me a bad person who couldn't change because I didn't want to change, and that I was bringing the school's name into question."

"And that was it?"

"Of course not. My parents were going to get an attorney involved but under advice that came from the school, they were told it wouldn't go far because I was seventeen which is the age of consent, as were the boys who did it. I was told if the case made it to court, I might have to testify against the boys and the school and that would destroy not just the school's reputation but mine and the accused boys' educational hopes."

"So what happened?"

"My parents spoke with them again. My father wanted to know if their parents would be informed, if there would be disciplinary action taken. But all they could say was that the encounter was consensual and that it was best for myself, the boys and the school that the matter be handled inhouse. If my parents wished to pursue legal action, I would have to take the stand and listen to them lie about me taking drugs, selling them, and breaking the rules in the school. However, it never even got that far. Like most abuse cases in boarding schools, the internal investigation was dragged out on promises that weren't kept. Basically, my parents were told in some way that if I continued to pursue it, I would be kicked off campus for lying, and I was so close to graduating that it would be a shame to ruin my education that way. Of course, by the time I graduated, I was no longer under them."

"And so, nothing was done."

"Exactly. They were under legal obligation to report the assault to the police but they never did. It was brushed under the rug and whenever asked, the rector would just turn it back, and ask why I never said anything at the time."

"All to save face."

She nodded, stubbing out her cigarette.

"Charlie Delaney. Did you ever approach him?"

"I did. I thought he might speak on my behalf but then..."

"The hazing?" Callie asked.

"It was just before I graduated. It was said to be a hazing but I know it wasn't. Someone had seen him talking to me, maybe they overheard. I don't know. I just know that he never said anything."

"He visited Katherine," Noah said.

"He did?" she asked.

Noah nodded. "Multiple times since you left and before she was... well, you know."

Isabella rose, glancing at her watch. "I'm afraid that's all I have time for. All I can tell you is if the Academy is behind Katherine's death, best of luck trying to get anyone to believe you."

They thanked her and exited.

As Noah and Callie were discussing what Isabella had shared with them on their way back to the Bronco, an urgent call came in from McKenzie.

CHAPTER 27

Wednesday, November 23, 2:50 p.m.

The drive back from Plattsburgh was long and arduous, the highway stretched out endlessly in front of them. For an hour, Noah had pushed the accelerator, watching the miles tick. As they hit the outskirts of town, he blared the siren, clearing traffic before them. They raced through the streets back to the home of the first victim's husband, Nicholas Evans.

McKenzie hadn't given them much in the way of details, only that they needed to get there as soon as possible. Noah had chewed the gristle of the case, finding it all a little hard to swallow. The process of elimination wasn't linear, it had taken them on a rollercoaster ride of twists and turns while offering little in the way of solid evidence or motive. Even though he had his theories, those wouldn't stand up in court.

Now, as they turned onto the quiet suburban street and pulled up to the house in Keene Valley, his heart rate quickened, and he felt a sense of dread. McKenzie and the forensics team were already inside.

Media vans lined the street, their satellite dishes pointed skyward, like giant antennae searching for a signal. Reporters and photographers bustled about, trying to get the best angle on the unfolding situation. Microphones and boom poles jutted out from the throng as they vied for position and to get the money shot.

"Geesh, they didn't waste any time getting here."

"Small towns. Word travels fast," Noah said. "Don't talk to them, just follow me in." He knew what it would be like as soon as they got out. Like a pack of vultures, they would swarm them. Even though squad cars had been positioned like a wall to keep them back and the home had been cordoned off with yellow police tape, that wouldn't stop them from pushing their luck.

Noah veered to the edge of the road and the two of them got out, making a strong beeline for the house. Almost immediately they were besieged by media, his face synonymous with law enforcement since the attention Luke's case had garnered.

"Mr. Sutherland. Mr. Sutherland. Can you tell us..."

"No comment."

They hurried up to the tape where a deputy lifted it to allow them to duck under before he shut down the wave of reporters behind them. Noah could hear them continuing to shout questions, hoping to glean some information about what was happening inside.

Noah had no idea, but was about to find out.

Ahead of them the house stood silent and foreboding, its windows covered by curtains to block reporters who were using long lens cameras. Inside it was a stark contrast to the frenzied activity outside. They passed by some members of the forensic team who were still working hard, examining the scene for any clues.

McKenzie was discussing evidence found.

"Good job. Log it. I want samples of everything." He glanced their way. "Ah, finally, did you take the scenic route?"

"Hilarious. What did you find?" Noah asked.

He led them over to an open door that was still being brushed down for prints. "Seems our suspect was hoping to off himself after we got that search warrant. We arrived to the sound of an engine. The smell of fumes was strong. The garage was locked. We entered through the door in the house and found Nicholas unresponsive, folded over on the floor beside his vehicle that was pumping out fumes. He wasn't coherent, and there was some blood in his nose. We called for an ambulance. They've taken him to Saranac. So far, he's still alive."

"You say he was outside of his vehicle?"

"Yeah. The garage was closed. That side door we just came through from the house was closed."

"Locked?"

"No. Only the garage door."

"Doesn't that strike you as odd?"

"What, because he wasn't found in the vehicle with a tube tucked inside? No. It doesn't take much for carbon monoxide to poison you. I'm thinking either he was already outside of the vehicle or he second-guessed his decision when he heard us arrive, and got out and only made it over to those steps before he collapsed. The only thing that was strange is that the vehicle wouldn't shut off. One of our guys turned the key and the engine was still going. Luckily one of the forensic guys knew a thing or two about engines and popped open the fuse box and took out the relay and then the engine shut off. I figure he screwed with the car, just in case he had second thoughts. He didn't want a plan B."

"Or someone screwed with it and he got out with the intention to figure it out. Was the hood already popped?"

"Don't know. I wasn't in here." McKenzie turned. "Bailey!"

One of the forensic team appeared in the doorway, outfitted in a full-body protective suit made of the lightweight, breathable material known as Tyvek.

"Was the hood already popped when you went to take out the relay?" Noah asked.

Bailey shrugged. "Not sure."

"Well, you would have felt the tension," Noah said.

"I can't recall. I just wanted to get in and out fast."

"Useless bugger," McKenzie said, turning back to the vehicle. "Anyway, doc says Nicholas might not pull through but he will keep us updated. I'm praying he does because I can't wait to see his face when we charge him for a double homicide."

"On what evidence?" Noah's voice was tinged with impatience.

McKenzie grinned, a glint in his eye as he beckoned Noah and Callie back into the house to a nearby table. Bagged up, ready to be logged, were multiple items.

"That unique colored rope tied off around Katherine and also used to hang Laura. We found it in his yard shed hanging up. It's cut at the end. I figure that will be a match." He reached for the next item which was a Glock 22. "You said he didn't have a license. Seems that didn't stop him from obtaining a gun on the black market. Serial number has been scratched off. Of course, we'll need to get ballistics involved to match the casing you found to this, but I figure it will be a match for the one used to kill Katherine."

"And what's this?" Noah asked, lifting a bag with a set of keys inside.

"Take a look."

Gloving up, he reached in and took them out to see the emblem for a Kia Sportage on the key fob.

"The damn thing was hanging up on the key rack. Imagine that."

"Yeah. Imagine that," Noah said, glancing over his shoulder toward the rack near the front entrance.

"My theory is Nicholas found out that Katherine was pregnant. They had a big fight. Probably wanted to know who the father was, or maybe she just told him outright. Then two days before she was pulled from the lake, she left and went and stayed at Nate Sawyer's place. We know it's his baby. So, husband loses it, kills Katherine and then follows up by stealing Sawyer's vehicle and killing Laura with the hope of pinning it on Sawyer."

Noah set the keys down, shaking his head. "No. It doesn't add up."

"Of course it does. Sutherland, the evidence is staring you in the face."

"That's what concerns me. How long has Nicholas had since the murders to get rid of these? You're telling me he kept the rope, and the keys to Sawyer's burnt-out SUV on his hook? And what about the gun? Where was that found?"

McKenzie stared back. He hesitated a moment before he replied. "In his closet."

Noah raised an eyebrow at him. Callie shook her head.

"Come on, McKenzie. You've been a detective long enough. How many cases have you worked where you've seen this amount of evidence all in one place? People throw guns, melt them down, dispose of them, they don't keep them in their closet. They sure as hell don't hang up the key to a stolen vehicle on the hook. No, he had plenty of time to dispose of these. He had to know he'd be the first person to be served with a search warrant. And then we have Sawyer saying he never saw Katherine in those days between the day she left and the night she was pulled from the lake — and by the look on his face when we told him Katherine was pregnant, he didn't know. She never went to his house."

"So, Katherine never told Sawyer and Nicholas killed her before she could," McKenzie replied. "It doesn't change anything."

Callie inspected the items while Noah browsed the kitchen, running a hand around the back of his neck and continuing, "Maybe. I mean, sure, it's plausible if he found out about her being pregnant, but why wait until she was walking the dog? Why not just kill her at the house?"

"Well, forensics is still taking a fine-tooth comb over this place. Perhaps he did."

"Then he plants the casing? No, the scene showed signs of a scuffle."

"That's conjecture," McKenzie said.

Noah eyed the room. Callie followed his gaze. "What is it?" Callie asked.

"Look at the chairs in the dining area."

All of them were tucked neatly under the table, barring one that was out.

"Anyone from the team touch that?" Noah asked.

McKenzie checked in with the forensics team and the deputies. None had. Noah ran his gloved fingers over the top of the chair, noting scrape marks. He picked it up and moved through the kitchen over to the door that led into the garage. He closed it and jammed the chair underneath the handle.

"Was the front door to the house locked?" Noah asked.

"It was."

"And the rear one open?"

"Closed but unlocked," McKenzie replied. "Look, Sutherland. Just admit it. You're pissed because I beat you to the punch."

"Don't let your ego cloud your judgment," Noah said,

removing the chair, taking it back to the dining area and discarding it in a manner as if he was in a hurry to get out. He then headed for the rear door.

"What the hell are you doing, Sutherland?" McKenzie shouted.

Noah walked backward, looking at the house and making his way over to the tree line. "You said the main garage door was locked but the one inside the house that leads into the garage was open or at least unlocked. Perhaps that's why Nicholas was out of his car. When he realized the engine wouldn't shut off, he got out to go into the house. He couldn't get into the house because a chair was jammed up behind the door and the garage was locked. Trapping him inside. All to make it look like a suicide. Now, you all arrive, spook whoever did this, and they pull the chair away but don't have time to put it back the way they found it. They exit through the rear and over to the tree line without being seen by those around the front," he said, pointing to the length of the house and how it could block anyone in the driveway or at the front door from seeing someone making a break for the trees.

"So, someone was already in the house and planted the evidence?" Callie asked.

McKenzie groaned. "Please. Would you listen to yourselves? This is our man. If he wakes up, I'm sure he'll give some sob story and if he doesn't, we have enough evidence to bury his ass."

"Yeah, maybe," Noah said. "But think about it. He's smart enough to work for a bank, organized enough to steal an SUV, clever enough to kill two people without anyone seeing him, but sloppy enough to keep the evidence that could send him away? C'mon!"

"It's not the dumbest thing I've seen a suspect do," McKenzie said, shrugging. "Besides, maybe he knew we were closing in on him and he opted to take the easy way out. It was only a matter of time before we would have figured it out."

"Well, that's the problem, McKenzie. Time. He had plenty of time to dispose of those items. Leaving them out in the open. No. I don't buy it."

"Like I said. Maybe he didn't expect to be caught because he planned on killing himself. You and I have both have had those calls where someone kills a person, calls 911, sits their ass down and waits for the boys in blue to show up and arrest them, or they take a gun and blow their brains out. It's called losing your mind, Noah, and I'm losing mine right now entertaining any other theory besides the one that is blatantly obvious."

"It's too obvious. Like someone wanted these items to be found. It's too clean. Besides, I did a preliminary sweep of the home back when we interviewed him. I never saw any gun in a closet."

"Then he had it stashed elsewhere with the intention of using it later. Maybe it was in his car. Maybe it wasn't even in the house. What matters is it's in there now. We'll soon find out if it was involved in Katherine's murder."

"Yeah, and while you're at it, maybe you can magically come up with a home pregnancy test and a video of them arguing about it."

McKenzie laughed and shook his head. "Sutherland, you talk about ego but maybe it's yours that is clouding your judgment. You're just pissed because I don't just have our man, I have the whole kit and kaboodle."

"What does that even mean?" Callie said. "Kaboodle?"

McKenzie groaned.

Noah continued, "If you do. Good. There is nothing more I want than to see whoever did this go away but that doesn't answer Lena's death."

"Maybe it's not related. Or if it is, she got too close. From what I hear, she did have a way of sticking her nose into things."

Noah jabbed a finger at him. "Watch your mouth."

"I will when you show me some damn respect. I've been at this longer than you!"

The two of them closed in on each other but Callie was quick to get between. "All right, fellas, all right, let's just let this play out. At least we'll get some answers."

"Yeah, even if they are wrong," Noah said, walking away.

Callie muttered something to McKenzie before hustling to catch up with him. "Hey hold up. Where are you going?"

"To see Charlie Delaney."

"You still think it's worth it now?"

"Yeah. I do. If not for this investigation, for the one that should have happened a year ago," he said, skirting around the house back to his vehicle. His mind was preoccupied by what he'd seen, his conversation with Isabella, and Lena when the phone rang.

It was Gretchen.

He had a mind to not answer but he knew she wouldn't have called him if it wasn't important. He tapped accept as he elbowed his way through the crowd like a fish going upstream. Reporters peppered him with questions. It was a chaotic scene, a whirlwind of activity and noise. "Gretchen. Can I call you back?'

She muttered something but he couldn't hear it.

Noah turned, losing his cool, and told the media to back off before he got into the Bronco and slammed the door shut, sealing out the ruckus.

"Sorry. What were you saying?"

"It's Ethan. Noah. You need to come by."

"Is he okay?"

"He's safe. Mia too but he needs his father, not some old lady."

He clenched his eyes shut. "I'm right in the middle of..."

"Listen to me, boy. I will always go to bat for you. You're my blood and I'm not one for telling you what to do but this is one time you need to listen or you will lose your kids." He glanced out at the crowd, his mind churning over before he answered to say he would be there in ten minutes.

CHAPTER 28

Wednesday, November 23, 3:10 p.m.

Noah took a deep breath as he climbed out of the Bronco.

Gretchen was standing at the window, waiting for him. She still lived in the same house that she and his uncle Patrick had built thirty years ago. It was a rustic private property nestled in a clearing located beside Echo Lake just off Mount Whitney Road.

Standing tall and proud amidst the lush greenery of the forest, the five-bedroom abode was a charming retreat worth millions now and would have netted Gretchen a tidy profit, but she refused to sell it. Even though she was getting on in age and it would have made sense for her to move into a small condo, it wouldn't happen. Her words, as he could remember them, were something to the effect of they would have to carry her out in a coffin before she let the place go.

It wasn't all stubbornness; it was nostalgia and love that kept her there.

The truth was it was a physical tie to Patrick who had tragically passed away in his sleep two years after Noah lost his mother to an aneurysm.

The exterior of the house was a stunning blend of natural materials, featuring a mix of sturdy wooden beams, rugged stone accents and traditional shingles. The roof had a steep pitch, creating a striking silhouette against the clear blue sky.

The wraparound porch, which added to the allure of the property, was full of comfortable seating that invited guests to relax and take in the tranquil scenery.

As Noah approached the house across a cobblestone walkway flanked by rows of colorful wildflowers, he eyed her.

"He's around the back, Noah," Gretchen said, waiting at the door.

"And Mia?"

"She's with me."

He nodded and skirted around the house past a charming wooden shed that housed outdoor equipment. Ahead of him, he spotted Ethan sitting on the dock, his arms wrapped around his knees. Ethan glanced over his shoulder as his father approached, his eyes red from crying, before looking back out.

Noah sidled up beside him, standing there for a second and looking out across the water that shimmered in the afternoon sunlight. The gentle rustling of the reeds was soothing but even nature couldn't ease the pain of a fourteen-year-old boy. Noah glanced down and exhaled softly as he sat beside his son.

He said nothing for a good couple of minutes.

Too often people were in a rush to speak, to fill the silence when all that was needed was someone to be present. Sometimes words weren't required.

Finally, he spoke softly. "I know how much it hurts, son. I wish I didn't but I do. I was only eighteen when I lost your grandmother. My mom. It was sudden too. I never got to say goodbye. Greatest pain I've ever felt. Thirty years later, I still grieve."

Ethan lifted his eyes. "I never met her."

"I know. She would have loved to meet you, to see how tall you've grown, how much you are becoming your own person."

Ethan turned to him, tears streaming down his face. "Why did this have to happen, Dad? Why did mom have to die?"

Noah put a comforting arm around his son. "I really wish I had the answer, son. But what I do know is that pain never really leaves you. It just becomes a little less sharp over time."

"I don't want to feel this."

"I know. We grieve because we loved someone. Grief doesn't end because love doesn't end. We just miss the person. All that changes is how we carry, feel and express that grief. I know that might not make much sense right now but eventually it will."

"What happened to mom?"

Noah knew Ethan would have questions, and he would do his best to answer them honestly. He deserved to know the truth about how she died, but in that moment, he couldn't say she was murdered, even if that was what he believed.

"We're still investigating. We don't have all the details yet. But what I do know is that we'll get through this together. I won't lie. I can't promise it will be easy or that pain will be gone tomorrow, next week or even in a few months, but I'll be here for you."

"I keep thinking about one of the last conversations I had with her. I was angry."

"Over what?"

"It doesn't matter now."

"Listen to me. What happened, happened. It was not your fault. You are not to blame. And I don't want you to beat yourself up over what you didn't or did say. Your mom loved you and that's all you need to hold here," he said, placing a hand on his kid's heart. "Let me tell you something I've never told anyone. Hours before my mother collapsed, I had an argument with her. It was over my father. As much as she supported my decision to leave for the military, she tried to get me to understand that my father only wanted the best for me. I couldn't see it back then. I said a few choice words I shouldn't have." Noah dipped his chin then raised it. "I can't change that now but I sure as heck blamed myself for those words after she was gone." He paused. "I only learned after my mother passed that she had gone to bat for me and tried to get my father to understand my decision."

Ethan nodded.

Noah gripped his son tightly. "Even though her life was cut short, I know your mom was grateful for every year she got with you and she understood you. She knows you loved her. Okay?" Ethan wept, leaning into his father. Noah choked up, a few tears rolling down his cheeks.

He wasn't sure how long he sat there with Ethan, only that in time, he heard movement behind him and looked back to see Mia. Not far behind her was Gretchen, a strained smile on her face. Noah motioned for his daughter to join them. She hurried over and sat, and he wrapped his arms around her too. He sat there holding them, staring out across the water until their tears ran dry.

CHAPTER 29

Wednesday, November 23, 5:20 p.m.

In the eyes of McKenzie, the investigation was in the bag and because Rivera felt he had a strong case, mentioning the pursuit of other avenues might have only created contention.

Noah on the other hand wasn't convinced. He felt like they were only holding a portion of the puzzle and a disputable one at that.

Despite his track record, they were walking a fine line returning to High Peaks Academy but Callie trusted his instincts.

As they entered the bustling dining hall at the private boarding school, the unmistakable aroma of chili and freshly baked cornbread attacked their nostrils. The dining hall was alive with the sound of student chatter, laughter and the scraping of cutlery against bowls.

The hall itself was large and spacious with a high ceiling and long wooden tables lined up parallel to each other. The walls were adorned with colorful posters and pictures and there was a large stained-glass window depicting Jesus at the Last Supper on either end to allow the natural light to stream in.

At the far back of the hall there was a serving area with a long counter and stainless-steel metal pans filled with steaming chili, and near that, wicker baskets of cornbread. The school dining staff, dressed in neat white uniforms, were standing behind the counter, serving up generous portions to students.

"I think we should have informed the rector about our arrival," Callie said.

"By the sounds of the previous interaction, I'm not sure he would be too happy to see us again."

As they threaded their way through a sea of students, they noticed that many were eagerly devouring their meals, while others were lost in conversation with their peers. A few caught their eye, muttering to one another. A uniform always garnered a different response. Shock, smiles, a weary glance.

Their attention locked on to the teenage boy who they'd been directed to by a staff member. He was sitting by himself at a small table in a corner of the hall. It was hard to tell how tall he was but it was clear he wasn't very imposing. He had a lean and lanky build that suggested he didn't spend much time on sports or physical activity. His dark hair was styled in a messy but modern tousled look with a little too much upfront. Noah noted the typical preppy attire with neatly pressed khaki pants and a collared shirt. His shoes were polished and well-maintained, and he had a book open on the table while he ate, indicating he took studying seriously.

"Charlie Delaney?" Noah asked.

He glanced up with a suspicious expression. "Who's asking?"

"Investigator Sutherland from State."

"Why aren't you in uniform?"

Noah glanced at Callie then back at him. "Because she is."

That wasn't the reason. BCI investigators wore plainclothes.

"You here about Katherine?"

"That among other things."

"What do you want from me?"

"Just to talk."

"No one told me you were coming." Charlie shifted nervously in his seat, he glanced across the room to a table where a group of older teenagers were talking and eyeballing him. Noah noticed two of them were the same boys he'd seen in Hawthorne's office on the first day when he arrived.

"No one needed to," Noah replied. "Is there somewhere else you'd feel comfortable chatting?" Noah could sense Charlie's unease and noted the constant glances at the others.

"And give them more reason to talk?" He glanced off to his left again toward the same table before he got up. "Why not? It's not like it can get any worse."

As the three of them made their way out of the busy dining hall, they passed through a long, brightly lit hallway. The walls were lined with lockers and there were a few posters hanging sporadically, and a white banner crossing the hall with the words: Academy Dance – Get Your Ticket.

The sound of chatter and laughter faded away as they turned a corner. They passed multiple classrooms. Charlie shifted his book bag over his shoulder, glancing at them out the corner of his eye before leading them through a set of doors into a library. As they entered, the scent of old books and polished wood filled their nostrils. It was quiet with only a few students scattered throughout, browsing, studying or reading quietly.

The first thing that caught Noah's attention was the vast collection of books that filled the shelves and lined the walls. The library was spacious, two floors with high ceilings. Charlie led them down an aisle past sections devoted to every genre imaginable. He eyed rows of textbooks, biographies, fiction, non-fiction, reference books and many more. The aisle was wide enough to accommodate several people at once.

Callie raised her eyebrows, noting how far back Charlie was leading them.

The lighting above them was subdued with soft yellow lights that cast a warm glow over wooden tables and chairs arranged throughout the room. There were a few reading lamps set strategically for those who wanted to read with more light.

Dotted over the walls were posters that were informative, displaying the Dewey decimal system, the hours of operation and inspirational quotes or book recommendations. A few had photographs of authors and advertised events that were coming up at the school.

"This should do," Charlie said, taking a seat at a table.

"You have many friends, Charlie? A girlfriend, perhaps?" Noah asked.

"What kind of questions are those?" He wiped food from the corner of his lips with his hand. Despite his smart appearance, Noah got a sense that he didn't have much luck with girls and that he was awkward in social situations by the way he blushed and stumbled over his words.

"Just curious."

"Um. I do okay."

Noah nodded, a smile dancing at the corner of his mouth. "I get a sense you aren't like the others. You carry yourself with a degree of respect."

He shrugged.

"Isabella Perez. You familiar with her?"

His eyes bounced between Callie and Noah. "Um. Yeah. And?"

"Well, it's just that she told us one heck of a story about a night here at the Academy. In the laundry room. You remember that night?"

"Um. I..."

Noah wanted to gauge his reaction. He could see his knee bouncing up and down, the way he was avoiding eye contact, the fidgeting, the sweat beading at his temples and the repeated um phrases — all the telltale signs of nervousness were there.

"Go on."

"I heard about it."

"That's it?"

"Um. Yeah," he replied, running a hand around his neck. "There were rumors going around."

"About?"

"Her."

"So, you weren't there?"

"Me? Um. No. I..." Someone nearby dropped several books on the floor, and that got Charlie's attention. His gaze darted off over Noah's shoulder. A short, pretty girl appeared, apologized and began restacking a shelf.

"You seem nervous, Charlie," Callie said.

"Do I?"

Noah decided to shift gears. "That's interesting what you've told us, you see because we recently got our hands on some of Katherine Evans' records. You know, the residential counselor you used to go to."

There were ways to suggest they were privy to information she had without saying they had it or lying. It was all a matter of extending a piece of rope and seeing how much they would take to hang themselves. The clever ones were careful. They closed up from the get-go; others told them to speak to their lawyer. It was the shy nervous ones that had a habit of rambling. Noah could see he was minutes from getting something out of him.

All the color in Charlie's face washed out.

His voice dropped to a whisper as he leaned forward. "Look. I don't know what Isabella or anyone else said but I can tell you I never laid a hand on her that night."

"I get a sense you didn't," Noah replied. "And... Katherine?"

"I saw her. Yeah."

"After the hazing that went wrong or was that event something more?" Callie asked, eager to know the answer to a question she'd posed to Hawthorne. Charlie kept glancing off down the aisle as if he was expecting company. He bit down on his lower lip.

"Adam Tomlin, Joshua Whelan, Ricky Patel and Benjamin Kim. Were they there that night? The night Isabella was raped?" Noah asked.

He nodded.

"Was it consensual?" Callie asked.

He shook his head, a strong no. "I didn't know they were going to do that to her. They never told me. Heck, I didn't get invites out to those things that often. They said there would be other girls there." He shrugged.

"So, you watched while they assaulted her?"

There was a commotion near the front of the library. Noah heard Hawthorne's voice. "Where are they?" He knew they had only minutes before their conversation would be shut down.

"It wasn't a hazing, was it?" Noah asked.

"No."

"It was a warning after you went and spoke with Katherine, correct?"

"Detectives. Detectives!" Hawthorne bellowed as he marched toward them down the aisle. Noah nudged Callie to stall him. Callie got up and headed towards Hawthorne, acting as a buffer. It bought him a few seconds longer.

"Charlie. Why did they hurt you?"

"Because Isabella came to me and told me to speak up on

her behalf. To tell the truth. I told Katherine in confidence in the hope they wouldn't know but..."

"They found out," Noah said.

Charlie nodded.

"Do you know who killed Katherine and Laura?"

Before he got an answer, Hawthorne and two staff members were on them. "That's enough. Delaney, go back to the dining hall. I will speak with you later." Charlie got up looking all timid. He eyed Noah before shrugging on his backpack and sauntering away. Hawthorne was quick to speak, wagging a finger in the air. "You've stepped over the line. Now we have answered your questions. Been more than accommodating. But I will not have you blindside our students and interrogate them without an adult or lawyer present."

Noah rose. As he turned to face him, he noticed some of the older teens from the dining hall at the far end of the aisle near the front of the library. They stared back, smirks forming.

"That's fine. It was just a conversation. We're done here," Noah said, brushing past him and leaving with a much better picture. It wasn't the slam-dunk he wanted but he sure as hell had what he needed to continue in the direction they were heading.

CHAPTER 30

Wednesday, November 23, 6:00 p.m.

The tension in the room was thick enough to be cut with a knife.

Acting Sheriff Rivera sat at her desk in the cramped, dimly lit office, drumming her fingers on the wooden surface. Across from her sat a smug-looking McKenzie who was practically oozing confidence. Noah stood by a large and grimy window that overlooked the brightly illuminated parking lot. A few squad cars came and went, a continual turning over of deputies and correctional officers starting their shift or returning with lawbreakers.

The walls were a dull beige color with a few framed certificates and awards hanging on them. Callie sat near McKenzie, looking at him expectantly.

"So," said Rivera, breaking the silence. "What do we have so far, McKenzie?"

He leaned back in his chair, a small smile tugging at the

corner of his lips. "I think he's our man, sheriff. The evidence we found at his home is hard to deny. We're just waiting on the lab results to confirm."

Rivera raised an eyebrow. "The husband?"

"Nicholas Evans, yes, ma'am," McKenzie replied. "We weren't able to rule him out. Both murders occurred after work hours. He has no concrete alibi for his whereabouts except that he was at home. He never reported Katherine missing and with his history with his wife and previous communication with Laura — based on her cell records in the days following Katherine's death — I have to wonder if Laura confronted him over Katherine's death and he snapped."

"That communication is open to debate," Noah said, turning away from the window, his expression serious.

Rivera frowned. "What do you mean, Noah?"

"We don't know what their conversations were about. If Nicholas told us the truth, there were more stresses in Katherine's life than him. Sheriff, I'm not saying what has been found needs to be ignored, I just don't think we should be focused solely on him. I think there's something bigger going on here."

"Like?"

Noah hesitated for a moment before speaking. "Last year, there was an assault at the Academy. A student named Isabella Perez said she was sexually assaulted by several teens. Isabella saw the nurse at the time, Laura Summers, and told Katherine Evans, the residential counselor. From what we've been able to tell, nothing was filed with the police and the accused never had any official charges brought against them. Today, we met with Charlie Delaney — a boy who admits to being there on the night of the assault. He said he told Katherine that the assault occurred. It wasn't long after that she was let go. Months later, she tried to get journalist Nate Sawyer involved and then went missing. Sawyer says he met with Rector Hawthorne the night Katherine was pulled from the lake, Hawthorne denies it."

"What are you saying?"

"I don't think the school is being honest with us. I think the two murders were related to that assault."

"An assault that could only be confirmed by our two dead women."

"More than that. We have the boy's confession."

"That's debatable," McKenzie said.

Callie was quick to throw in her two cents. "We've been doing some digging, and we've found some discrepancies in their statements. We think that they covered up the incident and now with the involvement of a journalist, someone from the school is tying up loose ends."

"Then why hasn't Sawyer been killed?"

Noah was quick to answer that. "He's already made headlines for sexual harassment. The DNA test came back as positive. He was the father of Katherine's unborn child. I think someone wants people to believe he was involved or maybe working hand-in-hand with Nicholas, hence the reason his SUV was stolen and the keys were found at the Evans home."

Rivera leaned back in her chair, tapping her pen against the table. "I see. And what do you propose we do?"

Noah took a step forward, his voice low and urgent. "I think we interview those students, pin down their whereabouts on the days in question, and verify where Hawthorne and the rest of the staff members were, because Sawyer refuses to change his story about that meeting which according to Hawthorne never happened."

Rivera sighed. "Look, I understand your concerns, Noah. Maybe more interviewing is warranted, but you should have considered that ahead of time. I've already had a complaint from the rector about you two talking to Charlie Delaney without an adult or lawyer present. I don't want to make things worse by poking around without good reason and then have them lawyer up and then we won't get anything if we have to go in that direction. Right now, the ship isn't pointing that way."

Noah stabbed a finger at the floor. "That's exactly my point. Someone wants it pointed in another direction."

"And we will find out. Let's focus on what we have here with Nicholas Evans, and leave the Academy alone for now."

Noah opened his mouth to argue, but Rivera held up a hand to stop him. "That's final, Noah. I won't have you jeopardizing this case because of some hunch. Stick to the facts, and the evidence we have, and let's see what becomes of that first."

"And in the meantime, what? Someone else dies?"

She narrowed her eyes at him. "This needs more time."

"We are running out of time."

She took a deep breath. "And maybe the death of your ex-wife is influencing your decisions. Do I need to contact State and have them assign someone else?"

He threw up his hands. "You want to go that route, that's fine by me," he said, turning and heading out the door, leaving it wide open. Callie was up in his shadow. They had made it about halfway down the hallway when Callie spoke up.

"Is that it? You're just going to walk?"

Noah turned, throwing his hands in the air. "What do you expect from me?"

"To stay the course and see this through to the end no matter what the outcome is."

McKenzie approached from behind her. "You're wasting your breath, Thorne. Sutherland can't. He won't. Because just like all those State guys that roll in and roll out. The first sign of opposition or a fuckup and they jump ship to let someone else deal with the blowback, just like he did in the Alman case."

Noah approached him, his brow knit together. "You don't

have a damn clue what happened because if you did, you wouldn't put all your eggs in the same basket regarding Evans."

"See, that's the thing, Noah, all the eggs are in the basket. I didn't put them in there. You're the only one that is ignoring that."

"I'm not ignoring them; I'm asking why they are together at the same time."

"Aye, it's called being guilty."

Noah shook his head and walked off, shaking a finger at him. "Tomorrow, you can lay it all out to the next State investigator. Just make sure you get forensics on that gun to see if they can recover the serial number."

"They're already on it."

"Good."

Every firearm had a serial number that was issued to identify it with the owner. It was stamped into the metal frame of the weapon using powerful dies that would drive the numbers deep into the steel. Most guns on the black market had their serial numbers deleted to avoid them being traced. However, forensics had improved. Just like many criminals didn't realize a hard drive that was wiped could be recovered, most were unaware that erasing a serial number didn't mean it was truly gone. There were numerous physical and chemical processes that were used to restore or enhance the damaged number. It wasn't bulletproof but in recent years they'd had a lot of success with the Magnaflux method, chemical and electrochemical etching, and ultrasonic cavitation.

He marched away. Callie took off after him.

"McKenzie has a point."

"Then follow it."

"And you? Why are you scared to get it wrong?"

"I can answer that in two words," McKenzie said. Noah glanced over his shoulder. "Hugh Sutherland. Am I right, Noah?

Must be difficult living up to his expectations and standing in the shadow of your brother."

"Save the condescending comments for someone who gives a shit. You'll get to close this case and bask in the glory; you'll just do it with a different State investigator."

"Aye. Will do."

Callie took off after him.

"And what if he's wrong?" she said. "If Evans and Sawyer weren't involved, they need our help. You know there is more to this than just an affair or a pregnancy. You walk away now, there is a chance they will do time and another innocent person will be screwed."

"They were screwed by association from the moment Isabella was assaulted."

"So, you believe her?"

"Callie. I don't know what part of our conversation with Isabella you missed but it doesn't matter what is believed, only what will hold up in a court," he said, glancing past her to McKenzie. "And right now, McKenzie thinks he's holding the golden goose even if it could be the wrong one," he added, his voice growing louder by the second.

"Which it's not," McKenzie said, answering while drawing water into a paper cup. He chugged it back, confident and at peace.

Callie moved around Noah, stopping ahead of him for but a few seconds to say, "After we thought we had those responsible for Luke's murder, I was ready to walk. I believed you didn't want to accept the truth. You never passed the buck. You stayed the course. What's so different now?"

"It was family."

"And Lena wasn't?"

She walked away, leaving him chewing it over.

Noah glanced back to see McKenzie lift his cup of water,

smirk and amble off in the opposite direction. Several deputies who'd been eavesdropping returned to tapping away on keyboards and answering phones.

HE HATED the thought of seeing her again but he had to know. Thirty minutes later, Noah shivered as he walked through the door to what he liked to refer to as purgatory for the dead. The stainless-steel morgue in the Medical Examiner's Office was uninviting and cold. The sterile scent of disinfectant and the hum of the fluorescent lights made him queasy.

Dr. Adelaide Chambers was perched on a stool over a body. She had a serious expression. Her white lab coat was pristine, her gloved hands poised as she examined an unknown deceased male.

"Noah Sutherland."

"Good memory."

"No. Names I remember, faces not so much," she said. "I'm not sure if it's because they all look the same when they come in here or my brain is on the blink with age. I think it's a little of both," she said, dropping a tool. It clattered in a steel bowl. "I was told that Lena was your ex. I'm sorry for your loss. I gather you want an update on the autopsy."

Noah nodded; his throat tight with emotion. He hadn't just lost his former wife, he'd lost a close friend, a confidant. Despite their separation, that had never stopped them from being open with one another. Lena had earned that right. She had become accustomed to the nuances in his tone. There was little he could hide from her.

"Do you want to see her?"

"Let's start with the facts."

Chambers crossed the room and lifted a tablet. She tapped a

few times, swiped, then began. “Cause of death was exposure to fentanyl.”

“Fentanyl? She never drowned?”

“No. No water in the lungs. She was dead long before she went in the river.”

His thoughts went back to the car stuck in neutral.

If she had been driving and swerved to avoid an oncoming vehicle or — God forbid — tried to take her life, the gear would have been in drive. Had Teresa lied to him? He’d come across numerous liars in his line of work. Teresa never struck him as someone who had a reason to. Though she could have.

“Teresa said she let her go,” Noah muttered.

“Sorry?” Chambers asked.

“Nothing.”

Chambers crossed the room. “We’ve had a number of cases of drug users dying from it. Doesn’t take much. 0.25 milligrams. It can be very lethal in small doses.”

“But she didn’t take drugs. I was married to her for years.”

“I’m not suggesting that she did when you knew her, but what about after that?”

“Not that I know. I mean, anything’s possible but she seemed content, she never struck me as the type who would do that. Not Lena. Our kids meant more to her than a high.”

“Well if she was using, she wouldn’t have known. Fentanyl is often used as a cutting agent, basically a filler for heroin. And nowadays it’s nearly impossible to tell if drugs have been laced with fentanyl until it’s too late. We used to get very few cases but there seems to be one in here every week. Accidental overdose. It’s sad to see people go out that way.”

“So that’s it? Nothing else?”

“There were marks on her body. Around her neck, suggesting strangulation but...”

"It could have come from someone holding her face and forcing her to take fentanyl?"

She nodded. "Yes."

"Let me see her."

"Are you sure?"

He nodded, unable to find words to convey how he was feeling. Chambers crossed the room filled with rows of metal tables, each covered in white sheets. Noah tried not to look too closely, though his eyes kept wandering to the covered forms, wondering who they were and what had led them here. Chambers pulled on a compartment and dragged out a rolling table.

Noah approached as she lifted the sheet, revealing Lena. Noah took a deep breath, trying to control his emotions as he looked down at her lifeless body. As Chambers pointed out the areas on the chest and neck that were bruised, he barely heard her, he was lost in grief.

After a few more minutes, Noah thanked the M.E. and left the morgue, his mind racing with memories of his last days with her. Conversations were both good and bad. He couldn't believe she was gone, and the sterile atmosphere of the hospital only made his loss feel more surreal. As he staggered back into the daylight, Noah leaned against the wall, feeling the world spinning.

His gag reflex kicked in and he spat on the ground.

Nearby, someone working for the hospital was perched on a low wall. "Let me guess? You had the pasta. Canteen food will do that. That's why I bring my own," she said, taking a bite of her sandwich.

Noah looked up at her, wiping his mouth, then something clicked in his mind. "Of course," he muttered. Like dominoes falling one after the other, it began to make sense.

He took out his phone and made a call to the Academy.

CHAPTER 31

Wednesday, November 23, 7:40 p.m.

Home was a welcome reprieve from the madness of the investigation.

Surrounded by the scent of fresh paint and the hum of the TV playing in the background, Callie took out a cold bottle of Chardonnay from the fridge and pulled the cork. She poured a quarter of a glass. Not too much. Not too little. Just enough to take the edge off. She didn't want to awake the next day with a heavy head. She saved those humdingers for her days off.

She glanced at the TV as she put the bottle back.

Local news was running the story of Katherine Evans and Laura Summers now that the media had managed to obtain names. So far, they had little information to go on regarding the deaths as local PD, County and State were tight-lipped. However, that didn't stop theories swirling of a serial killer on the loose since the discovery of Lena.

She leaned back against the kitchen island, taking a sip and listening as the reporter interviewed several neighbors, folks who had met, known or lived near the women. The comments were mostly the same — shock, disbelief and fear. Some mentioned buying a gun for the first time, others were scared to go out.

Comments were as varied as the rumors.

With a third death potentially being linked to the other two, and occurring so close in time to the others, High Peaks had now become the mecca for weirdos and oddballs. Callie shook her head as a reporter thirsty for even a smidgen of titillating information interviewed the head of a paranormal group. "Don't you feel this is a little disrespectful to the families?"

"We're just trying to help. We understand people don't believe in the spirit world but they will when we reveal the name of who's behind this."

Callie shook her head as she set the wine glass down and went back to applying the neutral-colored paint to the wall with the roller. She'd thrown down tarps to prevent damage to the hardwood floors. It was therapeutic to her as she found herself lost in the repetitive motion of painting.

A knock at the door interrupted her thoughts. As she stepped down off the ladder, a large dollop of paint landed on her face. She smeared it with the back of her forearm trying to wipe it away, but only made it worse. "Ugh," she groaned. "I'm coming," she said at the sound of another loud knock.

Peering through the peephole, she was greeted by the sight of Noah on the other side. She pulled the door wide. He looked apologetic.

"Sorry. I should have called first."

"No. It's okay, I was just… painting."

"I see." He pointed to her face.

She wiped it again which apparently only made it worse, as

Noah smirked. Callie shifted awkwardly from one foot to the next. "Come on in," she said, moving to one side. As he passed, she noticed flowers at his side.

"Who's the lucky girl?"

"Oh, uh. A housewarming gift," he said, handing them to her. They were beautiful, familiar, but very odd.

"Strange. I always thought florists wrapped them." She was noting the soil dangling from the ends.

"That's exactly what I said."

Callie set them down, smiling. "They look familiar."

"I would hope so. Getting them out of that hanging basket was a bitch, but Simon, your neighbor, eventually gave me a hand."

She smiled as Noah wiped mud from his hands on a rag.

"Hope he didn't screw you over."

"Forty bucks, but what can you do at this hour with all the stores closed?"

Callie laughed as she sifted through a cupboard for a vase. Noah's gaze roamed the room. "You eaten?" he asked.

"Not yet," she said, setting the flowers in the vase.

"You up for going out?"

"Uh. Not exactly in the mood for dashing around, after today."

"I hear you. Just I know a good Chinese place."

She nodded. "We can order in."

"Okay."

~

FORTY MINUTES LATER, with the Chinese food laid out on the table, Callie poured a little more wine. "You don't drink, right?"

"As of a day ago, I would have said no. I'll have some."

"You sure?"

He nodded and she poured a glass. "So, this is the new place you were talking about. For some reason I thought you were referring to the housing development over in Fawn Valley."

"Not on my wages. No, this place does the job."

"It's nice. Though I thought it was a new build."

"It is," she said, serving up some of the Chinese onto a plate.

"So, why paint it?"

She sat down, a smile forming, then shrugged. "You're going to think it's odd."

"Fire away."

"It's a habit I picked up from my mother. Every few months she would get bored of the layout and color of the walls and felt she needed to change things up. So, she would drag me and my sister down to the paint shop to pick out new colors. Drove our father nuts but it kept life interesting or at least our house."

"You said your mother was a..." he reached for the word.

"Psychologist. One of the best. At least if her accolades are anything to go by."

"So even psychologists are a little weird."

She laughed.

It didn't take long for them to segue into a discussion about the case after another segment rolled out on the TV. He twisted in his seat to view some of the shots from earlier that day of media outside the Evans home.

"Everyone's got their theories," he said.

"To be expected."

"What's yours?"

"You're asking me?"

He nodded; his mouth full of rice.

Callie picked at her food. "I think that I'm every bit as confused as the rest of the town. Theories get us nowhere. Facts. That I can work with."

Noah leaned back, wiping his lips with a napkin. "I went

back to the sites this evening after having a visit with the medical examiner. You know — the Evans home, and the tree."

"Wait. You went to see the medical examiner?"

"It was fentanyl. The cause of Lena's death."

Callie gave an incredulous expression.

Noah dug a fork into his food, picking at it. "I don't buy drug use for one minute. I also don't think her death is connected to the others."

"Why not?"

"When I talked with Maggie, she said Lena didn't know Nate Sawyer. It was long before her time, and although she wrote the first article about the woman pulled from the lake, her name wasn't on it. Carl McNeal took it over, edited her work and attached his name. So, if the one who murdered Katherine and Laura took offense to the media, it would have been with Carl or Nate. Nate was flying solo with his journalism business and was the one threatening to expose High Peaks Academy."

"And yet Nate is still alive. In fact, you would have thought that if it was related to what was covered up by the faculty, he would have been targeted first. It almost seems like a missed opportunity. I mean, there was more chance of him getting the word out to the public than Katherine."

"Unless the killer wanted it pinned on him. Sawyer was already dealing with an allegation of his own. Killing him might have only bolstered whatever he had written already."

"So then if Nicholas is innocent, why take him out?"

"I'm not sure right now. A fall guy, perhaps. He's the only other person that in the eyes of the law might have a motive to kill both women."

Callie took a sip of wine. "So you don't think it ends there?"

"What?"

"Well, you said to Rivera that someone might kill again."

"Might."

"No. You seemed pretty sure that if we focused too much on Nicholas, that someone else could be targeted. That would imply whoever did this isn't done. Sawyer is inside. Nicholas is at the hospital. So, who else?"

"I don't know. I just don't think they're finished."

"You must have a theory."

He shrugged, glancing back at the TV. "Like you said, theories lead us nowhere. Only facts do."

"Then where are the facts leading us?"

Noah took his glass and wandered over to the French doors that led out to the balcony. Callie's fourth floor apartment didn't have a clear view of the town or anything but trees for that matter, as it was nestled in Adirondack State Park. "We have an assault that was confirmed by one of the boys alleged to have been there. So, I've been thinking a lot about gain and loss. You know — who had the most to gain from the murders of Katherine and Laura. And with both of them alive, what would the perpetrator stand to lose?"

Callie chimed in. "Both women had knowledge of the assault on Isabella and the alleged hazing. If Isabella was telling the truth, someone from the Academy would have every reason to want to keep that quiet. That's why there is no police report of her assault. If it got out that they never reported the assault to police, the backlash from that alone would be the end of the school's reputation. No one would trust them, let alone send their kids there."

"But is that enough to murder two people?" Noah asked, looking back at her. "Countless private boarding schools over the years have been exposed for sexual misconduct."

Callie mused. "Yes, but not until decades later when the statute of limitations was past."

"So why wait? If they felt that Katherine and Laura were a

threat, they could have acted sooner," Noah said. "No, I don't buy it."

Callie took a sip of her drink before saying, "The Academy felt the matter was handled. It was only when Charlie Delaney started seeing Katherine that she would have brought it up for a second time, and this time it wouldn't have just been the alleged assault on Isabella but what happened to him too."

Noah shifted his weight from one foot to the next. "So, Hawthorne gives Katherine an option."

Callie nodded. "It might have been career suicide taking a private school that has been around for decades to court, especially when accusations were leveled at her. So she exited. Then two months pass."

"Exactly," he said. "The Academy thought they were out of the woods. However, the next time the matter would have been brought up, was when Sawyer got involved. Now they realize this isn't going away and not only are they dealing with sexual assault, but also Charlie's attack and the unfair dismissal of an employee. That's one hell of a dark cloud to live under. And to top it off, Katherine is now willing to lose her career for the sake of the truth."

Callie stared at him. "So, she's murdered and they follow through with Laura."

"Go on," Noah said, encouraging her to follow that same train of logic.

"By this point Sawyer is inside but there is no way of knowing if he's going down for it, so an attempt is made on Nicholas and they opt to pin the evidence on him." She shook her head and ran a hand over her blonde hair. "No. Something's not right here."

"What?" he asked.

"All right. Just humor me on this one. We know that Hawthorne doesn't have an alibi for the night Katherine was found dead. Okay. If Hawthorne was behind it, let's say he kills Katherine, he follows up with Laura and makes sure Sawyer's stolen SUV is seen. He then sets fire to it so it could be found and linked back to Sawyer. However, Sawyer was inside when that fire occurred, leading us to believe that it couldn't have been him. That's also backed up by the stolen vehicle report Sawyer filed and CCTV footage that wouldn't have given him enough time to do the murder. So instead of leaving the keys in the vehicle, Hawthorne or someone from the Academy plants them at Nicholas' place along with the rest of the evidence, knowing full well that Nicholas was the only other person that Katherine might have talked to about the assaults, but that's the problem..."

Noah smiled. He could tell she was beginning to realize what he had discovered and why he'd refused to believe that it was Nicholas. "Keep going," Noah said. It was a simple matter of connecting the dots and applying common sense.

"If Hawthorne is responsible for the murders, he couldn't have known who Katherine told. She may have told countless people. So, killing Nicholas wouldn't have helped. In fact, it might have worked against the Academy because they would have known that we would have looked into Katherine's background, spoke with Nicholas, learned about the dismissal and the alleged interference with children. We found no report had been filed, let alone the alleged assault on Isabella. And that alone would have opened up a can of worms he didn't want."

"Exactly. It would have ended up with the result Hawthorne didn't want in the first place, which was for no one to know about what was covered up. An adult would think about that. A teen? Maybe not so much. Isabella was straightforward. Charlie didn't deny it."

They exchanged a contemplative stare.

"And there are only three other people who really knew

about it: Hawthorne, Charlie and Isabella. You think they might be targeted next?" He didn't even need to answer it. The penny dropped. "You think it's the boys who murdered them?"

Noah nodded.

"But there were four of them. You honestly think they're all involved?"

"Remember, Thorne, we are dealing with a theory here. Let's not get ahead of ourselves." He reached for a pen and piece of paper. "You got a map of the area?"

"Yeah. One second."

She returned a moment later and helped him clear off the table so he could spread it out. Noah unfolded the map. He circled the places where Katherine and Laura were found, and the Evans home, and then drew a red line back to the Academy. "Connery Pond is nine minutes away for Laura. Pulpit Rock is fourteen minutes away for Katherine. The Evans residence in Keene is twenty minutes. Nate Sawyer's residence is ten minutes." Noah turned to his scrap of paper and jotted down the names of the victims. "Here's what dawned on me. Katherine Evans, Laura Summers, and even if we include Nicholas Evans, who still hasn't regained consciousness at the hospital. All of their deaths occurred within a very specific time frame. Okay, we don't know exactly what time Katherine died at, but if we go on the timeline of Laura's abduction based on her run, and then we take the incident at the Evans house, which we have McKenzie's logbook to thank for that. Then we take the time of when the farmer saw the SUV on fire. All three, four if you include the site where Sawyer's SUV was found, are within thirty minutes' driving distance of the Academy. Based on the estimated time of death for Lena, she doesn't fall into the timeline as she was located at Split Rock Falls, a forty-minute one-way drive from here, which is less than an hour and a half if you race back. Now I called the Academy tonight to find out when everyone eats in the dining hall. They said between five-thirty and six-thirty. That's an hour window. Plenty of time for them to do what needs to be done and get back without anyone noticing they are gone."

"We saw people eating elsewhere — in the library."

"Exactly," he replied, nodding. Noah continued. "And I'm pretty sure unless they knew to leave their phones behind, we'll soon have a record of where their phones pinged. There is a chance it will match these locations. However, chances are if this is correct, and all four are involved, they may have left them behind with one or two of the other teens."

"So they would have an alibi," she said.

"Exactly. Phones stay at the Academy, and the word of two other students. It's busy. You saw it. Students were coming and going. Some were eating outside, in the library, walking down the hallway."

"But surely all four wouldn't go along with it."

"If Charlie and Isabella are to be believed, they sexually assaulted a girl, Callie. They've already proven what they are willing to do together to get what they want. They have the most to lose. This isn't just about the loss of a school's reputation, no, it's their entire lives. The only question is who out of them committed the murders."

"Do you have an idea?"

He chuckled. "I wish I knew that much."

"Okay, so we have motive and opportunity but what links them to the crimes?"

"That rope for one. Nicholas and Katherine weren't climbers. There's no gear in their home related to that. But at the Academy. They have wilderness staff. Access to gear for climbing and rope courses. Hawthorne said it himself the first day I visited him. So, when I phoned the school, I asked to speak with Dalton Mathers."

"The expedition leader."

"You got it."

"He confirmed they use a specific rope. Mammut 9.5 Crag Dry. It's not your run-of-the-mill rope you pick up from a local Walmart. We're talking three hundred dollars or more. He emailed me a photo. It's a match."

"All right, so maybe it connects the school to the murders. What, so you think the teens' DNA might be on it?"

"That's what we'll have to wait on a lab to confirm. Of course, we'd need to get a DNA sample for them. However, in the meantime we know from the medical examiner there was red fiber found on the rope that was wrapped around Katherine that could be connected to a vehicle, a home or clothing."

"That's why you were pushing to go back to the school."

"At that time. No. I just figured that they needed a closer look."

Callie got up, set her drink down and snagged up her jacket. "Right, well, we need to alert Isabella, Charlie and Hawthorne immediately."

CHAPTER 32

Wednesday, November 23, 8:40 p.m.

Answers came fast and furious.

Noah's theory began to solidify as a call from McKenzie came in on their way over to the Academy. He knew immediately from his subdued voice that he was having some difficulty telling him. "Forensics got back to me on the gun. They managed to recover the serial number."

"And?"

"It's registered to a Nathan Tomlin."

Callie glanced over. Both of them instantly made the connection.

"Adam Tomlin's father. Sonofabitch! Look, McKenzie, I called the school and spoke to the wilderness expedition teacher. That rope at the Evans residence."

"Is a match. I know." McKenzie paused for a second. "You were right."

"We both were to some extent, we just weren't able to

connect the dots until now," Noah said. The Bronco raced through the winding roads of the Adirondacks, his heart pounding in his chest as he pressed harder on the gas. With his window partially cracked, he could hear the sound of the wind rushing past, and fall leaves rustling on the road as the Bronco blazed a way through them.

"Is Thorne with you?" McKenzie said, his voice piping out through the speakers of Noah's Bronco.

"I'm here," she replied.

"Good. I tried to contact Hawthorne to get him to pull in the students so we could speak with them but no one is picking up."

Callie replied, "We're nearly there anyway. You should—"

"Yeah, yeah, I'm already getting in the cruiser," McKenzie cut her off.

As they sped toward the Academy, a growing sense of dread crept up his throat. The darkness of the night only added to the uneasy feeling in his gut. The headlights from the Bronco illuminated the road ahead, the shadows cast by the trees seemed to be creeping closer with every passing second. As they came around a bend in the road, they got an answer to why Hawthorne hadn't answered the phone.

Off in the distance, Noah saw a tongue of flames flickering in the darkness, and the sky was lit up by an orange glow. As they got closer, he could see the source of the fire. It was the Academy.

"McKenzie. I need you to ring a number for me. She's not picking up. Try to get hold of Isabella Perez. If you get no answer after a few tries, contact Plattsburgh Police and have them head over to her workplace to detain her." He reeled off the cell and address. "Also send deputies our way."

"Why?"

"The school is ablaze."

He hung up as he swerved around a sharp bend, the tires

screeching as the Bronco struggled to maintain its grip on the road. Noah felt his heart skip a beat, but he regained control of the vehicle. The wind was picking up, he could feel it shaking the vehicle harder as they sped up the long driveway that cut through the trees. Muddied leaves slapped against the windshield as rain began to fall, slashing the night.

The urgency of the situation was not lost on him; as he got closer, he could see the fire was bad. Fortunately, someone had called the fire department as fire trucks were already on scene, their lights flashing widely. But it was clear from the outset that they were struggling to contain the inferno that was chewing through the main building.

The sense of impending doom was almost overwhelming. Noah's mind raced as they got closer to three fire trucks parked haphazardly around the building, their flashing lights illuminating the area. Thick black smoke billowed out of the windows and doorways and the sound of crackling flames could be heard even as they made their approach. It was utter chaos.

The acrid smell of burning paper, plastic and wood filled the air, making it difficult to breathe as they stopped and got out. Noah coughed hard and covered his nose with his sleeve, his eyes stinging from the smoke. The heat from the flames was intense; Noah could feel sweat beading on his forehead.

As he approached the fire chief, he could see firefighters in full gear moving around the building, carrying hoses and other equipment. They were shouting orders back and forth, trying to coordinate their efforts to bring the blaze under control.

The sound of water spraying onto the flames was intense, accompanied by the hiss of steam as it evaporated under the immense heat. Glass exploded from on high and firefighters backed off as shards rained down on them. Others moved in, breaking glass to create ventilation and gain access to the building.

Despite the chaos, the crew moved with a sense of purpose and determination. They were focused on the task, using all their training and expertise to try and save the building and the life of anyone trapped inside.

Under the glow of orange, he scanned faces.

"Callie. Go that way. See if you can find Adam and his pals or someone who knows where they are."

She gave a thumbs-up.

As Noah moved around the perimeter of the building, threading his way through students looking on in horror, he could see flames licking out of the windows, hungrily consuming decades of history and everything in their path. The sound grew louder, punctured by the occasional explosion as electrical equipment or gas lines ignited.

Eyeing the crowd of students gathered outside, he caught sight of a familiar face. It was Mrs. Perkins. She looked just as worried as the rest of the onlookers, holding on to a few students like a mother hen. Noah worked his way through, his heart racing. "Mrs. Perkins," he said, trying to keep his voice steady. "Have you seen Rector Hawthorne or Charlie Delaney?"

She shook her head. "I'm sorry, I haven't."

He nodded, his mind racing with possibilities. He needed to find them, and fast. "Thank you," he replied before quickly turning and moving through the crowd. Heading toward one of the ambulances that had arrived was the vice administrator. "Ms. Garcia," he said, his voice urgent. He raised a hand so she could identify him among the slew of people. She glanced back as he edged his way out. "I'm looking for Hawthorne and Charlie Delaney. Have you seen them?"

Her face was etched with worry. "Earlier. They were together in his office," she said. "They were talking before the fire broke out. I had to step out to help with a couple of students that were fighting in the hall."

Almost immediately, he began to conclude what might have happened. Had Adam and his cohorts decided to set the school ablaze, possibly to destroy whatever files were in the building or worse — kill Hawthorne and Delaney?

"I need your help," he said. "I'm looking for a few students, I think they might have been involved in something serious."

Garcia nodded, offering back an expression of concern. "Of course. Who?"

Noah rattled off the names, keeping his voice low. "I just need to speak with them," he said, not wanting to reveal too much. The truth was despite being sure that he was heading in the right direction, there was a slim chance that he could be jumping the gun. "As soon as you see them, let me know right away."

She nodded again. Her eyes scanned the crowd as she began speaking with the teachers. He turned to go, his thoughts shifting to Hawthorne and Charlie. He spotted Callie across the crowd; they exchanged a glance and she lifted her hands to indicate no luck. Noah continued the search. He spent close to ten minutes before his heart sank when he saw them being taken out of the burning building on stretchers. Both had oxygen masks over their face and were wrapped in crumpled space blankets.

Noah rushed over, working his way through the crowd.

"Hold up!" He took out his badge to show the EMTs. It was clear Hawthorne was unconscious, while Charlie was still alert. Without thinking he stopped them. "Charlie, what happened?" he asked urgently.

Charlie lifted his oxygen mask, his face blackened by smoke, a picture of pain and fear. "Joshua Whelan trapped us in the office, poured gasoline under the door and started the fire," he said, his voice wavering and hoarse. He coughed hard.

Noah's mind reeled at the news. He remembered on his first

visit to the Academy, the two older teens passed him as he came out of Hawthorne's office after being warned that they might be expelled. "How do you know it was him?" he asked, trying to keep his voice calm.

Charlie met his gaze, his face filled with a mixture of pain and guilt. "I… I heard him through the door," he said, his voice barely above a whisper. "As we were trying to get out, he said I shouldn't have said anything."

Noah's mind tried to piece together what had happened. If Joshua had started the fire, and was trying to cover their tracks so there would be no proof, where was he now?

Noah turned to the EMTs. "Go. Get them to the hospital," he said, his voice urgent as Charlie placed the oxygen mask back over his face and closed his eyes. Noah only hoped the two of them survived, and they managed to locate the teens before they continued their rampage. Behind, in the distance, he saw a fleet of squad cars coming up the driveway. He figured it wouldn't be long before they found the teens and…

Crack.

Noah immediately turned towards the sound of a gunshot and saw the chaos that followed. Panicked students fled in every direction, others dropped to the ground. The situation escalated even faster as he saw Callie engaging.

With quick thinking and decisive action, Noah pulled his service pistol and took off, telling others to move back as he hurried through the crowd to reach Callie who was already ahead of him and had opened fire on a car.

Noah hurried to provide backup.

"Show me your hands!" Callie bellowed.

The driver and passenger doors were wide open on a Ford Mustang.

In the back there were two students; the other two had fled around the building toward the forest. By now the other deputies had arrived on scene, lights and sirens blaring. Noah directed one of the deputies to secure the two students from the back of the Mustang while he and Callie took off pursuing the other two — Adam and Joshua.

The chase led them toward the dense tree line as multiple rounds were fired by one of the teens. Despite their efforts, the two teens were able to evade them and disappeared into the thicket of trees which made up a sliver of the Sentinel Range Wilderness, a mammoth swath of dense forest that covered over 23,000 acres.

"Wait," Noah shouted to Callie. "It's too dangerous. They aren't going anywhere."

It would be nearly impossible to find them on their own and at night. They'd need to bring in more officers, highly trained search crews and helicopters with forward FLIR.

The wilderness was too vast.

As Noah turned back to the Academy that was ablaze, he shifted gears quickly, formulating a plan to have State and County officers set a perimeter. They would set up roadblocks within a ten-mile radius. It would be a massive operation, but they needed to catch the suspects before they could cause any more harm.

CHAPTER 33

Thursday, November 24, 10:40 a.m.

Truth tellers and liars — the world was full of them.

Some were willing to fall on their sword while others would go to their grave with secrets. The world was full of both for all manner of reasons — shame, guilt, pride, anger or just straight-up stupidity. Although many would speculate about the liars, it usually boiled down to self-preservation, a more palatable version of cowardice.

As the sun rose over the Sentinel Range Wilderness the next morning, casting a golden hue across the forest floor, Noah and Callie trudged towards a clearing about three miles in from where they last saw the teens.

Search efforts continued throughout the night but were limited to securing the roadways around the vast wilderness and the use of technology, including drones and FLIR cameras on helicopters to track the suspects who had fled deep into the woods.

It was safer for law enforcement to wait until early light before closing the net. Knowing the teens were armed and more than liable to use deadly force, safety was paramount both for deputies and K-9s.

As soon as light broke and they received confirmation from eyes in the sky on the location of the two, using a thermographic camera, a slew of highly trained law enforcement geared up, ready for a violent standoff. The intention was to secure and arrest but neutralizing the threat was also on the table.

The forest was dense and quiet, its thick canopy of trees blocking out some of the sunlight. As the investigators made their way through the underbrush, they could hear the sound of their own footsteps crunching on fallen leaves and twigs beneath them. Occasionally, a radio squawked as officers communicated with the eyes in the sky. It was a coordinated effort. With the anticipation of the unexpected, a tense atmosphere formed among them.

A SWAT team spearheaded the operation, taking the lead.

At one point as they got closer to the location, Noah and Callie were told to hold back until they received confirmation that it was safe to move in.

Minutes felt like hours as they waited in a preserve known best by hikers who explored it for the trails and remote experience.

Static came over the radio followed by a voice. "All secure."

A sense of relief flooded Noah's chest as they moved towards a small clearing only to find a pair of bodies lying on the ground near a small meandering brook.

As they approached the scene, Noah felt no sense of triumph. Like the others he was exhausted, physically and emotionally drained by the events of the past week.

It became clear that both suspects had died from a self-inflicted gunshot wound. There was only one gun, a 44 revolver nearby. A heavyset imposing man, a lieutenant from Adirondack County, strolled toward them. He was wearing a heavy-duty tactical helmet, body armor, gloves, boots and holding an M4 rifle.

"You should see this," he said, handing them a cell phone that was open on a 25-minute video. Noah snapped on blue latex gloves, took it and hit play. The self-filmed video confirmed their guilt, as well as the fact that the other two boys who had been with them were only guilty of the sexual assault of Isabella.

A sense of relief mixed with sadness came over him. It was good that the suspects were no longer a threat and that justice would be served, but the fact that multiple lives had been wiped out was a tragedy.

"They took the easy way out," Callie said.

"No. It might seem that way but I don't think they wanted to die or they would have done it sooner. I imagine they just couldn't face the music or the looks on their parents' faces once they had their day in court and were staring at a lifetime behind bars."

"You sound like you've dealt with this before," Callie said.

"It happens all over the country. Stalkers who kill and then kill themselves, murder-suicide, abductors who shoot themselves after being cornered, and shooters that go on a rampage only to take their life before they can be held accountable."

"It doesn't feel like justice."

"Maybe not for these two. But it will save a lot of tax dollars," he said, bagging the evidence. "And there are still the other two teens we arrested."

In the eerie silence of the forest, the investigators worked quickly to gather evidence and document the scene. They knew they would need to piece together the suspects' movements in the days and hours leading up to their deaths to assist them in closing out the case.

As they turned and made their way back to the command center established at the school, which had all but been destroyed by the blaze, Noah noticed the other members of the police force looked just as tired as he felt. They had all worked tirelessly throughout the night, driven by a determination to bring justice to the victims.

"Do you think they will release the video footage?" Callie asked.

"No. They'll tell media that they brought in a forensic psychologist and a leading expert in threat assessment and after an extensive amount of discussion and forms filled out, they were advised that the release of the recordings would only fall into the motivation of why these boys did it."

"For notoriety?"

He nodded. "Though it's clear from their past that being known wasn't the reason. They wanted the past to stay buried. That was it. My thought is that once they realized they were in too deep, that people were talking, and the heat was back on, they reacted with little thought to the repercussions. That will be confirmed by the other two once they realize they are an accessory to murder. Their defense lawyer will get them plea deals, a reduced sentence where they'll only be tried for a sexual assault and they'll be back out within less than ten years. And hell, depending on what judge they get, they might just get probation for telling the truth. That, Thorne, is the revolving door of justice."

Callie nodded as they trudged out.

"And Lena? They admitted to Katherine, Laura and the attack on Nicholas but nothing about Lena."

"That's because they weren't involved. Like I said, the timelines don't match up. They only had a small window to leave the boarding school. The MO also doesn't match. The other three were an attempt to look like suicide."

"But wasn't hers?"

"Gear in neutral. Cause of death, fentanyl. No. She wasn't driving that car when it went over."

"So, you think Teresa Barkley and the others killed her and are lying."

He nodded. "For now, that's all we have to go on unless evidence proves otherwise."

"What about Hawthorne?"

"He'll see his day in court."

As they left behind the wilderness, Noah couldn't help feeling a sense of sadness and frustration. He couldn't help feeling that Teresa was genuinely confused when she'd heard that Lena was dead. The liars who took secrets to prison or the grave could be very convincing. Not every case was closed cleanly. Justice came in many forms, sometimes within weeks or months, other times years later on the heels of DNA evidence or a jailhouse confession.

Emerging from the tree line back onto the grounds of the once illustrious Academy, Noah was exhausted, his mind numb from the harrowing events of the previous night. The scene of devastation before them was hard to take in.

The historic private boarding school lay in ruins.

The once-grand building was now a smoldering pile of ash and rubble, its walls and roof collapsed in on themselves. The air was still thick with the acrid smell of smoke, and the ground littered with charred debris — scorched desks, broken chairs and shattered windows.

Fortunately, no one lost their life. The quick actions of teachers and students combined with the fire department's efforts offered a smidgen of hope.

"Hey guys," McKenzie said, his voice loud as he jogged over. "I've got some good news. Nicholas Evans awoke late last night.

He's going to pull through. The doctors said his blood was saturated with carbon monoxide and he was minutes from dying if I hadn't pulled him out of there."

"That's good, McKenzie. You saved a life. Well done," Noah said, patting him on the shoulder, knowing how much his ego needed stroking. "And Delaney and Hawthorne?"

"Alive." McKenzie fell in step. "By the way, I heard the news through the radio. Cowardly bastards. Well, at least we have the other two. They're denying any involvement in the murders. Their lawyers arrived this morning."

"Of course," Callie said.

McKenzie continued. "But I'm sure they'll sing a different tune when the defense sees that video and they are faced with Delaney's and Perez's statements." He jabbed a finger in the air. "Oh, and those red unknown fibers from the rope the M.E. found, well it looks like they'll be a match to the carpet in the Ford Mustang belonging to Joshua Whelan. Yeah, these teens weren't exactly bright." He sniffed hard. "Throw in the restored serial number of Adam Tomlin's father's gun and I can see Ricky Patel and Benjamin Kim folding like a cheap suit."

They walked on.

"Sounds like you've had a busy morning," Noah remarked.

McKenzie grinned. "Time and tide wait for no man."

"Perez okay?" Noah asked.

"Aye, she was at work. Safe and sound."

"Good." Noah opened the door on his Bronco and climbed in. Every fiber of his muscles ached from the cold.

"Where are you going?"

Noah glanced at him as he slammed the door closed. "Home. To bed. To get some shut-eye."

"But I thought—" He waved back at the scene.

"That I wanted to close the case? It's already in the bag. Literally." Noah handed him the bagged evidence out of the window. "You just need to work your magic in the interview room. Make a convincing argument. That shouldn't be too hard for a veteran like yourself. I mean, you saved a life, right? The rest should be a walk in the park," Noah said, firing up the engine.

McKenzie glanced at Callie as if she might stick around.

"Don't look at me. I've been up all night too. Your shift has just started, mine's over."

"I worked late last night."

"Late. Yeah. We worked all night." She motioned to Noah. "Can I catch a ride?"

"Jump in."

"But... but..." McKenzie said. "The paperwork. I thought we were partners?"

"We are. In some parallel universe."

"Noah. C'mon, lad."

"Like you said — us State guys roll in and roll out. This is me rolling out."

"I was just yanking your chain..."

"Smile, McKenzie. You're at the helm. You've got this. Oh, and before I forget... Happy Thanksgiving," Noah said, winking at him as he reversed, swung the Bronco around and left him behind, grumbling in a plume of grit.

Callie nudged him on the way out. "You are a devil."

"Always need a little yin and yang." He pulled out onto the highway, yawning as a bright sun bathed his face. "How are you spending Thanksgiving, Thorne?"

"My sister is back in town."

"From California?"

"Yeah. Not sure for how long, so I'll be catching up with her. You?"

He took a deep breath, realizing where he'd agreed to go. "Hugh Sutherland's."

She snorted as she twisted open a bottle of water and brought it up to her lips. "Best of luck with that," she muttered before she let out a tired laugh.

CHAPTER 34

Thursday, November 24, 6:30 p.m.

Thanksgiving felt like the Last Supper.

Twelve of them were in attendance: Noah and his two kids, Kerri and her two, Ray and Gretchen, Maddie and her significant other, Jake Randall, a man they all had yet to know. Then there was Hugh at the end of the table like some high priest overseeing his flock. To his direct right was Maggie Coleman from the newspaper, a close friend of the family who he'd invited to join them, a kind gesture since she was a widow.

The room was filled with a warm glow from candlelight. The smell of roast turkey, stuffing and mashed potatoes wafted through the air. On the surface it all looked idyllic, but the tension in the room was palpable.

Noah couldn't help but feel the weight of Luke's absence at the table, never mind the loss of his ex. He had yet to tell anyone how she died, only that it was an open case. The pain was still raw and would be felt for months. His children who sat sullenly at the table felt the same way. It was hard to be thankful when so much had been lost.

The silence was broken only by the sound of silverware clinking against the plates and the occasional cough. Hugh, a stern but well-meaning man, attempted to keep the conversation flowing, but his efforts were met with stony silence from all barring Maggie.

Noah scooped potato into his mouth and stared at Ray across from him. The last time they had spoken, his older brother had attempted suicide. Then there was the discovery of the debt and the money he'd been spending like water to feed his gambling addiction. Noah had paid off the debt, but the awkwardness of the situation hung heavily in the air. Ray promised to pay him back but Noah wasn't holding out hope for that. His attempt at taking his life was a topic that not even Hugh had been privy to. It would remain a secret between Ray, Maddie and himself.

His sister gulped wine like it was going out of fashion, her gaze bouncing between them.

Forks scraped against plates and the soft whispers of Kerri's children could be heard as they exchanged furtive glances with his own two. They now had something in common. Both had tragically lost a parent under circumstances that weren't natural.

No child should have experienced that.

Noah's heart ached as he looked around the table and considered how much damage had been done. Everyone had been affected by loss in some way. He only wished it could be different.

"More wine?" Hugh asked, his eyebrows raising as he screeched his chair back and dabbed the corner of his lips with a napkin. The room erupted with a hearty yes, almost at once, as if numbing themselves as fast as they could might delude them into thinking that the meal was anything but awkward.

"You know, Dad, I'll get it," Noah said. "Sit. Chat."

Chat? The word sounded foreign.

"No, it's fine. I have to use the washroom, anyway," he said. If Noah wasn't mistaken, even his own father looked a little out of his comfort zone.

"You think I could get some more pop, Dad?" Ethan asked.

"Sure, buddy."

Noah took his glass and headed out into the kitchen, away from the rabble. He checked the fridge but they were out. Hugh was returning with two bottles of a reserve Pinot Noir, a favorite of his. "You out of pop?"

"No, there's some more in the garage." He went to walk by him but stopped short. "Noah. Um. About the funeral for Lena. I'll take care of all the cost involved."

"You don't have to do that. The Grayson's said it would be handled."

"No. I insist. I'll phone and speak to Doug. Lena was a part of this family. It's the least I can do." He let out a heavy sigh as if burdened by a weight he couldn't verbalize. "I'm sorry, Noah," he said before walking back into the dining room. Something about the way he said it struck Noah as odd. Sorry generally wasn't in Hugh Sutherland's vocabulary. He certainly hadn't heard it in the years he'd been alive.

Perplexed, he pushed it from his mind and strolled into the garage. Inside it was immaculately clean and tidy, just the way his father liked it. The walls were lined with tools, and there was a workbench to the right side of the room.

As he walked towards the fridge, Noah glanced at the gleaming red truck parked on the right side and a sleek black BMW that sat next to it. The floor was spotless, and the air was filled with the faint smell of motor oil and gasoline.

Just as he was taking out the pop, he heard the sound of the door opening behind him. He turned to find Kerri standing in the doorway.

She looked worried, and he could tell that she had something important to say. "What is it?" he asked, his voice low. She cast a glance over her shoulder and then approached him, tucking a strand of hair behind her ear.

"After our last conversation, I did a bit more digging," she said, her voice barely above a whisper. "I found out whose name is on the LLC. It's owned by a man named Luther Ashford. You familiar with him?"

"Huh. Well. I think I have a good idea," he replied, thinking of the Ashford Royale, the casino that was managed by Gabriel Ironwood.

"A powerful family, Noah. More money than they know what to do with."

"Which would explain why he was willing to offer the waterfront property rent free."

Kerri looked troubled, she cast her eyes down then looked back at him.

"What is it?"

"The LLC buys and sells properties. It has several owners; your father is one of them."

"What?" He felt his heart sink. He had suspected something was amiss with the property, but this only confirmed his suspicion.

She continued, "I know. Why would he be involved in that kind of real estate and what is his connection to the Ashford family?"

A conversation with Gabriel came back to Noah.

"What's to stop me from raiding your casino right now and arresting you?"

He replied confidently. "Nothing. By all means, if you think that's the way to handle this, do so. But have a conversation with your father first and see what happened to those who tried in the past."

"What are you going to do?" Kerri asked. She looked at him, her eyes searching his face, no doubt seeing Luke.

Noah paced for a moment or two, considering all options. "I don't know."

"You won't take the property, will you?" she asked. "Who knows what he's gotten himself tied up in?"

Noah hesitated, then sighed. "Those kids need a home of their own," he said, his voice determined. "They can't go back to Lena's rental. I can't stay at Gretchen's forever. And I've all but used up what money I had for Alicia's property."

He took a deep breath.

"So, you're taking it?"

"There's an old saying that goes, 'Keep your friends close and your enemies closer.'"

"But do you know who your enemy is?" she asked.

"That, I plan to find out."

Kerri looked at him for a moment longer, then nodded. "Okay," she said, her voice resigned. "But be careful, Noah. It's not just you now you have to think about," she said.

She nodded, then turned and walked back out.

Noah took out his phone and placed a call to Harland and Stafford.

"Suzanne Gilford, please."

A second or two later she came on the line.

"Noah. Good to hear your voice. Have you considered the offer?"

"Yes. I'll take it."

"Very good. I will make the arrangements to have the keys ready for pickup here, tomorrow, how's that sound?"

"That works. Thank you."

He hung up and stood there for a few minutes longer before

returning and joining the others. As he sat down, he glanced across at his father, seeing him through new eyes. Suspicion swirled in his mind as memories of his conversation with Gabriel Ironwood came back to him. Noah knew that he had to be careful, and he was determined to do what was best for his family, but to understand how entangled his father had become and what had changed in the county since he'd been away, it would require some risk. *Lies* were the backbone of every criminal enterprise, *secrets* its currency, and now he was about to find out how deep the two went in High Peaks.

~

THANK YOU FOR READING

If you enjoyed that, read the next High Peaks Mystery Thriller called Her Final Hours.

Please take a second to leave a review, it's really appreciated.

Thanks kindly, Jack.

A PLEA

Thank you for reading Vanish from Sight. If you enjoyed the experience this book gave you, I would really appreciate it if you would consider leaving a review. It's a great way to support the book. Without reviews, an author's books are virtually invisible on the retail sites. It also lets me know what you liked. It also motivates me to write more books. You can leave a review by visiting the book's page. I would greatly appreciate it. It only takes a couple of seconds.

Thank you — **Jack Hunt**

VIP READERS TEAM

Thank you for buying In Vanish from Sight, published by Direct Response Publishing.

Go to the link below to receive special offers, bonus content, and news about new Jack Hunt's books. Sign up for the newsletter. http://www.jackhuntbooks.com/signup

ABOUT THE AUTHOR

Jack Hunt is the International Bestselling Author of over sixty novels. Jack lives on the East coast of North America. If you haven't joined ***Jack Hunt's Private Facebook Group*** just do a search on facebook to find it. This gives readers a way to chat with Jack, see cover reveals, enter contests and receive giveaways, and stay updated on upcoming releases. There is also his main facebook page below if you want to browse. facebook.com/jackhuntauthor

www.jackhuntbooks.com
jhuntauthor@gmail.com

Made in the USA
Columbia, SC
28 July 2024